ALL
HEART

MARA DABRISHUS

Dabrishus, Mara, 1981 -
All Heart / Mara Dabrishus

Editor: Erin Smith
Cover: iStock

ISBN: 0996187251
ISBN-13: 978-0996187251

www.maradabrishus.com

ALL
HEART
MARA DABRISHUS

For Mohammad.

Chapter One

Rain mists over Belmont Park, clouding the track in a fuzzy gray haze. I have to squint to make out the starting gate sitting in the chute, which is a long stretch away from my perch in the Blackbridge viewing box. Below me, the nearly empty grandstand cozies up to the muddy, sealed track. What's normally warm, harrowed dirt looks like a slab of cold concrete. Nine horses are about to go charging down that surface, punching through sticky slop with jockeys pumping away at their necks.

If Lighter decides to go into the gate, that is.

The colt bobs and weaves, scattering assistant starters like they weigh next to nothing. I can see his bombshell blond mane flipping over his neck through the gate, his copper body coiled between attendants that have hooked their arms under his butt, pushing his petulant self into the waiting nine hole. Lighter's head is up, ears flicking forward and back, my mom patting him softly on the hindquarters with the crop in gentle reminder.

Move forward. How hard can that be?

It's like he's purposely stalling, and I have to say he's actually helping us out because the colt's owner is so far nowhere to be found. There's only a flurry of texts on my phone that say *I'm coming, I swear, I'm coming,* but honestly? I'm starting to doubt that. I hunch into the rain and watch the assistants go for the towel, which they'll use to shutter out the world so Lighter can't see where they're aiming him. Dad grunts something about scheduling gate training to Paul, our assistant trainer, who nods with a somberness I feel all the way through my aching muscles.

Because that's what it's like working with Lighter. You put your all into it and then stand back and watch the mayhem as he decides how to put his lessons to chaotic use.

"Every time we train him in the gate, he goes right in. Put him in a race, and suddenly it's impossible." I shiver into my jacket. The wet is starting to soak through, so I'm even less in the mood for Lighter's antics. I'm not even down there dealing with him in person and already he's pushed me into complaining.

"Could be he enjoys the special attention."

The colt's owner leaps the viewing box rail behind me and lands with a slosh in the puddles at our feet. I afford him a raised eyebrow as he shoulders up next to me, all casual charm and smiles. The city boy has finally returned.

"Tore yourself away?" I ask, watching his enthusiasm slide into a grimace.

"I wore this suit to a group meeting, Juls," he says, motioning to his damp three-piece suit that is currently the best thing about standing out here in the rain. I give him the side-eye, because I still have to appreciate that suit, even if it does come with Beck being so late he's only saved by his colt's pigheadedness. "I was prepared.

It's just that I got paired up with people who actually care about things like grades and fair division of labor in group projects, which is stunning for a sophomore level business class. I'm not even sure what my own name is anymore."

Okay, maybe it's a good excuse this time. Maybe.

"It's Beckett Delaney," I remind him, grudgingly.

"Ah," he nods, squinting down at me, a sly smile climbing one side of his stupidly attractive mouth. He pushes his once-blond hair back with one hand, green eyes watching me warmly. "I had this feeling you would know."

I allow a smirk, and before Beck can capitalize on this small chink in my armor the announcer's voice rattles under the grandstand's rafters.

"We're almost all in line for this afternoon's Champagne Stakes. Waiting on Lamplighter to load and we'll be underway."

The announcer sounds amused as Lighter splays his front legs out in front of him and shifts enough of his weight against the assistant starters' arms that I know they're all cursing at him. Then, like he's gotten tired of making a scene, he bounces into the gate with a sassy tail swish. The assistant starters have to catch themselves before they nosedive into the mud.

"This must be what going mad feels like," I mutter to myself.

Beck laughs and throws an arm around my shoulders. I let it rest there, which still feels like a new development. Before the summer, I would have shrugged him off, elbowed him in the side, done something definitely less affectionate than let his warm, if equally damp, body lean into mine. And because it still feels so new, there's that rush of eagerness that floods me at his touch, fills me up to the point of flowing over, which makes me suck in a breath to keep it all down. It feels good having him here, with me at the track, like this is how we should always be when reality is not so kind most of the time.

"Would watching him run be as satisfying if he was totally well-mannered?"

I swing a look up at him, caught immediately in one of Beck's brilliant I-am-adorable smiles.

"Yes," I say flatly, pretending I'm not affected at all. We both know better, and Beck lets me know that when he presses a kiss to the side of my forehead, right there in front of the world, like a mark that says *this one is mine.*

Only we don't say that. Haven't said it at all.

Then the bell rings and the gate explodes open, releasing a field of two-year-old Thoroughbreds that startle and leap like deer flinging themselves clear of danger. Lighter takes one stride out of the gate and bobbles, like mud is not what he signed up for. Mom rises in the saddle for a split-second to collect him, but just like that the rest of the field is gone and Lighter falls to last, with ground to make up and eight horses to pass.

Great.

Mom gets to work, pushing him into the race. They pass two horses easily before Mom goes chilly still in the saddle, like she's hit cruise control. Only her hands move, shifting back and forth with Lighter's bobbing strides as he eats at the slippery ground, hovering mid-pack down the backstretch.

On the other side of the box, I feel my dad's telling silence. Lighter is too young for this scenario, and way too full of attitude to even begin to comprehend strategy. That he's even listening to Mom is a miracle.

Mom keeps Lighter on an outside track around the turn, the colt lengthening his stride as Mom opens her hands, giving him room to float toward the front on his own. There's a beat where it's just horses galloping, and another when the jockeys are all movement, shaking the reins and twirling crops. This is when I have to take a huge breath. Next to me, Beck tenses because this is the moment of truth.

Lighter goes bounding into the homestretch, Mom re-crossing her reins and pumping her arms up his neck. The reins flap loose, tighten, flap loose. She flips the crop up and swats Lighter's hindquarters once, twice, pushing him to engage.

Now.

The leader, a classy gray colt off a giant allowance win at Saratoga, begins to roll in earnest, pulling away from the pack by two lengths. On the outside, Lighter cavalierly pricks his ears and Mom rests her whip hand against his neck, flicking it past his eye to get the message across. This is not a fun morning ride, after all.

This is the Champagne Stakes.

The grandstand echoes in a clatter of encouragement, but I can barely hear it from the blood rushing in my ears. We are all shouting at the horses, like that will do anything to change the outcome.

"Get up!" I scream at the track, joining the crowd when the urge becomes too much. "Come on, Lighter. Get up there!"

With two bounds, Lighter goes from hanging out with the pack to strides ahead of them. It looks like all the other horses have slowed down, but it's really Lighter moving so much faster. Within a second, he pulls even with the gray. With another, he runs past him.

Then there's only air between him and the wire.

"Lamplighter has cruised to the lead, making it look easy today in the slop . . ."

The announcer's voice rattles over the steel beams of the grandstand. Beck lifts a fist in the air, celebratory already. Mom keeps at Lighter, waving the crop and working hard at teaching him a lesson until they splash past the finish pole and she can rise in the stirrups.

Lighter's ears are still pricked, his pale tail flicking behind him as they go streaming into the first turn with an outrider giving chase to bring them home.

"And who was worried that he couldn't rate?" Beck says to me on our way out of the box.

"I will give you a pass because you haven't seen that monster train every morning, but the answer is *everyone*," I reply, tipping my chin up at him in knowing rightness, because what would Beck really know? Outside of Dad's daily chats, Beck is mostly absent on the backside with school in session. It's mostly just me out there with Lighter now, Dad at the sidelines with his eyes on me like a hawk every morning as I wrestle with the colt. If Beck is there, he's escaped the city's stranglehold and looks distracted all the time, like he knows he needs to be somewhere else.

Like right now, actually.

And I get it. I do. We all have priorities. Our entire lives can't be made up of easy, sun-filled summers in Saratoga. After all, this is fall at Belmont. It's gray and wet and full of obligations, like work and training and school.

Or, in my case, the *lack* of school, which is something I'm trying to fix.

"I cannot wait to see you balance the track and NYU," Beck says, grabbing my hand as we wind our way toward the winner's circle. "You'll be putting us all to shame."

I open my mouth, and then quickly shut it, swallowing down what I need to say.

"Oh, I intend to be amazing," I tell him instead as we step out into the rain, losing my nerve entirely, telling myself that now is not the time for this conversation. Lighter is coming back to the grandstand a mud-streaked winner, and it's time for celebration. Not disappointment, although it's hard for me to think of it that way.

Ever since I went to work for Dad this summer, the track has become my life. I'm on Belmont's backside before the crack of dawn, working my fingers down to nubs before lunch, and exhausted by the time I hit my bed at dusk. That's life now. If NYU accepted me for spring semester, it would feel weird not to be out with the horses, making it work somehow.

So that's why I haven't applied.

I know. *I know.* I suck so much I'm making it a profession. But I've seen how Beck doesn't make this life work. He wants to be here, and can't. No matter how much he was there at Saratoga and the Outer Banks, he hasn't been here for Belmont since we all came back to New York with sand still in our shoes and sunburns healing on our necks. I remind myself for what feels like the trillionth time that he doesn't have to be here—he is, after all, the blue-blooded owner's son.

A month has passed since Saratoga, since our trip down south to the Outer Banks, and it's like everything has been reset. Beck is in the city, and I'm at Belmont. I think that's expected of Beck—it was what he did before, so why not now? Even with Blackbridge declaring bankruptcy, the family finances in total disarray, Beck still lives like he's always lived.

7

Careless. Always.

But I'm the trainer's daughter—meticulous, always involved, with horses in my less-than-blue blood. So I'm not applying to NYU, not since I came home from the Outer Banks with the track on my mind. The horses have always been my life, and it took being away from them to make me realize that they're the only thing I want. NYU, with its clustered buildings sitting in the middle of a city that doesn't know what to do with a horse except hitch it up to the front end of a carriage, isn't going to get me any closer to that goal.

I know I should still apply. I should still entertain the option. Beck and Bri are in the city, waiting for me, and I want to be there with them. I do. But . . . maybe I shouldn't be.

Maybe I should be right here, where I've always been.

"I'll have a visitation schedule. It will be NYU, the track, Kali, then your apartment at Columbia," I declare, because I suck. God, I do. I really do. I can't find the nerve to disappoint the people closest to me, so I'll just lie to them instead. Great, July. Good work.

"I don't know about that last part," Beck says offhandedly, which brings my fantasy train to a screeching halt. I hazard a look up at him, wondering what he means. He opens his mouth and shuts it again as he walks, looking pained as he tries again because he knows how it sounds. Beck isn't an idiot. "It's just that if you came to my place, you would die a little inside, Juls. Three guys living in a small space? You would never want to see me again after you saw that mess. You'd run screaming for the hills."

That . . . sounds like a crappy excuse.

I swallow the lump that's formed swiftly in my throat along with the question that wants to stick in my mouth, begging to be asked. So, I'm not invited then? Why? Sure, I haven't been to see him in the city yet because playing pseudo-assistant trainer full-time every day for my Dad gives me no time at all to be social, but in my fantasy NYU life, I'd have plenty of opportunity to slip into Beck's city apartment, live like a college student with a boyfriend, just being utterly *normal*.

And now I'm not even invited?

My fantasy self is insulted, right before I realize that real life me should be equally annoyed.

Before I can say a word, Lighter goes rollicking into the circle, sweeping up every concern I might have with his owner and replacing it with his jubilant self. His whole body is a wash of mud trickling over his dark copper coat in slick clumps. Mom flicks her crop a few times in the air, trying to dislodge the persistent mud, before tossing it to her valet. Gus leads the colt in a tight circle in front of the group clustering around him, waiting for everyone to get in line so the photographers—bedecked in shiny rain slickers—can do their job.

Lighter chews at his bit, shows the whites of his eyes as he strains to look everywhere at once, ears flicking every which way. Mom leans to pat his neck as she grins for the photo. I can't help watching her out of the corner of my eye, even as I smile hard as the cameras flash.

Mom flew in yesterday to ride Lighter, dropping everything and getting on a plane the second Dad asked because Pilar is still recovering from her fall last month. I would love to say that it's been an amazing twenty-four hours since Mom's plane touched the tarmac at LaGuardia, but I think we all know I'd be lying through my teeth. Because Dad had the brilliant idea to invite her to stay at the house, I am shocked we all survived to see Lighter's race. Of course, Martina hasn't seen it at all, because she refused to walk over from the backside. Martina's appearance at Lighter's Hopeful Stakes was the beginning and end of her olive branch to Mom.

And me? Here I am, in the winner's circle at Mom's booted feet as she laughs and scrubs at Lighter's mane. A necklace of dirty goggles hangs around her neck, her silks stained brown and wet through. She looks so happy, and I wonder if this is all it really takes. Four years of wondering how to get her back, and the solution turned out to be simple. Offer Mom a spectacular ride, and she shows up with bells on.

Mom jumps off of Lighter, who barely notices she's left his back. He's looking at something off in the distance that only Lighter seems to think is interesting, and then lets loose a riotous whinny, his ribs shaking with it. Mom laughs and slaps the colt's shoulder before collecting her saddle to go weigh in. As she passes, she does a hesitant little stop in front of me, looking at me like she just remembered I was there.

"We've got an amazing horse, don't you think?" she asks me, and I tilt my head to the side, considering the word *we*.

"Sure do," I say, and she smiles at me, big and brilliant, before taking off for the scales.

Gus shoots me a look as he walks past with Lighter. I give him a pressed-lip smile and shrug, like what can you do?

～⌒

The test barn is right in the thick of Belmont Park's Millionaire's Row, where Count Fleet Road hits Man o' War Avenue. Here the grass is greenest, where the biggest barns sport the widest, tree-shaded courtyards. The trainers here earn their keep, consistently winning Belmont's biggest races. It would make sense to plop the test barn in the middle of their home turf. For the sake of convenience, I suppose. Wouldn't want to walk too far to get home after your winning horse has their blood and urine sampled. That would just be asking too much.

We've ticked blood off of Lighter's list, but urine is proving to be a challenge. It's one more thing Lighter refuses to do on cue, so we wait. Rain patters on the test barn roof, dripping off the eaves. I huddle just inside and watch the barn next door—a sweeping thing that has its own indoor galloping ring, with speakers attached to each curved wall so the Thoroughbreds can listen to Mozart during morning works when it's too cold to go outside.

Or so I've heard. Dad never made it into Millionaire's Row. Maybe he would have with one or two more years training for Blackbridge, but now? Not likely. Can't exactly do that when Blackbridge is closing up shop.

There's a little whoop of excitement inside the test barn, and I turn to see what the commotion is about. Beck appears around the corner, hands in his pockets and a sly grin on his face.

"Finally," he says, as Gus leads Lighter past him, the colt all high-stepping theatrics. "Guess he was a little shy."

"Shy?" I ask, raising an eyebrow. "Lighter?"

We both watch Lighter fling his head up the second he leaves the barn, like he's surprised that it's still wet outside and he's being asked to walk in it. Two more steps out onto Count Fleet Road and Lighter goes up onto his hind legs, formally lodging his protest. Gus just waits him out, gets him moving the second Lighter's hooves scrape back to earth.

"Must not be too tired," Beck observes, and maybe he really isn't. Lighter dashed away from a field of promising two-year-olds like they were second rate runners, but the slop and the distance would tire out any young horse—even Lighter.

"I think he keeps a special energy reserve for being a pain in the ass," I say, and mean it.

Beck laughs.

"And here I thought you were warming up to him." He nudges me into the rain so we can follow Lighter home. "A dual grade one winner doesn't get any respect around here."

"I am warming up to him," I say, eager to correct Beck when he's wrong. "He still takes great pride in making my life difficult."

"What does a guy have to do to get on your good side, Juls?" Beck asks, casting me a sideways look as we follow Lighter and Gus down Secretariat Avenue through Belmont's backside on the way to Barn 27. I pretend to look like I'm giving this great thought.

"Do what I say, for starters," I decide.

"Being around me all the time must be staggeringly difficult for you," he says, which is such a dare. He winks at me, just to drive it home. I don't say *but I haven't been around you much this month, so how would I know?* I trap that impulse and shove it away, because no matter how true it is we're riding the high of Lighter's win and it's not right. It's not the time to give that thought a voice.

Like NYU, a traitorous little part of me thinks. It's not time for that, either.

I wrinkle my nose, a cool raindrop slapping on my skin. "I make special allowances sometimes."

"Aw, July," Beck says, pulling me into his side. I stumble into him, shallow puddle water sloshing over the tips of my shoes. "No one has ever called me *special* before."

"Really?" I ask, regaining my balance by grabbing onto the back of his suit jacket. "How has that not happened?"

"Depends," Beck replies brightly. "If you mean *important*-special, no. If you mean *eats paste*-special, I would expect that only from you."

I blink up at him, letting myself marvel that Beck somehow became mine.

Of course, I haven't told Beck. The *you're mine* part. How do you tell someone that when you only see half of their life? A month has passed and I haven't even seen where he lives. That seems crazy, right? It's jump the gun, break through the gates, false start sort of behavior. Never mind the part where we've known each other for-ever, because all of that feels like it was left in another life, shucked off like an old husk. Beck and I are new again, which leaves me grasping for how to act. The same? Different? Both?

How would I even manage to act both?

Beck narrows his eyes at me.

"Are you having an aneurysm? I was expecting a witty remark by now." He ducks to look into my eyes, and I think *same. Act the same. You can do this.*

"I suppose I wouldn't put eating paste past you." I shrug. "I imagine your mom got a lot of concerned notes from your kinder-garten teacher."

"There she is," Beck sighs, looking up at the falling, silvery rain. "I was beginning to worry for a minute."

I scoff and dive under the cover of Barn 27's dry shedrow, all evenly raked lines in the dirt aisle. Soft dust clouds rise up around

Lighter's hooves as Gus walks him past the office, where Martina stands in the doorway with her arms crossed, observing our return with a cool sort of detachment. Her dark hair is slicked back into a no-fuss ponytail, jeans streaked with dirt, and boots muddy around the heels. For the first time in what seems like ages, I can look down at my dress and say I've finally out-styled my sister.

"I was expecting you back sooner," Martina says by way of any sort of greeting or congratulations. Our grade one winner walking down the aisle doesn't even faze her.

"We were waiting for Lighter to pee," Beck says to her. "You can't rush greatness, Martina."

She just looks at him from her perch on the doorjamb, unamused.

"You should have come with us," I say, knowing immediately what Martina will think of the word *should*. "It was an impressive race."

"I watched it," Martina says pointedly. "From the warmth and silence of the office."

I don't know about warmth, with the storm breezing through the barn. But silence? We've got that in spades. I cast a look down the aisle that sweeps around the corner of Barn 27, at the telling lack of horses nosing at hay nets or hanging their necks out into the aisle to get a look around. The same can be said for all the stalls running up the opposite side of the shedrow.

Empty, empty, a running stretch of nothing. We put all of the Blackbridge horses on vans to the sales pavilion at Keeneland in Kentucky only days ago, holding only three back: Galaxy Collision, Quark Star, and Lighter. They're Breeders' Cup-bound. All the rest are gone.

Well, almost gone. As soon as the gavel falls in the auction house this weekend, they'll be off to new homes. Plenty will come right back to Belmont, working under new trainers and different riders. I'll watch them breeze in the mornings, wondering what could have been had Delaney not invested in the wrong funds. Money seems to be so quickly lost in racing, and it takes the horses right along with it.

The empty stalls stretch out in front of me. Call me crazy, but I think I might have more time for Kali if things around here don't pick up. Of course, if they don't, we're all so screwed.

"Can't get much more silent than this." Beck looks down the shedrow, similar thoughts on the brain. We're all thinking it—Dad needs new owners, stat. Delaney won't be flush with horses again for a while, if ever. And Beck, with his trust fund going to Ivy League tuition? Please. I know he can hardly keep on top of Lighter's insurance, so it's not like he's going to add any more horses to the barn. The horse he has he should sell and he knows it, but now Lighter is a dual grade one winner staring down the Breeders' Cup Juvenile.

There's no way Beck is going to sell.

"It will pick up," Martina says, waving a hand at Barn 27 flippantly, and I wonder when she decided to be so optimistic.

"It would pick up if we were over on Millionaire's Row," I say. "Easy. But here?"

Barn 27 is roughly adjacent to The Hole—Belmont Park's eastern edge that slopes down toward the Hempstead Turnpike. The barns there routinely flood in storms like this, and no one is listening to classical music while they work their horses on inside tracks, that's for sure. Our barn doesn't have it so bad. It's surrounded by a green lawn, thick clusters of trees congregating along its sides. We can take horses out to graze on well-clipped grass, letting them act like horses under supervision.

Still, no classical music.

"I didn't start managing this place so Dad could drive it into the ground," Martina sniffs, shooting me a look from the doorway. "Give me some credit, July. There are owners on the hook. Just let me reel them in."

"There are owners?"

She huffs, like I've offended her great talents.

"Of course," she says. "This morning, yours truly bagged Khalid Sahadi."

"The Power-T guy?" Beck asks, which means nothing to me because it is vastly apparent I live under a rock. He sees my lack of understanding and nudges me. "Flavored tea and antioxidants, Juls. What's not to love?"

"He loves horses, too." Martina looks immensely pleased with herself as she points a finger at me. "He's moving an entire string to the east coast, and Dad is training them. Tomorrow there will be some big changes around here, mark my words."

I am stunned. Truly. Maybe having Martina out of disability law and in our barn is a good thing after all.

Beck throws an arm over my shoulders. "Martina, our savior. Who would have thought?"

Not I, that's for sure. But then, I didn't think Lighter would be a grade one winner, Kali would be all mine, or I'd get a little thrill up my spine each time Beck gives me a certain look, like he's thirsty for something. I wouldn't have thought Mom would be riding at Belmont Park, or Martina would be standing here in boots and dirt-streaked jeans, that I'd be applying for college. These are the things I couldn't have anticipated, and with the barn primed to fill up again with different horses, different owners, I feel a little dizzy with the newness.

But that's a good thing, right?

Gus and Lighter round the corner of the shedrow, coming back down to us. Lighter is all coiled energy, even more full of himself after his big win as he yanks at Gus's tattooed arm. Gus keeps him moving, a clatter of hooves and swiveling ears all the way into the colt's stall. Only a small beat of time passes before there's a thud, Gus grunting out a firm *pendejo* and rubbing his shoulder on his way out of the stall. Lighter immediately hangs his head over the stall guard after him, pricking his ears at us like he's the face of innocence.

"That colt," is all Gus says on his way past us. He shakes his head, but his dark eyes glitter happily, like he wouldn't wish for anything else.

Some things never change.

Chapter Two

Rain patters on the windshield, sluicing down the glass and flicking into thin air when the wiper blades go flashing by, the steady *thump-thump* the only noise in the car. Martina stares stonily ahead at Mom's car in front of us as we drive home from the track, where we've left our tiny contingent of horses bedded down for the night. My sister is a lesson in utter silence that has me tapping my fingers against the steering wheel, fiddling with the vents, and trying not to notice how deeply angry she is about this arrangement.

I get it. I do. But you know what? I don't have any say in the matter, so it's not like I was the one who told Mom *yes, sure, of course you can stay with us!* That was Dad, he of the easily-persuaded parental philosophies. I'm just along for the ride here, just like Martina.

So I don't know why I'm getting Martina's attitude.

"You know, it's not all bad," I try, casting around for something that will draw Martina out of her stoic glare through the window. She turns her head slightly, giving me a look out of the corner of her eye. I know through this look my best option is to stop trying, that there's no hope getting her to meet me halfway. But I continue, because what do I have to lose?

"It's not like Mom is staying for the duration," I say, finding the path forward. "Just for the meet and then she'll be back in California, we'll have our lives back, and after the Breeders' Cup we'll have Pilar on Lighter so there won't be a need for Mom to come back."

Martina snorts out a laugh.

"What?"

"I can't believe you're trying to sell me on this by saying it won't last long," Martina tells me, crossing her arms and straightening her spine, shoving her shoulders back and letting out a long-suffering sigh. "Any amount of time is too much time. If you care to remember, Mom doesn't live with us anymore. She made her decision. That she's using us as a hotel is insulting."

"I don't think she thinks of it quite like that . . ."

"She wouldn't," Martina grumbles. "Since when is Mom at all self-aware enough to realize what she's doing?"

There was a time when I would have said not at all, but now? I'm not so sure. I know what Mom regrets, but I also know she's not nearly ready to figure out how to fix things the right way. Instead of letting things progress at our pace, she's barging in, trying to insert herself into our lives in one fell swoop. It looks like a takeover, but with her stuff in the guest room and her toiletry bag on the bathroom counter it's just so obviously temporary. Like she can't even commit to making us welcome her back, open arms and all.

Then there's the obvious. If we didn't have Lighter, would she even be here? If Pilar gets the ride back, will Mom show up just for us instead of a horse?

I can't answer that, but I know what Martina's thinking—all of this isn't enough. Mom isn't trying hard enough, so she's digging in her heels.

"She's trying," I say, which is definitely the truth. I can't fault Mom for that, because for so many years that was all I wanted. I've wanted to move forward, even when I couldn't, even when I was stuck and spinning my wheels. This feels like forward motion, so shouldn't I be glad?

"You shouldn't just roll over and accept her minimum amount of effort," Martina says. "Four years, July. And she came back for a horse, not us."

Up ahead, Mom's rental car turns into our driveway, the garage door lifting. Mom parks in Dad's empty spot while he's gone to the auctions at Keeneland, chatting up the new owners Martina found and looking at prospects to fill up Barn 27. I know Martina desperately wanted to go with him, anything to avoid this fate, but she's needed at Barn 27 because she's the manager, the person who keeps it all together. That person can't just leave when their mother shows up in town.

Mom pops out of the rental car, throws a grin at us like she just can't wait to spend quality time alone with her girls.

Martina glowers and I make myself smile at Mom as I pull my car into the garage next to hers, the wipers still beating out their steady *thump-thump*.

"One month," Martina mutters to herself as she unfolds out of her seat and slams the door in her wake. She doesn't give Mom the time of day as she walks toward the door to the house, leaving Mom with a paralyzed smile on her face, the one that stays there when she knows she shouldn't be smiling. When there's no reason to smile at all.

I watch them both head into the house, Shady's little black body twirling around their legs in welcome, insistent cat meows trilling over the sound of my car's engine. Martina looks back at me, narrows her eyes in that silent question because I'm not getting out of the car. I'm not even turning the engine off.

What the hell are you doing?

Let me see. Either I can go inside the house and play peace-keeper between my clueless mother and my resolutely angry sister, or I could back out of this garage and leave. My thoughts skitter back to Kali, back to the barn, and before I know it I've got the gear shift in reverse and I'm giving the car gas.

Martina's eyes widen when she realizes.

"July!" she calls, but I'm already halfway up the driveway. I'm on the road. I'm putting the car back into drive and I'm already gone.

~~

When I get to Woodfield Equestrian Center, my car dips into the first pothole with a splash. I lurch out of it, bumping across the gravel lot into the first open spot I see. It's Saturday night lesson time, and therefore the place is a hive of activity. The three-aisle barn shines like a beacon in the encroaching autumn darkness, light spilling from all three open doorways. Further out, the empty out-door arena glistens with muddy footing. The indoor will be packed as a consequence, full of pony lessons and adult amateurs trying to find the time to ride in the rain.

The second I park the car, I reach into the backseat for my

duffel bag and haul it into my lap. I'm still wearing my dress from the race, which isn't exactly barn appropriate. The good news is it's so easily fixed.

I pop open the door and make a dash through the rain, bag banging awkwardly against my hip. When I turn the corner into the open doorway, I'm presented with the haunches of a cross-tied warmblood. The mare tilts her head, rolls one large brown eye back to give me a good look, but otherwise stands still. No crisis, she seems to think, so she shifts to rest on three feet and lets her ears flop. Madeline, her owner, lifts onto the tips of her toes to see over the mare's neck and smiles at me.

Madeline and I have ridden together at Woodfield since we were little kids doing stupid things on the horses out in the back paddock. Riding the school's star schoolmaster, Gideon, together bareback, inevitably falling off into a patch of something thorny, breaking tailbones and fingers and toes—it was all in a day's adventure at Woodfield. We don't get to see each other much anymore, with the racetrack taking up my life. But now I have Kali, so that's starting to change.

"I don't think I've ever seen anyone ride in a dress around here," she says, getting an eyeful of my knobby, pale knees.

"Don't hold your breath," I say, pointing to the duffel. "Is Lisa around?"

"Up in the indoor," Madeline says, dropping back onto her heels. "She's booked, though."

I catch a glance at the whiteboard listing lesson times, the names beside each thirty-minute block. My name is slotted in on Mondays and Tuesdays—dark days at Belmont, otherwise known as when the horses don't race. Free rides don't get listed on the board, but I haven't freely ridden Kali unsupervised by Lisa since I led the filly into her stall at Woodfield. Probably because everyone is a little leery of a Thoroughbred straight off the racetrack. Riders give Kali a wide berth in the arena, like they're afraid any stray cluck to their own horses will drive Kali into a wild fit of speed.

But I know my horse well enough to know she isn't liable to do anything wild or speedy. Kali was a failure on the track for a reason, mainly because she didn't feel the need to go fast when it counted. So what if I ride her unsupervised? That's practically all we ever did for over a year on the track and in the galloping fields.

"Come on, Cricket," Madeline croons to the mare, who is much, much larger than a cricket. Nevertheless, it's her name. The mare sighs deeply and lifts a foot for cleaning. I duck under the cross-ties and up into the enclosed boarder's tack room. It takes a few minutes to yank off the dress and pull on my riding clothes. By the time I'm presentable to be around horses, Madeline has Cricket's saddle resting in the dip of her back, her fingers nimbly working at the girth as Cricket sweeps her ears back, swishing her tail with a characteristic snap.

"Hey, wait for me," I tell Madeline, and she looks up from her hands with a frown on her face.

"But Lisa . . ."

"Is booked," I finish for her. "I know. Wait for me, okay?"

Madeline tilts her head at me, narrowing her eyes as I jog down to Kali's stall with the filly's saddle in my arms and her bridle hanging over my shoulder.

Kali comes up to the stall guard at the sound of my feet, stretching her long, chestnut neck into the aisle and pricking her ears like two eager satellite dishes honing in on me. I scrub my short fingernails against the whorl of hair in the center of her fore-head, and let myself into her stall, where I can clip her halter onto the line we've attached to the bars separating stall from aisle. Race-horses don't cross-tie, so I do what Kali's used to—tacking her up in her stall.

"Seriously, July," Madeline says, leading Cricket down the aisle and stopping in front of Kali's stall. She peers in at me with her wide blue eyes. "Is this the best idea?"

"I've ridden Kali many, many, *many* times," I say, patting the filly on the neck as her ears swivel toward Cricket, nostrils widening to get a good sniff of the other mare.

Madeline just raises an eyebrow at me.

"It will be okay," I promise, unclipping the stall guard and clip-ping it back on itself, leading Kali from the stall. The filly shivers excitedly, looking up and down the stall and swinging her attention to Cricket as Madeline shrugs her shoulders.

"It's your funeral," she says in that blasé way of hers.

And that's fine. I just need something familiar right now, even though this, too, is different. Kali is in her royal blue saddle pad and brand new tack instead of my exercise saddle and nylon bridle she would have been wearing at the track. Kali even looks different, more filled out already without her daily workout and racetrack diet.

It looks good on her, like she's taking to this new life like a hog to mud. It puts me at ease—the knowledge that my filly is settling in here. Maybe she'll bring me with her.

"You know," Madeline says as we lead our horses out of the barn, the wet gravel slushing around hooves that scrape in the muck. "I'm taking Cricket with me to Jericho in the spring."

"You're taking the leap?" I ask, surprised, because Madeline has been here forever. Jericho College is just up the road, where she's a freshman. It also features heavily in my internet browser history ever since I discovered it had an equestrian studies program. There's something crazy about going to school just to learn more about horses, but it's also incredibly tempting.

"Yeah," Madeline says with a shrug. "Why not, you know? The trainer there is top notch, and I'll have more time to spend with Cricket."

"Did you tell Lisa yet?"

Madeline gives me an impish smile. "She helped me film our application video yesterday."

Oh. She laughs.

"Sorry," she says, scrunching up her nose. "Looks like I won't be around here much longer."

"And you're like the last person I know here," I sigh, looking at the familiar surroundings which are packed with unfamiliar people. I reach out and put my hand on Kali's shoulder, giving her a pat that is more meant for me than it is for her.

"So why aren't you applying?" Madeline says.

"To Jericho?" I ask, and she raises one of those perfect eyebrows. "I guess I hadn't thought about it. It's not like I could take Kali anyway. She's too green for them to do anything with."

Lies. All lies. I am thinking about it, but part of me just can't pull the trigger. If I do, NYU is really gone. I'm really not doing it, and part of me likes thinking about that fantasy life I'm never going to live.

"They take green horses," Madeline points out, like I knew she would. "They'd probably even take you—racehorse girl though you are."

I groan, mock offended. "Hey."

She grins at me as we get to the indoor arena. "Think about it. I'll help you do the video and everything."

Grabbing the handle to the indoor, she pokes her head inside and calls, "Door!"

She slides the giant door to the side, revealing three horses in the massive indoor. One is a young kid on a lunge line circling around Travis—the barn's second trainer—and the other two are older students. One goes cantering around the short end of the arena, her pelvis tipping easily to the horse's gait, while the other struggles to convince Gideon to trot.

"Come on." Lisa prods at Gideon's rider, who blows a breath like moving shouldn't be *this* difficult. "Don't let him get away with that."

The girl thumps Gideon on the sides and the gelding lifts into a heartless trot, tipping his ears back in surveillance. Lisa is about to tell the girl to use the whip when she notices us, tipping her chin up when she sees me with Kali.

"You know what you're doing, I hope," she calls across the arena.

"Of course," I call back.

Lisa's is a face schooled into complete stillness, so it's impossible to tell what she thinks. Gideon falls back into an unmotivated walk and she's forced to get after her student again. Madeline springs off the mounting block, landing lightly in Cricket's saddle. The two move off, giving me room to jump up on Kali.

The filly moves off into an energetic walk before I have time to leave the mounting block. I leap, getting a leg over her back and collecting the reins as Kali enters the fray of the indoor with her ears pricked so far forward they're almost touching. She blows out a huffing breath, her walk so fast she easily overtakes Cricket and puts Gideon in her sights.

And it's perfect. I sink into her movements, letting myself follow her as I feel for her mouth. Kali drops her head, flicks her ears back at me like she's reminded I'm up there.

"That's right, remember me?" I ask her, collecting the reins on the second turn around the arena. The cantering horse goes skipping past us on the inside, and Kali throws her head up, frothy spittle from her working the bit flinging up into the air, landing on her mane and my chest. She dances to the side, giving the cantering horse the side-eye. I sink my weight down, push her into connection.

Remember me, Kali.

The filly lowers her head again, and I ask her to trot to keep her on the business of us instead of the cantering horse, Gideon doing his start-stop tricks, Madeline and Cricket taking their time on the buckle, and the kid lunging around Travis with his long whip trailing in the dirt. There's so much to be distracted by—so much newness she's being expected to take at face value instead of gawking and staring in confusion. I can feel the shivering excitement in her, from all of this activity she hasn't been near in weeks of private lessons.

She picks up the gait, lifts her head excitedly as I rise and fall in the saddle. Her head is up, ears twisting this way and that, following the cantering horse as it comes around again, a steady three-beat *thump thump thump* of hooves in dirt. Her ears sweep back when the noise approaches, gets louder, goes streaming past on her inside.

I give her just a sliver of space, and then try to find her, get her attention off the cantering horse before it comes around again.

Thump thump thump.

Kali full-on shivers and lifts. I know what's about to happen—have felt it more times than I can count on the track. The shift from two-beat to real speed. But this isn't a racetrack, and Kali isn't going for flat out run. Not here in the indoor, at any rate. She rises and falls into a canter, striking out so beautifully, so collected and smooth I let her keep going. I sit the rocking, tilt into it, find her mouth and turn her into a twenty-meter circle at the far end of the arena. Kali follows me, lets me guide her into a bend.

It's not dressage. Not really. It's an off track Thoroughbred cantering in a circle, bending just enough to look nice. Although it isn't important, because it's Kali showing me it doesn't matter where she is. Track or indoor, Belmont or Woodfield. She's still Kali, and we're on this new path together.

I let out a breath I didn't know I was holding, and sip in a new one. The filly settles into a gentle three-beat, her hooves shushing into the thick carpet of dirt. Her head comes down, and her body rounds, her ears tipping back just enough to let me know she's listening. Out of the corner of my eye, I catch a smile flickering across Lisa's face.

Then the observation room door slams shut, the noise banging through the indoor. Kali is underneath me and then she's not. She's a plunge of copper and lifted hooves as she leaps away from danger and I'm left with nothing but air between me and the ground.

I sail into the dirt, landing with a hard thunk over the reverberations of hooves thundering far from me. Tipping my head back in the dirt, I can see an upside-down image of Kali going straight for the indoor wall, twisting and leaping out of a head-on collision in a feat of athleticism I would be grateful for if she weren't headed straight for Travis and the little girl on the lunge line. My heart unlodges from my chest, heading straight up my throat.

The lunging lesson horse shies hard, dumping the girl at its feet and bumping into the cantering horse, who stumbles to the side and flings its rider over its neck before righting itself and careening off to the center of the arena, where Lisa is standing with her arms out.

I push my hands into the dirt, my muscles telling me to lay back down right now. I ignore them, rolling onto my knees just as I see Madeline do a flying leap off Cricket, leading her into a corner as Kali goes bucking by, hooves slicing through the air. Shoving to my feet in time to see Lisa catch the other loose horse, I turn my attention to Kali, who zooms past me in a whirl of chestnut mane and whipping tail. She takes a sharp turn, her head high until she lowers it to buck again.

It occurs to me that my filly is having fun now, taking the spook to new heights.

"Kali!" I yell, waving her down. The filly looks at me, all bright brown eyes and mischief sparkling along her edges. She huffs a snort and falls into an extended trot, floating over the ground right up to me. Then she stops and puts her head down, depositing herself in my hands like she's had enough here and would like to go back to her stall now.

"If you think you're getting treats after this, you are so sadly mistaken," I inform her.

Kali only chews the bit, looks at me expectantly while I pull the reins over her head. Behind her, I see Travis assessing his student. The girl is hunched in on herself, stunned tears streaking her cheeks. The other rider is already up, limping toward her horse. Gideon carts his student around in a wide circle, not even remotely interested. Madeline sorts out Cricket and jumps back on because she hadn't even gotten through her warm up before Kali went berserk.

We made it all of ten minutes before imploding. I look up at Kali, who's pricked her ears at the scene, nostrils blown wide as she takes deep breaths like she can smell the dimming chaos in the dust she kicked up.

"July." Lisa walks up to me, taking my elbow and steering me toward the door. Kali goes high-stepping with us, snorting with each stride like she's hot under the collar and expecting something. "Go put your horse away and come see me after I finish this lesson."

I open my mouth, only to find excuses piling up on my tongue. *Kali's green yet; she's still figuring things out; she's just starting to learn; horses spook at loud noises all the time.* It's all true, but it's not helpful. So I only nod and lead Kali out of the indoor, and I swear I can practically hear the collective, relieved exhale we leave in our wake.

∿

I take my time dragging myself out of Kali's stall. The filly has her nose buried in her hay, her coat is pristine, and her feet immaculate. There's nothing to do except watch her hoover up scraggly alfalfa strands, munching and swishing her tail. Madeline puts Cricket into cross-ties outside Kali's stall, the big mare taking the opportunity to press her nose against the bars as Madeline roots for the mare's halter.

"Leese is free," Madeline says, almost off-handedly as she sorts out the halter and starts working on Cricket's bridle. "You and I both know you don't want her to come to you."

I definitely know. Time is paramount in the lesson world, and you don't keep a trainer waiting. As much as I know I need to haul myself back to the indoor to hear Lisa out about Kali—most likely even me—I'm not exactly relishing it.

I scrub my short nails against Kali's neck and leave her stall, meeting Madeline's apologetic shrug.

"It was just a spook, Juls. No one died."

I smile half-heartedly and walk up to the indoor, letting myself in and catching the end of Lisa's speech to her student about impulsion, drive, forward momentum.

"You have to anticipate him." Lisa's voice drifts over to me. "Every few strides you have to check in and give him guidance, otherwise he's going to do things his way."

I feel like it's a speech ready-made for me—for Beck and Mom and Martina. Impulsion, drive, forward momentum. Anticipate, check in, give guidance. Otherwise it all falls apart. Never before has lesson terminology hit so close to home, and I wonder just what I should have really been paying attention to during all of those years' worth of Lisa's lessons.

The student nods, all head bobbles, and leaps off Gideon with a grunting sigh. She's worked too hard getting him to go, and her legs are wobbly. I remember those days, being mystified that I even needed to ask for forward when I was always around horses that seemed so naturally inclined toward speed.

Now maybe I've got a little too much of it. It's almost hilarious, because it's Kali.

Lisa catches my eye and comes over. The indoor is empty in the lull between lessons, and I think of the little girl curled up in the dirt.

"Is the girl okay?" I blurt out. Lisa squints like she's trying to remember which girl I'm referring to in a sea of girls. The barn is crawling with us.

"Fine," Lisa says. "Shaken up, to be sure, but everyone falls. How's your back?"

"Probably bruised." I feel a twinge deep in the muscles, and can already envision ibuprofen in my future. Lisa only nods.

"I can't have you free-riding Kali on busy indoor days until we get more training into her," Lisa says, launching into the speech I knew I'd hear. The *she's not ready* speech. I find myself nodding, because it's Lisa's barn and Lisa's my trainer. She may not have taught me the nuts and bolts of riding, but she is responsible for many years of finesse. Every twitch of my fingers on the reins, every shift of a muscle just so—Lisa made that happen. And if she says no free-riding Kali in the indoor, no free-riding Kali in the indoor.

"What about the outdoor?" I ask, because there has to be some leeway.

Lisa just gives me a look I know so well. "I know you've ridden this filly day in and day out for who knows how long, but this isn't the racetrack. It's a dressage barn. Until Kali is settled in and settled down, I don't want you riding her unsupervised on my property. Is that clear?"

"Technically speaking," I start, trying to wiggle my way to more freedom, "I was riding supervised just now."

Lisa just waves a hand in the air like she doesn't want to hear it. "You know you can always take Kali back to the track if you want to play by your own rules, July. This is what I'm asking. If you can't comply . . ."

"I can comply," I say immediately, letting all my hopes deflate. I can ride Kali under Lisa's hawk-eye gaze, work on her ground manners every other day of the week.

Lisa just shakes her head at me and draws me into a hug, wrapping her arms around my shoulders. "I know you were waiting a long time for this," she says against my hair. "Don't get impatient. Kali will get there on her own time, and you will, too."

I sigh and lift my hands, resting them lightly on her back as she pulls away when the door opens with her next student. Lisa pats my arm and turns her full attention to her next charge, leaving me to slip back to my car, hardly noticing the misting rain as I fall into the driver's seat and gaze through the wet windshield at the barn, its *Save Woodfield!* banner still stretched across its long, weathered side.

There was a time I would have given anything to see Diver—the gray gelding who was never mine—happily tucked into one of Woodfield's stalls. I wanted it so badly I could see that future in crystal clear color. He'd been meant for a place like this, and I was going to give it to him.

Instead it's Kali, still baby-new and confused by what we want of her. All we ever asked of her was speed, speed, speed and now it's extend, collect, bend. No wonder she's confused.

Don't get impatient.

No kidding.

I tell myself to pull it together as I push the key into the ignition. I only have a house sitting on the land mine of Martina and Mom to go back to, and think I'm going to need all the patience I can get.

Chapter Three

I shiver into my jacket as I canter Maggie around the far turn of the Belmont training track. To my outside, Quark Star and his regular jockey, Jorge Velazquez, jog down the rail. Jorge is perched on Star's shifting shoulders, reins bridged against his withers to give the colt something to push against. Every so often Star leaps into an eager canter, wondering when we're going to go already. And like clockwork, Jorge pulls him back into a steady trot.

Impatience shimmers over every line of Star's body, and I get it; I do. The colt hasn't raced since winning the Travers Stakes at Saratoga, well over a month ago. We could have run him back in the Jockey Club Gold Cup yesterday against older horses, but the colt was blowing hard after his work last week so we didn't enter him.

Hot Metal won that race going away, so maybe that was the right call. Star might be eager to run, but it doesn't mean he's necessarily ready. He's not peaking at the right time, and we have the Breeders' Cup Classic to think about. Wasting time and energy on the Gold Cup could have ruined our chances in California, and when our owner needs the purse money more than we do, you don't even dare think about running in the Gold Cup.

You wait for California.

"He's gonna need a blow out soon," Jorge yells over at me, pulling the colt back down into a jog after another attempt to launch into go. "This little bastard is trying to pull my arms off."

Star shakes out his pitch black mane and grunts, dropping his head and plowing forward into the turn. I keep Maggie close by, her rocking gait drifting us closer to his head so I can snatch the colt's bridle if he doesn't come down to a walk after the turn.

"You say that like there isn't a plan," I call to Jorge over the hoofbeats. He throws a stretching smile my way.

"All I know is it ain't your arms getting ripped off this morning," he says, sitting back in the saddle and closing his hands on the reins, asking Star to slow. The colt lifts his head, annoyed by the pressure, and resists for just a split second before I swoop up, snagging his bridle with my lead. Maggie shoulders close, ears tipped back as Star falls into a hyper-motivated walk toward the gap in the track.

Jorge eases up, loosens the reins when I've got a firm hold on Star's head.

"Is this it?" he asks me, pointing at Star. I squint at him, wondering what he's talking about until I realize.

There aren't any more horses to ride. It's just Galaxy and Star this morning. No one is waiting for us at the gap—not even Beck, which isn't a surprise. I'm trying to actively avoid thinking about his absence, about where he is instead and why I'm not invited there. It's too early for him to be anywhere other than dead asleep in his New York apartment, the city already raging at his windows.

"This is it," I tell him. "Lighter's walking the shedrow, Mom should be getting Galaxy ready, and now that Star has fought you around the track, your time here is complete."

Jorge whistles. "Three horses isn't a stable. Your dad knows that, right?"

"I'm told he's on it," I say, although who really knows what that means. Dad and freedom of information are definitely not synonymous. "There are owners on the hook and Khalid Sahadi has horses coming in today."

Jorge just gives me a look like he'll believe it when he sees it. Dad has been a private trainer so long it's easy to wonder if he still has the skills to talk his way into training for other people. Multiple people, even—people who definitely will be racing against each other. Public trainers usually have multiple owners, and the opposite is also true. Owners can send any horse they want to any trainer they want, fitting horse to trainer and switching them around at will. It's just more to be uncertain about in the long run, the wondering how long you're going to have a certain horse before it gets pulled out from under you. It's a business set up on results, not sentiment.

Maggie pricks her ears at Barn 27, where Gus stands outside with Mom, Galaxy Collision shining bronze in the morning sun between them. Jorge hops off Star and pulls the barn's exercise saddle off, gives the colt two hearty claps on his near-black shoulder before waggling his eyebrows at me and stalking off into the backside in search of his next ride. I hold a shifting Star while Gus boosts Mom onto Galaxy, the mare doing a quick clatter on gravel as I hand Star off to Gus.

Just your average day of playing musical horses.

I reach out and grab Galaxy's bridle, heading back out to the track with all of Martina's cutting glances digging into me from last night. Her face as I backed out of the garage is going to stay with me forever. The silence I returned home to may be even more so. I walked into the house as silent as the grave, Martina's door shut and locked, no matter my rattling at the doorknob. Mom just shrugged, her hands wringing together the only sign she was worried about it. Once Martina sequesters herself, that's it. There's no cajoling her back into the land of sanity. Best to just let her inner rage work it out until the coast is clear.

So I let her be. I shouldn't have, but I did. If I want to be honest, I shouldn't have abandoned her to Mom in the first place. But I did, and part of me isn't remotely sorry about it.

Mom slumps over Galaxy's withers, studying the rubber-coated reins in her hands like she doesn't know what to do with them. I don't say a word, because like hell I'm playing this game. Martina and Mom are adults, and they don't need a mediator.

"Last night was a little awkward," Mom finally says as the maple trees quiver above us, autumn breeze fluttering through the amber leaves. Maggie's ears sweep forward, and Galaxy huffs, shifts so she's prancing sideways with her nose pressed into my mare's neck. Mom nudges Galaxy, and the filly swings back around with a smooth slide of her haunches.

"I don't know what I was expecting," Mom continues, and it's an effort for me to not flagrantly roll my eyes. What had she imagined would happen? Open arms? Movie and popcorn night with the girls like when we were kids?

We're not kids anymore, and Mom isn't blind. At least, not physically.

"I'd say you know how Martina is," I say, leading Galaxy onto the track, "but you don't know, Mom. I think that's the point."

She swivels her attention to me, her hands gathering the reins. Galaxy collects, draws her nose in with just a hint of pressure.

"I thought we might be good after Saratoga," she says. I just blink at her, because really?

"Did you even talk to Martina at Saratoga?" I ask.

"Briefly," Mom says, and I wince, just imagining what happened. "It wasn't much, but it was still a start. I thought if I came back to ride Lighter in the Champagne, we could work on it. Start making up for lost time. I get it, July. This is all my fault, but I was hoping—"

"She'd just drop the years of resentment?" I cut in. "I can think of so many more big words to describe what Martina and I both feel about this situation, Mom."

That shuts her up for a full few minutes. Long enough that she doesn't speak to me when I let Galaxy go and peel off on Maggie, stopping the mare on the outside rail and turning her so I can watch my mother ride our best horse in the history of Blackbridge Farm through a two-minute lick.

I train my eyes on Mom's pink safety vest, watching her go galloping off down the middle of the track. The bay filly throws herself into the work, which is supposed to be a mile done in two minutes, hence the name. Mom has to keep a tight lid on Galaxy's momentum, counting seconds to satisfy the requirements of the work. Sixteen seconds per furlong, a full four seconds longer than your average solo breeze, when you're near racing speed with no one but yourself and the clock in your head. Galaxy isn't a full-out blur, but she's definitely pushing for more.

Mom won't give it to her, settling the filly and keeping her steady. I count the seconds on Maggie as they go skipping by mile markers, my mare tipping her ears back to listen diligently in case one of the words slipping out of my mouth is a command for go. When they wind back around into the backstretch, Mom standing in the irons and Galaxy slowing into the middle of the track, I cue Maggie up. The mare rocks onto her haunches from a stand-still, rolling into an eager canter and angling across the track so I can snag Galaxy's head and lean back, letting her know it's time to stop now.

With a bounce back into the saddle, Mom shifts the filly into a jigging trot and runs a hand over Galaxy's mane, looking down at the filly like she's just being clued in on what she's been missing.

Of course, it's a horse.

But then she surprises me.

"I just want to make everything better," she says, turning to me, her face open, naked hope. Like if she tried hard enough all the problems will slip away, the knots will untangle, Martina will suddenly stop holding onto her grudges and I'll be that girl Mom remembers. The one who would have done anything to see her again.

Well, that's not how the world works. I want to go forward with Mom, but it has to be at my pace.

"You can't expect to fix everything just by showing up," I tell her. "It's too late for that."

She nods, like she knows, deep down. Maybe she just needed reminding.

"I don't think I should leave," Mom announces on the way off the track. I blanch at her, swinging to face her so quickly that Maggie does a light sidestep, pushing Galaxy across the path and nearly into the fence. Galaxy pins her ears and kicks out a hind leg, her personal space violated. No one shoulders up against the queen. I nudge Maggie away, giving Galaxy her strutting room.

"Did you not hear me?" I ask, still floored. I'm pretty sure my jaw is hanging so far open I could swallow a fly and not realize.

"I heard you," Mom says. "But how am I supposed to keep showing up, being here for you girls, if I'm not here?"

Okay. Maybe I wasn't clear. Maybe none of this is clear and there's no hope in getting on the same page ever again, but I know if Mom stays here, Martina will move out. She won't show up at the barn anymore. She'll disappear into the city and I'll never see her again, just like before. That is the last thing I want to happen. I've just now gotten used to having her at the barn all the time, and we've all been better for it. Barn 27 is clean, controlled, organized—so many worlds better than when she wasn't there making it livable.

I can't have her fading into Manhattan again, ghosting in and out of our family.

"Smothering Martina with quality time is not going to get you on her good side," I tell her. "And rolling into town to ride a horse won't get you on mine."

She gapes at me, but I keep thinking about Martina, about her face when I backed out of the garage last night. I don't want to see that again about as much as I don't want to be caught between her rock and Mom's hard place. I'm sick of playing this game.

"Maybe you should think about going home," I tell her. Then I specify, because I don't want there to be any confusion. "To California."

"I thought I was doing things right," she sighs, ignoring my request as we walk through the backstretch, Galaxy Collision pricking her ears at every noise and movement, looking around with bright-eyed eagerness.

"No one's telling you to stop trying," I say, trying a different tactic. There has to be something that will punch its way through to her. "Just listen to us when we tell you what we need. That's all we're asking. You can't barge in."

Mom straightens her back, squares her shoulders and nods, like she's just heard an order from a trainer and she's going to follow it through to the letter. A little bit of me lightens at the thought, like she's taking orders from me—her daughter.

"I'll try to do that, July," she says, as though I've gotten through to her when I know there's no possible way. She'll disappear to California once the meet is done. Or maybe she'll keep letting herself be lured by the prospect of amazing rides on equally amazing horses. Lighter, Galaxy, on whatever we find next.

Less likely? That she'll do anything we just talked about. I know it, she knows it, Martina knows it. That's just how it is.

Wow, am I a boatload full of sunshine or what?

We turn the corner, Barn 27 tucked into the line of Belmont's shedrows. Its sides are still slicked with rain, puddles marking the entrance. The sight is so familiar my chest tightens just a little bit, like I'm turning the corner toward home.

Home, which has a giant 15-horse transport rig sitting in front of it.

It's a semi, dazzling white like its contents are too valuable for it to be seen dirty. Martina stands at the mouth of the shedrow, a clipboard in her hands and a frown on her face as she ticks at whatever papers she has in front of her with a cheap ballpoint pen.

Then Dad's SUV pulls up, someone I vaguely recognize in the passenger seat.

I ask Maggie to halt as Dad climbs out of the car, landing one of the nice shoes he wears right into a puddle. I wince for him, but Dad barely notices, shooting me a wide grin.

"There are my girls," he says, clapping his hands together and rubbing like this is the day he's been waiting for. I can practically feel Mom stiffen next to me. Galaxy does a little shifting dance underneath her, reacting like she always does to every tiny movement, to every shot of nerves that go from Mom to her. I gape at Dad as if he has two heads, mirroring Mom's expression so perfectly it would be hilarious if not for Martina's frown deepening into a set scowl. I duck my head and tighten my fingers on Galaxy's lead until my knuckles turn white.

He's just excited about the horses, I tell myself. That's it. Nothing more.

"Honestly, Rob," Mom shakes her head at him, his excitement lost on her. Gus comes out of the barn, raises one dark eyebrow at me before physically unclenching my hand from the leather line.

"Let's cool this girl out," Gus says, patting a hand against Galaxy's neck and looking up at Mom. "What do you say, Celia? Want to come with?"

Mom shakes out a nod, and they're off, giving the rig a wide berth as horses stream off of it. Grooms I haven't seen in days chatter at each other, wide smiles stretching across their faces as horse after horse is led into 27 like a current of swishing tails. Izzie leads a little plain bay filly past me, her black-and-blond hair swept into a messy ponytail as she points at the filly, mouthing, "You'll love this one."

A splotchy brown and white goat goes romping after them, sidestepping by the filly and head butting Izzie in the back of her legs. I can't help the double take I give them, but Izzie is all grins, giving the laughing smiles on Dad and the man that unfolds from the front seat of the SUV a run for their money. I narrow my eyes at Dad's new friend, wondering where I've seen him before.

He's got that football player physique, like he's deliberately sculpted himself into shape. His clothes are the nice kind—dress shirt tucked into slacks with a shiny belt and shoes giving off that new leather glow—so he's either an owner or he's been courting one. All of that aside, there's something about him that I just can't quite make fit. His smile widens when he looks at me, so I know it's not all in my head.

I know this man.

"Juls," Dad says to me as I leap off Maggie, leading the mare up to them. "You remember Leo, don't you?"

And it all falls right into place.

Chapter Four

The first thing Leo Reyes does is pull me into a hug, scrub a hand into my hair like that's totally appropriate behavior for someone who hasn't seen me since we were kids, and leaves me far more disheveled than I normally look after a morning on the backside. Dad just shakes his head at us like we're siblings getting into an adorable tousle, which for all I know is exactly what he thinks.

I push my hair back into place, and Maggie immediately shoves her nose against the side of my head and blows out a breath, wriggling her lips as if to help continue what Leo started. Maggie, though, I don't mind. Even as I duck out of her way and push my palm against her cheek in a silent *stop*.

Leo gives me an extra squeeze as though I'm a shiny new toy he can't wait to play with. His brown eyes sparkle, and there's too much product holding his black hair into a swishing style. Being near him is basically being trapped in a cloud of annoying boy cologne, which I'm pretty sure is going to cling to me for a few days after this experience.

I haven't seen Leo in years, not since his dad, Emilio Reyes, pulled up stakes at Belmont and moved his training operation from Barn 32 to Kentucky. Barn 27 was a public stable back then, and Leo was the fourteen-year-old popular kid—junior varsity everything—to my twelve-year-old tomboy.

Dad, of course, loved him. The number of times I found them rattling off statistics from sports that didn't involve horses, playing actual catch with a baseball and leather gloves, flat out ignoring the world to watch whatever football game graced the television was horrifying. Little Leo was practically Dad's third child, the son he never had, who could at least appreciate the finer aspects of baseball when Martina and I couldn't have cared less.

But then Dad got Blackbridge, and Leo moved to Louisville—never to be seen again until, apparently, now.

"This one just got to his internship semester at KRA," Dad explains to me. I arch an eyebrow at him. Kentucky Racing Academy is one of the few schools in the country that actively teaches Thoroughbred racing, from jockeying to training. So much of the sport is hands on, learn as you go from someone who knows everything. KRA takes a new path, which is one Leo has at least nearly finished if he's entering internship.

I know these things, because I considered applying before realizing Kentucky is kind of far away.

"I'm doing the training pathway," Leo supplies, answering my dubious squint and letting me go, taking his boy smell with him. "I was interning under my dad last month, but you can imagine how that turned out."

Back when our barn neighbored Leo's, his dad made the news for punching out one of his assistant trainers after one of their horses tested positive post-race. Obviously the assistant quit. The owner pulled his horse the next day. Emilio got slapped with a fifteen-day suspension, and I suffered through half a month of Leo wedged in our barn like it was his new home away from home.

Leo interning under his dad? I can only imagine the explosions. There's a reason Leo was around so much, and it's one I never wanted to dwell much on.

"I offered to bring him on for the rest of the semester," Dad says to me, which makes my stomach drop. Leo. Here. All the time. And *why?* "He'll shadow Paul, Martina, maybe even you, if you're willing."

He looks at me in that way I know to mean *you should be willing.* I'm too shocked to even nod along, agreeing to a new, swoosh-haired shadow persistently tagging along at my heels.

"If we're lucky," Dad says, "maybe we'll even keep him on as an assistant when he's done with the program."

Oh, dear god.

"I think there's a saying about chickens and eggs," I remind him, arching an eyebrow. Dad nods like he's heard me when I know he hasn't and pats Leo's shoulder, thumping it like he does with Beck—as though he's testing his balance. Leo wavers under the onslaught, but holds fast.

"I'll let you give him the grand tour," Dad tells me, nodding to the last of the horses swishing one conditioned tail as it walks into the shedrow. "I'm going to look into the new charges, if either of you needs me."

"Wait," I start, but he's gone, already into the barn like a kid rushing for the candy bins in a grocery store. Really, who can blame him? I feel the excitement, too. There's a fizzy feeling in my chest, like I'm about to pop from the activity scurrying around the barn. I'm itching to follow him, wanting to see the new horses, but Maggie is in my hands and Leo is at my side, bouncing on the tips of his toes.

"Looks like a fun time to join the crew," Leo observes from next to me. I roll my eyes over to him, because right. Leo. There's a barn tour or something I must now commence, as if Leo doesn't know our barn from the rafters to the dirt floor. I rustle up Maggie, who's been inspecting the blades of grass around the edge of the gravel yard.

"It's an exciting time to be alive, Leo," I tell him, deadpan.

"You know I missed it around here," he says after me as I walk Maggie into the barn, stripping her tack off and leading her back into her stall, where she immediately buries her nose in the hay. I give her a few pats, which she studiously ignores in favor of chewing, and leave her to it.

"You mean the pastoral Kentucky life didn't cut it?" I ask, letting myself out of Maggie's stall. Leo just looks at me like *of course* the Kentucky life didn't cut it.

"It all looks remarkably the same," Leo says, tagging along with me to the tack room, where I dump Maggie's saddle on its post and hang up her bridle. He stops in the doorway and frowns. "Wait, wait. This is cleaner than I was expecting."

"Martina took over the office," I say. "We needed reinforcements. It gave me time to organize."

"You organize?"

"With the best of them," I say, pushing back out of the tack room with Leo nipping at my heels.

"Who are you?" he asks my back. "I remember—"

"You remember a twelve-year-old," I remind him, stopping when I find Izzie in the bay filly's stall, her flash of blond peeking out from under the shiny fall of black hair down her back as she bends to remove one shipping bandage. I narrowly avoid getting clocked in the face when she tosses the balled up bandage out into the aisle.

"Nice aim, little lady," Leo says, and Izzie looks up quizzically, her mouth opening.

"Who's that?" Izzie asks me, and I smile.

"That's Leo," I say, waving a hand as though he's inconsequential while I pin my interest on the filly. "The real question is, who is this?"

"Hey," Leo starts, like he's actually offended. I roll my eyes and Izzie grins, already in on the game.

"This is Feather," she says, scrubbing her chipped pink nails into the filly's orderly black mane.

The goat bleats from the corner of the stall, twitching its short tail. Izzie jumps, like she's forgotten the filly has a friend. It's not unusual for racehorses to have companion animals—other horses, cats, goats, even the occasional pig. They're herd animals, and can get nervous being by themselves. We've had the occasional goat or barn cat in the past, so this is definitely something we'll all take in stride.

What's another animal, now that we're filling up the barn?

"And that's Betty."

"Betty the goat?" I raise an eyebrow.

"Feather has a friend. They're inseparable, or so I'm told," Izzie says as the filly crowds up to the stall door, nosing against my pockets in that way horses have who are spoiled, seeking treats and usually getting them.

"I've got nothing, baby girl," I tell the filly, pushing a hunk of black forelock aside to reveal a tiny white star. The filly butts me in the side, shoving me straight into Leo, who dances out of the way and immediately touches his hair—like he's afraid the sudden action might have mussed it.

I regain my balance just in time to catch Izzie hiding her smile by wiping the back of her hand against the pointy tip of her nose.

"These are all Khalid's horses?" I ask, because my father has characteristically left me in the dark like he always does, and there's no asking Martina for more info now. With most of the grooms and assistants gone while the Blackbridge horses were down in Keeneland, waiting for the gavel to fall, the gossip network suffered a debilitating knockout punch.

I'm clueless. And I really, deeply dislike that.

Izzie shrugs. "For today. We're expecting two more transports tomorrow, all with different owners. I heard one was a Wharton," Izzie tells me, leaving the stall.

Leo whistles, long and low. The Whartons are legendary Thoroughbred owners out of Saratoga—the kind you'd grovel to have in your barn. Izzie nods appreciably, then she stops and looks at me.

"Why don't you know about any of this?"

I grimace. "I only know about Khalid. Guess I got frozen out of the rest."

Izzie purses her lips, because of course she knows what's been going on down here while most of the grooms have been in Keeneland with the horses. It wouldn't take a rocket scientist to figure it out. "I'll call Pilar and make her get her butt back here. Broken arm or no, she can still play poker."

"As much good as venting sounds, it won't fix the problem," I say. "I just need to talk to Martina. I can't have the barn manager pissed at me, especially when we share a house. It's too crowded in there right now for us to not be speaking."

"Especially since you're about to have a house guest," Leo casually breaks in, bringing everything to a screeching halt.

"We're what?"

He blinks at me, his stupid gelled hair shining in the dim light that slants in through the barn windows.

"Roomies," he says, punching me lightly on the shoulder. "Did your dad not tell you?"

Izzie gapes at him, and I realize somewhat belatedly that I'm perfectly mirroring her. Then she shakes herself out of it and spins to me. "Who is this guy again?"

I groan.

"My worst nightmare."

∿

You will not believe this.

I hit the send button and the text goes zipping off to Bri's phone as I sit at the kitchen island, watching my mother pulling out all the stops. The whole kitchen smells like it used to before she left—cumin, oregano, garlic, the warmth of chili powder permeates the air and soaks into my clothes. Along the granite counter, a mess of ingredients is slowly turning into my mother's enchiladas, which I have a sharp memory of being mouthwatering.

Martina is upstairs. Leo sits next to me, eyeing my phone as it lights up with Bri's text. I snatch it away before he can be a jerk and read it.

Beck, Lighter, Martina, or your mom?

Bri Wagner knows me so well. A big piece of me wishes I could just walk out of the house and troop across the front yard to her door, walk in without knocking like we always used to do, and fall down on her bed with the day's news falling out of my mouth. I can't do that now because I'd only find an empty room. Bri has a new room in the city, in one of the NYU dorms, and can I just say I wish she'd decided to commute?

I stare at her text, realizing she needs updates on all four. Except then there's the fifth problem.

I turn to Leo and lift my phone.

"Say hello to Bri, Leo."

He looks up from his phone, face drawn into confusion, and I snap a photo.

"Wait, that was horrible." Leo jumps to snag the phone. I shift away just as fast, jumping off the stool and shipping the photo off to Bri before he can do anything about it. Bri's response is immediate.

What is Leo Reyes doing in your house?

He lives here now, I text back.

What?!

Leo looks up at the ceiling like he's holding in his urge to let out a deep, suffering sigh.

"God, is this what little sisters are like?"

"Yes," Martina says from the hallway, lured out by hunger, perhaps. She ignores Mom's tentative smile, makes a beeline for the fridge, and pulls out the bottle of filtered water, pouring herself a glass. "Since you were not burdened with siblings, you're free to adopt mine."

"Low, Martina," I scoff, weathering the look she sends me just fine.

Mom clears her throat as she puts dinner in the oven, like she has something to say. It dies before it can reach her mouth when Martina turns a glare onto her, full force. That's apparently all it takes for Mom's resolve to go shivering back into a corner, and I honestly don't blame her. She's not used to this. She hasn't run up against it as much as I have, but that's entirely of her own doing.

Why do I have to keep reminding myself?

Dad bops out of his office, the condition book for Belmont's fall meet open in one hand and a stack of paperwork in the other. His glasses have slipped down his nose, and he's not paying any attention at all to the stalemate happening in the kitchen. When he looks up, he pins his attention on Leo and lifts the book.

"New horses, new races to consider," he says, and Martina rolls her eyes so hard I can feel her disdain fill the room, reaching out to strangle him. Dad acts like he doesn't notice, since that's the smartest move to make right now, and plops the book and papers in front of Leo.

"Study up," he advises. "We've got a fleet of horses to start tomorrow, and the majority are past starters."

"Yes, sir," Leo says, like the kiss-up I always knew he was, and picks up the condition book as though he actually intends to read it cover-to-cover. A bubble of disappointment rises up my throat, since Dad never throws the condition book at me with expectations to pick a race. I've only been playing Leo's part since June, being there every day, but then what am I supposed to expect? I haven't been able to commit fully to the barn, with my Jericho application still floating unfinished in my computer. My thoughts are on Beck, Kali, and college. I have bigger things to think about than frustrate myself over my father's favoritism.

If I want the assistant trainer gig that Leo seems lined up so easily for, I'll actually have to start doing something about it.

Like commit. Fully.

Bri has been on me non-stop about NYU, and I've held fast to this fiction I'm still applying when I haven't been able to say a word about Jericho. Applications are due by early December for spring semester, and I've tortured myself through so many essays about my passions in life, influential female characters in fiction, embarrassing moments that have made me stronger, times I've found my voice—whatever that means. No wonder I didn't do this last year—the whole process makes my stomach hurt. I wish I had Bri here to help, which is a non-starter. And I can't vent to her about it because then I'll have to experience her disappointment that it's not going to be NYU; it can't be. All of our big plans are no longer just deferred, but dead.

My phone buzzes again, Bri's text floating on its face.

You've got your application in, right?

It's like she has some scary sixth sense.

Working on it.

I push away from the kitchen island wordlessly, leaving my family and our unexpected houseguest to the discomfort of waiting for dinner to bake. My messy room greets me at the top of the stairs. Shady is curled up on the unmade bed like a black throw pillow, ribcage rising and falling in sleep. I grab my laptop and fall onto the bed. Shady stretches and yawns, goes straight back to sleep as I open up my browser, which takes me immediately to my last viewed page—Jericho College.

A horse leaps across the website—the equestrian studies program on full display. For a second, I'm wildly envious of Madeline bringing Cricket to *college*. Being able to immerse yourself that way—of course that's what Madeline would do. Of course.

The tab for NYU sits next to Jericho. I click on it, looking over the half-finished application I haven't been able to convince myself to totally trash. It's gigantic. This has been my baby ever since I came back from North Carolina with Beck, and it's still nowhere close to done. The sheer magnitude of it seeps out of the computer, hits me with all of its unspoken promises. The city, the people, the crush of noise and smells, the temptation of being close to my people, who are so far away from my horses.

Falling back in my pillows, I shift back to the Jericho website, to the horse leaping over my nearly done application. I read through everything I've written, wondering if this doesn't make me a horrible friend, a horrible girlfriend, choosing the horses over human beings I care about. Maybe I'm doing what Mom would do, but then maybe I'm also doing this for myself, not anyone else.

This is for me. Me and Kali.

Scrolling to the bottom of the page, I hit submit and watch the page blink to white. A message pops up to let me know I've gone and done what I didn't think possible only a month ago.

"Thank you for submitting your application for admission to Jericho College!"

My heart is beating way too fast, and I close the laptop, making myself take a few deep breaths. Shady cracks her eyes open, watches me out of the narrow slits. I pull her into my lap and tell myself to calm down. It's only college. It's only my entire future. It's just one decision in a life full of giant decisions. What's to worry about? If I don't get in, NYU is still waiting for me, off in the city. And there's always the track, offering up all of its real world opportunities.

The tantalizing smell of enchiladas wafts into my room, tugging me out of myself. It's the gentlest of reminders that not everything is as it should be, and I shouldn't forget it if I don't want to experience whiplash on my way back down to the kitchen. As if to remind me, Martina yells up the stairs.

"July! Dinner! Now!"

I wince as Shady abandons me with a quick leap, a rake of back claws on my knees, and runs out of the room with her tail in the air.

"July!"

"Okay!" I shout back, climbing off the bed and putting my laptop back on my desk, where it looks right at home in the chaos of clutter. Framed photos of Mom, Martina, and me cluster along the shelves. Printed post positions for Santa Anita pile up on the surface, Mom's name highlighted in yellow. It's almost jarring to realize this isn't my life anymore, not really.

Not when Mom is standing right downstairs.

"Juls!"

"Okay!" I shout back, and turn to step into my new life.

∼◡∽

Two weeks later, the track moves giant heaters into Barn 27 on the day of final breezes before the Breeders' Cup. All the big names are out on the training track, being put through the motions under exercise riders or the jockeys who will ride them on the big day. There's a crackle of excitement in the air, anticipation. In a couple of days, the rigs will come for the horses. Those rigs will take them to JFK, and giant cargo planes will ship them across the country to Arcadia, California, where they'll all race under palm trees in the shadow of snow-capped mountains.

Lighter, Galaxy, and Star are going. They're peaking—utterly ready for the trip. We just have to breeze them first, but that doesn't involve me. I'm needed elsewhere, on other horses.

Barn 27 is nearly full. The transformation from dwindling, private Blackbridge barn to packed, public stable is mostly complete. Now it bustles with energy, with grooms and hot walkers, exercise riders coming in and out with horses hot and steaming from the track. There's a week left in the meet, and I can see my breath in the morning cold as I tack up Feather in the light of the barn fluorescents. The filly flicks her black-tipped ears back at me, monitoring me closely. I'm still new to her, even after two weeks of riding her every morning. She gives me the evil eye of distrust every time I come into her stall with the saddle.

Next to her, Betty the Goat bleats.

"She'll be fine," I tell Betty, who blinks big brown eyes at me. I pat the filly on the shoulder and untie her from the hook in the stall, turning her around to find Beck leaning against the stall opening.

A flutter starts up in my chest at the sight of him, because it's been too long. Two weeks too long. I take one look at Beck's bed-messed light brown hair and sagging jeans, knowing he just got out of bed, pulled on dirty clothes, and dragged himself here while still half-asleep. A screen-printed image of a unicorn peeks out from underneath his jacket, the words *Don't stop believing!* cheerfully written across it.

The first thing he does is look quizzically down at Betty.

"A goat?" he asks, because he's been city-bound with never-ending classes and a chronic inability to wake up early enough for works, so knowing about Betty? Not so much.

Betty the Goat shimmies underneath the stall guard and lifts onto her hind legs, firmly butting Beck in the hip. He yelps and sidesteps, which is enough to wring a laugh out of me. Beck's presence fills me with a sad kind of optimism; like he's here, so I should be thrilled. I try to nip that feeling in the bud. It doesn't work at all, because it's already blossomed, become an encroaching worry.

"Goats happen sometimes," I tell him through the smile that spontaneously appears on my face anyway, despite all the uncertainty that eats away at me. It's like treacherous magic, there unbidden and insistent on staying, wiping the problems away even as I have to remind myself that city-bound Beck won't be around much until winter break. That's a fact I'll have to live with if we keep doing this, like all the others I can't seem to make sense of.

"I wish someone had told me," Beck says, pulling the hem of his jacket out of Betty's chewing mouth. "I would have worn something nicer for her to gnaw on."

And just like that my grin falls at the edges, because I don't want to allow him that kind of passive-aggression. "You're free to visit whenever you want," I tell him, wondering if he even remembers casually forbidding me from ever visiting him in the city. "It's an open door policy around here. Just in case you've forgotten."

He gives me this blank look I've come to understand is his attempt to veer away from understanding what I'm saying. Like if he feigns ignorance, there's nothing wrong. Nothing needs to be addressed.

"You may not realize this, Juls, but I have a deep yearning to visit the barn while being unmolested by a goat at the same time," he says, pulling his jacket out of Betty's mouth while deftly stepping around everything I've put between us.

I just stare at him, amazed.

"Seriously, July."

"Honestly, Beckett," I mimic through a sigh, leading Feather up to him and undoing the stall guard, trying to walk past him and failing because he grabs me by my waist, pulling me until I'm resting there against him with Feather at my back.

"Hey," he says against my hair, a soft tinge to his voice when I know he feels bad about something and is trying to make it right. "I know I'm not around enough."

It's not exactly an apology, because Beck hasn't been known to throw those around. It's also not a promise that things will change, that I'll get an invite into his world on the other side of the river—the one I know absolutely nothing about. It's just a statement of fact, simple, to the point, out there so we can stare at it and agree not to touch it because it's too messy to unravel and fix. I don't even know what to say except lean into him a little harder, let him know I've heard him.

Feather crowds close to us, inserting herself into the scene and breathing warmly into our necks. Beck groans, the moment broken.

"Horses," he sighs, shaking his head at Feather as I lift myself off of him and lead the filly into the aisle. "Speaking of, where's the devil horse?"

"Already on his way down to the track," I tell him. "Mom is firmly planted in the saddle."

Beck nods. "Have I mentioned this is weird? Your mom on my

horse?"

"At least a dozen times," I say. "I give you credit for continually refusing to believe this is happening."

"I felt better with Pilar on him, honestly," he says, giving me a leg up onto Feather when I wordlessly turn and lift my foot, wiggling it at him.

"Pilar still has her arm in a cast," I say, settling in the saddle and gathering Feather's reins. The filly heaves a big breath of air, ribcage rising and falling. "Then there might be rehab," I continue. "I'd say she'll be back by December, at the earliest."

I try not to feel too guilty as I say it, because it was a fall off of Kali that broke Pilar's arm, knocking her off of rides for who knows how long. For a jockey, riding is life. It's what they do. Not riding is sitting around, unemployable and functionally disabled. I know it wasn't really Kali's fault Pilar is grounded, but I miss seeing her every day. Now that Mom is riding Lighter—has been around the entire Belmont meet without talk of going back to California—I worry. I want Pilar to have a place here when she's riding again.

More to the point, I don't want Mom to push her out. Pilar already can't stand coming to the track when she can't ride. The last time I saw her was weeks ago, when she was on her way out, insisting the whole place made her jumpy with need.

"Well, the good news is I own all of Lighter," Beck says. "When she comes back, send her to me. I'll have her risking her neck on him in no time flat."

"You say the nicest things," I tell him, leaning over Feather's shoulder. The filly halts by the gap in the training track's outer rail, pricking her ears at the activity and snorting milky breaths into the air.

"I realize." Beck puts a hand on the filly's neck and kisses me. "Just think how lucky you are."

I laugh and nudge Feather onto the track, pushing Beck to the back of my mind and the filly to the forefront.

Feather moves lightly down the outside rail, walking with an airy lift to her steps as she jigs under me, mane fanning up off her red-brown neck. The training track is a hive of activity, horses blowing out dragon-breath snorts as they go slipping by through the October mist. The filly lowers her head and does a happy plunge, kicking out her hind legs in an exuberant celebration at the freedom to move, to run.

"In a minute," I tell her, lifting her out of another head-dipping plunge and setting my heels to her sides, asking for a systematic jog.

Feather lifts her head, tucking her chin in toward her chest, her tail going up and her legs settling into that old two-beat rhythm. I lift off her back, because it's easier for me not to have to post my way across the track.

Ahead of me, I see Lighter's pale blond tail slip through the mist like a silver wisp. Mom's electric pink safety vest materializes next. The colt's head is up, eager to jump into something. They're warming up for the breeze, still beating through a jog before they'll turn around and warm up going the right way around the track.

Feather pricks her ears at the colt, shifting her attention to Lighter before she diverts it to the sudden materialization of a breezing horse on the rail. She spooks—hard—skittering to the left and then rearing up on her hind legs. I grab a hunk of mane as she comes down and twists, like she's preparing to bolt in the opposite direction. I pull her around, turning her in a circle and pushing her forward, getting her attention back on business.

Which is not easy, let me tell you. She's a jumping mass of nerves, her head craned nearly to my face on the way around the turn.

I let her shift into a canter, pull her into the bend in the rail, and make her think about something else other than the horses in the mist. One thing I've learned about this filly in the past two weeks is she's nervous—always watching out for something she can't see and overreacting when she finally sees it. Doesn't matter if it's a real threat or not. If it's moving, Feather will be taking off in the opposite direction.

Which means I'm always on my toes when I'm on her.

I turn the filly around on the backstretch and cue her into a canter, taking her down the middle of the track while leaving the inside open for horses breezing down the rail. The fog thickens in front of me, so suddenly milky white around us I can only see a few horse-lengths ahead of me, just enough to keep the track open and dangerous enough for a filly like Feather to freak out at the drop of a hat.

But that's on me—her potential freak out, that is.

At the finish pole, I push Feather into a gallop. She lifts, stretches, goes into flight mode. I bend just so at the knees, feel the pull of wind on my clothes and on my arms as I feel the filly's mouth all the way down the reins. There's a rumble of thundering hooves underneath me, each slip-slide of muscle rubbing through my jeans and boots as I bend over the filly's withers and sight through her ears down the track.

Feather huffs, pricks her ears as I ask for her to change leads in the turn. She hesitates a fraction, just as Lighter goes blowing by on my inside, all golden sheen and electric pink.

Instead of changing leads, Feather leaps. I tighten my fingers on the reins, shifting my weight back as she jumps again and lands in full gallop, chasing after Lighter in a way that looks like she's trying to run him down but is definitely more panicked craziness.

"Whoa," I try, tugging her back down as she runs flat into the backstretch. She pops her hind legs up, letting me know she feels the weight I'm putting on the reins and isn't in favor of it. I ride through one, two bucks.

It's the third that puts me on the ground.

I land with a plume of dirt, the air squeezing right out of me, leaving my lungs burning. The milky mist closes around Feather, and I dimly wonder if anyone even saw the fall, if the alarm for a loose horse will even sound.

It doesn't. That's just great. I roll over onto my knees and sit up so I can yell.

"Loose horse!"

I scream it so loudly my voice breaks, snapping like a twig under a boot. I swallow and scream it again, getting my shaky legs underneath me to stand. Sitting on the track in the mist is about the stupidest thing someone can do around here. I need to get off the track. I see the outside rail's dirty white beam in the shifting fog so I head for it just as the alarm blares to life.

"July?"

I turn around, peering into the drifting white when Lighter appears, the fog parting for him in a sweep that curls back in on itself as he trots toward me. Mom nods to the outer rail.

"The gap is just up a ways," she says, tugging Lighter into a walk. The colt is sweat-stained, his mane flicked back off his forehead and froth around his lips. A white ring of happy excitement circles his eyes, all the morning's action written in the ways he rolls them. Then Mom seems to put two and two together.

"Where's Feather?"

"You tell me?" I ask. "Here I thought she'd be a piece of cake, and turns out she's worse than Lighter."

Lighter side-steps right into me, Mom's boot digging into my shoulder. Then he gives a hard thwack of his tail, blond strands whipping through the air and raking down my arm. I wince and I push him right back. The colt yanks his head up, swivels his ears around as if he expected better behavior from me.

Yeah, right. Keep dreaming, buddy.

"There you are."

I hear Dad's voice, disembodied, coming from the gap. I squint through the fog, seeing only outlines at first and then worried faces. Dad, Leo, and Beck stand at the rail, identical expressions mirroring over them. Curiosity, concern. Mainly, I wonder what Leo and Beck have been talking about since I set foot on the track. Beck's inability to get to the track has put off their introduction, which has to work in my favor because god only knows what those two will get up to together.

For now they're just standing next to each other, giving me twin looks.

There's a group of horses leaving through the gap, and we have to wait our turn just as a thunder of hooves on the inside of us announces Feather—a bay streak cutting through fog—and an outrider surging quick next to her on the outside. Twisting around to keep my eyes on them, I see the outrider snag her reins as they're swallowed up by white.

Beck whistles.

"Got a live one there," he says to no one in particular. I completely agree.

"Makes Lighter seem half sane in comparison," I say, ducking under the rail.

"Those are fighting words," Beck says, brushing some of the track dirt off my shirt. "We all know Lighter's the problem child of the barn, July. Don't steal his thunder."

"I wish it weren't the case, but my bruises tell another story." I stretch, feeling my back muscles protest. It wasn't too long ago that Kali dumped me in the dirt, and now Feather. I'm way overdue for a broken bone at this point.

"What hurts?" Beck asks.

"Can I say everything and still be taken seriously later?" I ask.

Beck tilts his head at me. "I think you know better than to ask that question, Juls."

I groan, and he pulls me into a hug, wrapping his arms around my shoulders. "There, there," he says, like he's almost offering real comfort. "I'm sure you'll be back on Lighter in no time."

I snort, but don't make any move to push him off. Beck takes that opportunity to duck down, pressing his lips against mine. A soft, feel better kiss. This is the real comfort. Sometimes, in my blind stumbling to figure out how we're really going about this, it's hard to know for sure. I lean into him, letting his warmth sink into me. Then I catch Leo looking at us like he can't quite compute what's going on.

"Have something to share with the class, Leo?" I ask him, catching Beck's mouth quirk.

"I have been gone way too long," Leo says, shaking his head and rubbing his eyes, like proof of my not being twelve anymore is tiring for him. That's fine with me, because living with him has been tiring since the first second it started happening. Sharing a bathroom with Leo is about as horrifying as it sounds. I'm forced to live with all of his boy products, which make his hair as glossy as Star's coat before a race.

Mom walks Lighter off the track, heading back to Barn 27 as the outrider arrives with Feather. The filly is all wild eyes, face shot through with suspicion.

"Someone missing a horse?" the outrider calls to us.

"Thanks, Tom," Dad tells the outrider, thumping Leo on the shoulder in wordless command to retrieve Feather. Leo scurries under the rail and takes Feather's bridle, walking her after Lighter. Feather has her head craned up, eye rolling down to give Leo a thorough look over. Lighter is doing a fast jig, head twisted around so he can keep an eye on Feather. The two look like they could both fall apart at any second.

"Quite the pair." Beck breaks the silence, and Dad just shakes his head.

"We'll send her out with a partner next time to get her mind on business. Next horse, Juls," he says, which lets me know it's time to stop complaining and get back to work. We've got a flight to California in two days, and a whole barn full of horses to work in the meantime.

Which means there's no time to even think, just the way I like it.

Chapter Five

California is all sun, which pours down out of the sky with an intense yellow brightness that layers over Santa Anita Park like a vibrant blanket. The turf course glows emerald. The palm trees pop and sway back and forth, rustling against a brilliant blue sky that doesn't seem to understand what clouds are, since I've not seen one up there since we arrived. Acting as a backdrop are the San Gabriel Mountains—a hazy range of blue-green peaks that crawl toward the track in gentle, upside-down v's.

I take a deep breath, matching Maggie perfectly. My mare has had her ears pricked all morning, her nostrils flared and an extra jig to her step. I can't help but feel like I've been doing the same, eager to inhale it all in one giant gulp of air.

Next to me, Mom laughs, leaning forward to run a hand over Star's mane. The big near-black colt is finished with his jog, but doesn't look quite convinced of that fact. He swings his hindquarters around and jigs underneath Mom, unwilling to come down to a simple walk.

"I knew you'd love it here," she says to me. "You've got

California girl written all over you."

"Seriously?" I ask, unable to hide the disbelief that crosses my face in one quick flash. Besides, California girl? Hardly. I have New York in my blood, and it's not as though California has been very kind to me. No matter how beautiful it is, California has never been a subject of sweet feelings. It housed my wayward mother for four years, after all.

Can't think very kindly about a place after that.

Still, Mom is beaming—utterly in her element—and I can see she's really back on her home turf. She's comfortable here, with the sun absorbing into her shiny black hair and soaking into her honey dark skin. I just have to look at her and feel like I'm getting a sunburn.

So no, definitely not a California girl. I'm more the girl who agonized over California for four years and has no idea what to do now that I'm here.

"I'm happy you're here, July," Mom turns that beaming smile on me, and I feel the megawatts of it more warmly than the sun. She's been like this ever since we got here, like *finally* she's got her family here with her. Like she always dreamed and never once tried to make happen.

No wonder Martina stayed in New York. This is getting a little hard to swallow, even for me, but I don't call her on it. I just press my lips into a smile and tap Maggie with my heels, hustling us past Clockers' Corner along the outside rail at the head of the home-stretch, where Beck immediately catches my eye.

Beck, who should be back in New York, is here, in California.

My mouth drops open, and I catch his grin through the shifting crowd.

"What are you doing here already?" I ask, lifting in the saddle to see him over Star's head. Beck wasn't planning on getting in until later in the week, just in time to fall asleep before the first of the big races start up on Friday. I'd come to accept that as basic fact, and now here he is, acting like this was the plan the whole time.

"Getting coffee," is his response, which he knows isn't the one I'm looking for. I shoot him a look as we walk past. He grins at me and lifts a coffee cup in salute to our passing by.

I settle back into the saddle, narrowly missing Mom's knowing smile.

"Don't start," I warn her, and she shakes her head, like she would never assume.

"Wouldn't even try, July," she tells me as we wind our way through the Santa Anita backside, which is all dirt paths and dingy barns—similar to nearly every other barn area I've ever visited.

"It's just," Mom starts, and then stops when I shoot her a glare. She chews the insides of her cheeks a second before she turns back to me, confidence renewed because this is California. What can't she do here?

"I hope you realize he's in love with you," she tells me, the sincerity in her voice throwing me for a loop. "Probably since the summer with the shampoo."

Maggie lurches to a halt, confused by my sudden insistence on acting like dead weight. Star dances a pirouette away from us, and I have to shock myself into moving Maggie forward, bumping her with my heels.

"That's . . ." I start, having no idea how to finish. Insane? Maybe the truth? I don't know where Beck lands on this issue because he certainly hasn't told me and I haven't asked. I don't know where

I land on this issue because I'm too afraid to look. People seem to leave so easily, whether or not you love them. Probably more often if you do. Maybe it's better not to ever know.

"You guys are playing at something," Mom says. "Your father brought me up to speed. I think we both know he has no helpful pointers, so I just want you to know—"

"Oh my god," I groan, closing my eyes and letting Maggie guide us for a few seconds down the path to Barn 89. She knows the way better than I do anyway.

"If you need to talk to someone," Mom continues on, like this is normal and appreciated. I don't need a relationship talk from my mother of all people, the woman who decided to skip out of my life before relationships were vague things I might have one day. I open my eyes, cast a sideways glance at the blush rushing up her skin. Good. At least that makes two of us who are deeply embarrassed right now.

"About . . ." Mom trails off, waving one gloved hand in the air like she can conjure the words without speaking them and I'll immediately understand, saving us both from this conversation. "About relationships, and boys, and . . . consequences."

"Consequences?" I nearly shout, and she immediately ducks her head. "What are you even talking about?"

"You know what I'm talking about," she starts back at me, her honey-colored skin flaming to pink along her cheeks, like she's flushed from the work when that isn't it at all. "Don't make me say it."

"You're my *mom*," I tell her. "And I'm not an idiot. I know what happens in relationships. *Consequences* is not how I would have put it. We haven't even done *that* yet, so you don't need to worry about becoming a grandparent any time soon."

"Well," Mom huffs, deflating in the saddle. "I just notice how happy he seems to make you, and how little he's genuinely with you, Juls. I want to make sure that *you're* sure, is all. If you've talked at all about what you are to each other before making that kind of commitment."

"Commitment," I echo. She sighs.

"Relationships involve work, July," she insists. "I'm sure you've figured that out by now. You're incredibly cute together, but sometimes it looks like you've swallowed a frog when he's around."

"I have no idea what that means," I tell her.

"It means don't be afraid to tell him how you feel," she says. "Too many things end because no one is willing to be honest, and I don't want to see that happen to you. I'd like to see you be happy."

"I am happy," I say, trying the words on for size. They're stilted coming out of my mouth, like there's something missing. I must look like I've swallowed a frog again, because Mom pats me on the knee as we sidle up to Barn 89.

"Talk," she advises, pinning me with those dark brown eyes of hers. "What do you have to lose?"

She bounces off Star, leaving me holding onto his bridle as Gus comes out of the barn to collect the colt. Mom pulls her saddle off his back and heads for her next ride, leaving me behind with Gus, who looks up at me and squints.

"What's with you?" he asks. I glare down at him.

"What do you mean?"

"You just look like—"

"I swallowed a frog?"

He tilts his head at me. "Is that a reference I'm supposed to understand?"

I let out a breath.

"Nope," I say, jumping off of Maggie and leading her past him into the barn, suddenly eager to get out of the sun. When did it get this hot? "Not at all."

∿

The Clockers' Corner is part breakfast nook, part gossip ring. It butts up against the track, its happy green table umbrellas shading trainers discussing potential rides with jockeys' agents, gamblers studying the day's *Daily Racing Form* with cigarettes perched between stained fingers, and curious onlookers straining for a view of the big Breeders' Cup horses. Anyone who watches the Santa Anita morning works and wants the inside scoop—or a simple coffee—heads right here.

Since it's the Breeders' Cup, The Corner is packed up to the rail and I have to elbow my way up to Beck, who hands me a paper cup of coffee. I take it thankfully, the warm bitterness sliding over my tongue and down my throat. I practically groan against the lid, while Beck narrows his eyes at me.

"Calm down, jitterbug," he says, a smile quirking up his mouth as he watches me. "It's not *that* good."

"You haven't been here since five in the morning," I tell him, swallowing another mouthful. "It's amazing."

"Guess I'll have to take your word for it," he says, watching me with a sparkle in his eyes. I lick my lips and look away, down at the coffee cupped in my hands.

"I didn't think you were coming in today," I say, pushing the words out there. See, I can talk to Beck. Even if they're the least charged words I can find.

"Late last night, actually," he says, and I tilt my head at him, wondering at his ability to sneak into Los Angeles without telling me. "Figured this could be my first and last Breeders' Cup as an owner, so who am I to miss the post-position draw?"

"Getting nervous, huh?" I accuse, poking him in the shoulder, meeting hard muscle through a worn out T-shirt advertising propane, like it was something he found for free one day and decided to keep forever.

He laughs, shaking his head. "You cut to the heart of things, don't you?"

"You own the only undefeated colt in the Juvy field," I say, catching sight of the front of the *Form* as one of the gamblers rifles through pages, the front story a big color image of Lighter, collected and ears pricked forward as he flies across the finish line at Belmont. I remember Dad talking to the reporter for the story, shooing me away from his office while Lighter stood outside Barn 27 and abjectly refused to load into the rig that would take him to the airport.

"If you weren't nervous, something would be wrong."

Beck plays with the cardboard cozy wrapped around his paper cup, twisting it all the way around as he nods and lets out a breath. Finally he smiles at me. "Good," he says, "because I didn't come here early for Lighter, you know?"

"Do I?" I ask, my mouth going tacky. I swallow around my sticky tongue and try to look as though I'm not shivering out of my skin. I don't know why talking about us makes me so incredibly petrified, why I can't seem to wrap my mouth around words that need to be said. Mom is right—I need to talk, but all I can do is stand

and stare, waiting for the universe to make my decisions for me.

"I hope so," Beck says, looking out at the busy track and then back at me, like he's antsy before he slides a hand over my hip, pulling me up to him despite the crush of people.

"Juls," he says, low enough for only me to hear. "I came here for you. That's obvious, right?"

The heat of the day seems to condense on my spine, superheating until my entire skin seems to burst with a rosy shiver when my body presses up against his. My initial reaction?

Want. I want to roll around in this feeling forever, and Beck seems happy enough to indulge me if the way he's looking at me is any indication at all. I think I've figured out enough facets of him to know exactly what he's thinking.

"Let's get out of here," he says, leaning into me and hand tightening on my hip. Another shot of warmth goes gliding down to my fingertips. We're so close, hemmed in by the rail on one side and people on all the others. No one at all is paying attention to us, which has to be the upside of Santa Anita. If we did this at Belmont, the whole place would probably collectively roll its eyes.

Here we're close to anonymous, even if we've got the favorite in the Breeders' Cup Juvenile—one of the most anticipated races of the whole event.

Suddenly, Mom's advice comes roaring back into my thoughts. *Love. Talk.* I can feel the urge to say something come bubbling out of my throat, because I know she's right. But when the words get to the tip of my tongue I swallow them back down, afraid they're going to come out like a garbled mess. Afraid whatever I do manage to say will be met with one of Beck's raised eyebrows—and not the good kind.

The *consequences* kind, where everything ends because he's the owner's son and I'm the trainer's daughter and what the hell were we even thinking?

Beck looks down at me, and I desperately need to figure out what to do that is not falling all over myself trying to tell him what I need to say.

So instead I say nothing, and lift up to his mouth. His lips part against mine, hand lifting to dive into my track-tangled hair. I pull back before he can get caught up in it, bite back the words on my tongue, and replace them with something else.

Something less daring, but no less true.

"Yeah," I say, breathy. "Let's get out of here."

"Four hours?" Beck asks, aghast. Like if I'd told him it took all afternoon to stick a bunch of numbered rocks in a bottle and shake them out one after the other until each horse has a spot in the starting gate of eleven races then there's no way he would have come to LA early.

Except, of course, there's me. He came here for me. The feeling is still warm and fuzzy in my chest, threatening to overwhelm me. Beck Delaney is willing to sit through four hours of Breeders' Cup post selections because he wanted to be with me. That's something. It's a light at the end of this tunnel we've been in all autumn.

I smile—just a little—and lift the thick book the officials provided us several days ago, its glossy purple cover glistening in the hotel lights. Within it is all one could ever possibly need to know about the Breeders' Cup, down to the times for sunset and sunrise.

It truly takes attention to detail to a new level.

"Even better, it starts in about two hours," I say, checking the glowing alarm clock on the nightstand as I sit cross-legged on Beck's king-sized bed. He's sprawled out next to me, feet dangling off the bed and arms covering his eyes. This is where we ended up after leaving the track, laughing and talking, kissing and breathing each other in because when else do we have the time? "Then they interview the trainers for an eon about strategy. On the plus side, there will be hors d'oeuvres and an open bar."

Beck groans.

"What do you think the chances are you can flirt your way into procuring champagne?" I ask, still studying the book.

"I'm having a change of heart," he says. "Let's stay here instead."

My snort of indignation tells him all he needs to know. Then I poke his thigh to drive the point home.

"No, sir. You represent Lamplighter, therefore you will be there. If I have to dress you myself and drag you."

He laughs. "Everything you just said sounds utterly compelling. How exactly do you imagine you're going to pull that off?"

I shoot him a look over the book. "Do you doubt my commitment?"

"No," he shrugs, "but you're a girl, Juls. I think I outweigh you by at least fifty pounds."

I scoff. "Like I would let a little thing like weight difference get in my way."

He pulls his arms from his face, pushing himself up on his elbows.

"Juls," he says, like he greatly pities me. "You keep talking like you have even the slightest of chances. We both know that's not the case."

I study him appraisingly, then slap the book closed, dropping it by our legs.

"Beckett, you act like there's going to be some sort of physical altercation," I say, sidling next to him and bracing two hands on his chest, throwing a leg over his hips and resting gently in his lap. "I think you're failing to take certain things into account, don't you?"

His mouth drops open, just slightly, and I smile winningly because *gotcha, Beck*. It's just too easy sometimes.

But then his hands come down, grip my waist, and I shriek as he flips us over. My head hits the mountain of pillows, the book goes flying off the bed and thunks against the wall. Through the screen of hair that has gotten into my face I see Beck there, grinning like a loon.

"What were you saying again?" he asks above me. "Something about a physical altercation?"

"You wish," I tell him.

"I do, actually," he says, so bald-faced that blood rushes up to my skin, goes singing down my spine to pool in my belly, burning hard enough to make me squirm. He puts a hand on my stomach to stop my wriggling, making a face like this is paining him.

"You are way more devious than I ever gave you credit for," he tells me, even though that's not what I'm trying to be, not really. I just want to figure out what we're doing, drum up the ability to spit the words out between us when every time I try I only come up empty.

But the way Beck's fingers clench on my waist sparks a thought. Actions speak louder than words, apparently. I can't believe it never occurred to me before.

I don't have to *say* anything.

Hooking my fingers into the front of his shirt, I tug just enough for him to understand what I want without having to voice it. This isn't rocket science, and I know what he wants because he at least said as much. I'm a little jealous of that, actually. The ability to just let yourself admit what you feel and wait for a reaction.

Well, if Beck is waiting for a reaction, he doesn't have to wait long. He falls into me, and I meet him halfway, pushing up and meeting his mouth. He drags his hands up from my waist to press into the bed on either side of my head, becoming a solid weight of warmth and muscle as he hovers above me. The hovering won't do, so I wriggle my way up against him.

Beck makes a noise against my lips that makes me smile before he pushes back onto his heels and looks down at me, mouth slack and eyes hooded. He sucks in a deep breath, and maybe I am pretty devious because I didn't know I was capable of this.

But then what is he doing, just sitting there?

"Okay?" I ask.

"Yeah," he says and then shakes his head, like he's at a loss for words. "I just . . ."

And silence. He stares at me like he's trying to work something out, torn between two very different options. I sit up, my legs tangled around his, wondering how hard this needs to be. Here we are, utterly alone, behind a locked door, on top of a giant bed, with two hours to spare. Could there ever be a better time?

I kiss him, feel his lips part against mine. His hands come up to frame my face, slip around into my hair. My heart is thumping rapidly, my fingers tingling as I press them against his chest. He pushes deeper, and I let him in, opening and thrilling and so willing to let everything fall back to the bed that I'm stunned when he pulls back.

There and gone, just like that.

Beck clambers off the bed, nearly falling off in his haste, and I sit there looking at him with surging adrenaline spiking into the incredibly embarrassed, what-is-even-happening range. Seriously, what *is* happening? Since when does Beck ever back down from a challenge? This isn't even a challenge. It's practically an invitation, and he's declined by purposefully falling off the bed.

Beck gets his feet underneath him and pushes his hands into his hair like he doesn't know what to do with them. His disheveled shirt rides up past the waistline of his jeans, showing off a narrow strip of boxers and an even narrower strip of skin.

I feel like an utter idiot.

"Shower," he says to me. I blink.

"Not together," he continues rapidly, and I narrow my eyes. "Separately. In our separate rooms. Then track."

"We'd be early," I say, pointing at the discarded book laying haphazardly on the floor. "The book says—"

"I remember what the book says," he interrupts me, and I glare at him, the realization sinking into me like a weight dropping in my stomach.

"Are you . . . kicking me out?" Those are words I can say, out loud, because I'm so aghast by what's happening. He opens and closes his mouth, which means his silence might as well say yes.

Shit.

"Fine." I say, anger flowing up so fast I have to get out of this room before I say something I'll wind up regretting. I scoot off the bed and pick up the book in one swift movement. "I guess I'll go get ready by myself. Should be grand."

He lets out a breath, like what I've just said is a relief even when he knows I'm pissed. He couldn't not know I'm pissed. He's known me too long to pretend otherwise.

I go to the door, Mom's advice swirling back down to cloud my thoughts.

That boy loves you. You need to talk to him.

With my hand on the door handle, I shoot a tentative look back, but Beck isn't looking at me. He's staring at the floor, hands on his narrow hips, like he's trying to work something out that's far too complicated for him. When he senses that I'm staring at him, he looks up.

"Juls," he starts, voice like a sigh.

I jump, not wanting to hear it. Because what if Mom's wrong?

Then I'll have made a fool out of myself. This whole thing would have been two people having fun, and I would have been the idiot making it more than what it was because I have yet to realize I'm just one in a long line of girls hopelessly attached to Beck Delaney. Who am I to think I'm any different? I'm a fling at the end of summer petering out under the pressures of real life, under the understanding that it was never going to keep going at all.

Like all the others, apparently.

"Actually," I jump over what he's about to say, bulldoze it in my attempt to put space between us. "Forget it. You're plenty capable of representing Lighter alone."

"Wait, what?" Beck asks, true astonishment lacing through his voice, his eyes widening. But how the hell can he think I'd just be okay with this decision? Does he not know me at all?

"I'm not going," I say, opening the door.

"Juls," he says, calling me back when I'm already halfway out of the room. "Wait. You know I want you at the draw. I didn't come here to—"

I stop, hand hard on the edge of the door as I look back at him. "No," I say between gritted teeth. "You don't want me *here*, so how could you possibly want me at the draw? I don't know what you want, but I do know you can't have this both ways. I'm either someone to you, or I'm not, Beck. I can't be both. So I'll make this simple. I don't want to be at the draw. Not right now, and not with you."

He looks like I've dropped a bomb at his feet, and maybe I have. Maybe this is me exploding. Beck swallows and doesn't say a word to stop me as I turn around and slip out of the hotel room. He doesn't call me back, doesn't say a damn word.

He just lets me go.

Chapter Six

The sun is just crawling over the mountains the next morning when Gus gives me a leg up onto Lighter. The colt erupts out of Barn 89 like the building's on fire and we all need to run for our lives. My foot finds a stirrup while I cling to the colt's mane in a death grip, planting my other boot in its iron. Gus has the reins in his fist, keeping Lighter tethered to reality if not the ground.

Honestly, I wish I was on Maggie this morning, but Mom is getting in last works on her other horses and, after all, *Lighter goes so nicely for July*. At least, that's what Mom said on her way to the big barns. The barns with racing's brand names that pop up in the Kentucky Derby year after year.

Those names.

So we're down a jockey this morning, and I'm the next best thing for Lighter's morning jog. Lighter, naturally, doesn't give a damn who's on him, even if it is his owner's maybe ex-girlfriend who can't seem to stop shivering. We're all extra weight, pressure on the reins, a nameless, faceless voice telling him what not to do.

Don't gallop clockwise, Lighter. Stop yanking my arms out of my sockets, Lighter. Maybe refrain from leaping into the air and flipping me over your shoulder, Lighter.

Lighter flicks his ears like chaotic satellite dishes as Gus leads us through the backside, the muscles under his tattooed arms bulging in effort to keep the colt straight and on all four hooves. I ride over Lighter's floating jig—not quite a walk, not quite a trot, just the happy dance of the hopelessly insane.

"You okay up there?" Gus asks me as the track comes into sight. Santa Anita is washed in yellow sun, horses peppering across the track in various stages of speed. The sound of hooves sinking into sand, striking the track in soft sighs and sharp bursts, makes Lighter even more of a trembling mess on our approach.

"Do I have a choice?" I ask, and Gus shoots me a wry smile.

"Fair point," he says, then slaps a hand against Lighter's muscled neck. "Give 'em hell."

He lets go, and Lighter bounds into an even trot before I have any time to ask. In any dressage arena, that would be met with an instant halt and a new ask—but this is the track. I'm just happy he didn't sideswipe anyone as he bounces his way down the furrowed dirt.

Jog in racetrack speak means *trot*. It's just an extended two-beat drumming around the track, designed to keep a horse fit until the next two-minute lick or breeze. Lighter is scheduled for once around before he gets his cool down and bath, slipping into a routine he knows so well that he could probably do it half asleep if there weren't people around to terrorize. What is life if not a steady succession of attempts to sink teeth into Gus's arm?

Lighter puts his head down and I bridge the reins, pressing

them into his withers so he can lean on himself instead of my hands. The colt does a steady one-two beat down the outside rail, acting professional up until there's something utterly scary but completely imaginary to panic about.

The second time Lighter skitters to the right and breaks into a riotous canter, I sigh and haul him back down.

"Cease," I hiss to the colt. Lighter flicks his ears back once and then brings them forward again, blowing hard at nothing and craning his head up high. We look like we're locked in a struggle for supremacy as we half-trot, half-lunge past the Clockers' Corner, where a few whistles greet us.

"Ride 'em, cowgirl!"

I grit my teeth, because I really don't need the commentary. Still, I swing a quick look to my left, find the rail utterly packed. Of course, there's Beck in the thick of it, leaning his forearms against the railing and keeping his face schooled to stillness as he watches me go by.

Because that's my life now. Get rejected by a boy, wake up and ride the same boy's colt. This is some sort of special hell, I swear.

Reddening, I pull my attention from the Clockers' Corner, from Beck altogether, because all I can see is his insistence that we not go that far, even though I *know* he wants to go that far. He said as much, after all. There's nothing like getting booted out of a hotel room after I've offered up everything, especially to Beck, the only person in the world who wanted all of me.

Or so I thought. Now all I can think about is the red hot flush of rejection.

And if he doesn't really want me, what is he doing?

What are *we* doing?

Lighter leaps, higher. His head twists around, and I see one white-ringed eye peering back at me like he's plotting my downfall. I put my heels to his sides and the colt explodes forward, taking off into the turn and into another lap that definitely wasn't planned, especially at speed.

There's a moment of gut-churning fear he's going to take me into the stream of horses coming onto the track, but even Lighter isn't so stupid. With a rain of dirt, he avoids a collision course, and I'm able to haul him to the side of the track, pulling him back down to a peppy walk that is less apocalyptic and more thrilled.

It's like Lighter's a toddler yelling *I want to do it again, Mom!*

"There's no way that's happening again," I tell him, and Lighter's ears sweep back, listening to me for half a second before he's back to surveying the track in all its brightening glory.

We're passing the Clockers' Corner again, Lighter's head bobbing up and down with each stride, like he's just oh-so proud of his ability to nearly get me killed, when I feel it.

Just the slightest bobble, like he's spending one too many thousandths of a stride favoring one leg over another. I frown down at him as a few more hoots tumble out of the Clockers' Corner.

I ignore the comments, letting myself sink into Lighter and shutting out the world as the colt jigs off the track. Outwardly, there doesn't seem to be anything wrong. Lighter is barely sweat-streaked. Barely blowing. Sure, he's still huffing from his excited tear around the far corner, but what horse wouldn't be? Especially Lighter.

Looking up, I catch Gus giving us a critical look. His arms are crossed over his chest, eyes narrowed in concentration as we come straight toward him. The second he opens his mouth, I really feel it. The colt takes one stilted stride and bobs his head, takes another and in that instant I'm off his back. When I bend to feel down his leg, intending to look for heat, Gus puts a hand on my arm, bringing me back up.

"Not here," is all he says to me, taking Lighter's reins and walking him back to Barn 89. Casting a look out at the track, at the teeming Clockers' Corner, I suddenly realize what he means. There are too many people watching, which means too many critical eyes on the favorite looking for weaknesses. There's money to be won or lost, and the favorite possibly coming up lame?

That's important information to have on the day before the race.

Spinning, I scurry into step behind Lighter. I can't drag my eyes away from his legs. There's barely any sign—although there wouldn't be much of one at a walk—and the longer I search for it the less obvious it seems. I try telling myself it could be nothing, just a little stiffness he's working his way through. Maybe he took a bad step on the turn, but that could be just as bad—a soft tissue injury or a bone bruise will end our year, no questions asked.

My heart starts to beat a little faster, and I jump when Beck jogs up next to me.

"Hey," he says, reaching out to touch my hand. I jerk away, and he stiffens, his jaw tightening as he backs off just enough to give me space and still ask his question. "What's the deal? Why aren't you up?"

I glance over at him distractedly, feeling my stomach clench.

"Don't know." I can afford him that much as we follow Gus into Barn 89.

The shedrow bursts with activity. It's not just our three horses here, after all. There are loads of runners in for the Breeders' Cup, and we lead Lighter into his stall to avoid blocking the busy aisle. We strip his tack, my saddle coming off in one fell swoop when Dad walks in the barn with Jorge and Galaxy, the big mare snorting and ready for the Distaff.

Dad takes one look at the situation and I see his face cloud over. Gone is the eager excitement that comes with the Breeders' Cup, replaced with an unspoken worry we're all clearly radiating. There's something wrong with Lighter. Exactly *what* remains a mystery.

What's worse? Maybe it's my fault, simply because he ran out on me in the turn. I try to tamp down on that impulse to blame myself. Horses are flighty—Lighter even more so—and easily damaged. If he can't run in the biggest race of his life because I couldn't hold his ridiculous self back from injury then that's all on me.

"What's happened?" Dad asks us as Gus swaps out the bridle for the colt's halter. Lighter throws his head up, meets the chain over his nose, and acquiesces, kicking a hind leg halfheartedly at the air.

"Didn't look good coming off the track," Gus says.

"Didn't feel right," I add, and Dad swings a look to me and lets out a whoosh of breath.

"Let's see it then," he says, motioning for Gus to take the colt out.

We follow the colt back outside, where Gus puts the colt through his paces. The whole backside seems to stop around Barn 89, and the back of my neck burns under the gaze of eyes on us as Lighter walks up and down the dirt path between barns.

Nothing.

"Pick it up," Dad says, watching the colt with the sort of intense scrutiny I feel coming from the rest of the backside. Gus tugs the lead shank once and picks up the pace. Lighter's head goes up, eyes rolling down at Gus as he bounces into a trot.

I see it. Just a slight tick in the colt's stride, like a split second of hesitation. Dad shakes his head and lifts a hand.

"That's enough," he says, and Gus pulls the colt back to a walk. Lighter rounds into the pressure on the chain wrapped over the noseband of the halter and slows to a halt, standing in the middle of the backside like a statue until he lifts his head and snorts, shooting us all a wild look, like he's saying, *what?*

"Soak the foot," Dad says to Gus, who's nodding silently, staring at the colt's hooves like they have some mysteries to give up. They do, actually, until we know what's wrong. "I'll get the vet out here for the full workup, but if it's the foot we might as well start now."

I suck in a breath.

"That mean what I think it means?" Beck asks me, sounding so blasé that my hackles rise fast enough for me to snap.

"It means we're not racing."

I know how I sound. Even if I didn't, the look Beck shoots me would tell me as much. But he wasn't the one riding Lighter when it happened. That was me, and to make matters worse I was distracted, thinking about Beck, and us, and about how I can't seem to get my feet underneath me while we stand on rocky ground.

That's on me, because I can't get my act together.

So Lighter not going in the Juvy? Also on me.

I just glare right back at Beck and stalk into the barn after Gus and Lighter, the colt holding his head low like he's bored with the whole thing, unaware anything has changed.

Unaware *everything* has changed.

∿

Normally, this is supposed to feel satisfying. The Breeders' Cup hums around me, the first day of races culminating in Galaxy Collision standing in the paddock while we wait for the lead up to the Distaff. A statue of Seabiscuit glows black in the middle of the outdoor walking ring, the pale yellow and green face of the Santa Anita grandstand stretching art deco lines behind us. The whole place looks like it has come perfectly manicured out of the 1940s, if not for the utterly modern crowd surging and lapping around the fences restricting it from the horses.

Our filly stands in the covered saddling paddock, gazing around at the goings on with curious, dark brown eyes. Galaxy barely moves a muscle as Dad tightens her overgirth, Leo on the other side of the filly to help the valet keep the saddle steady. Izzie holds the filly's lead, her two-toned hair swept into an intricate braid and her classic jeans swapped out for dress pants and a sleeveless shell. An apron with the filly's number on it drapes across her torso. Every so often, she sends me a sympathetic look because it's like the eagerness to be here has been sucked out of each of us.

Nearby, an NBC reporter is chatting with Beck about Lighter as the rest of his family clusters close. His dad, the great Lawrence Delaney, rests a hand on Beck's shoulder like he has to physically show his support. Beck's mom, Cynthia, and little sister, Olivia, stand to the side, their sweeping hats and perfectly done hair being used as a colorful background image. Beck's older brother,

Matthew, stands next to me, head bent toward his cell phone and eyes shaded with aviators. There's a small smile on his face, and he lets out a huffing laugh like he knows he shouldn't, but can't help himself.

"Your sister says I should bet your mom's horse," he tells me by way of explanation, still looking at the phone with that same smile firmly affixed to his face. "I'm fairly sure that's an insult."

"What did you do now?" I ask, still watching Galaxy, because the long-standing Martina and Matthew feud got boring ages ago.

Matthew sighs, even though he doesn't sound at all tired. It sounds far more satisfied than I would have expected. "Is there any one thing with Martina?"

"You're right," I nod. "It's really just a running list of grievances. She checks one off and adds one more. How she gets through her life is a mystery."

Matthew laughs, shrugging. "I keep inviting her to lunch. Call me an optimist."

"I'm starting to think you're as hopeless as she is."

"That's not far off the mark," he says, just as his phone starts to ring. "Ah, speak of the devil."

I raise an eyebrow, watching him saunter off to take the call, that smile still stretching, all Delaney boy who's pleased with something he's done. I narrow my eyes at this, trying to sniff out what doesn't seem right about it—besides a general sense of everything—when I hear Lighter's name.

"Like Rob said in the press conference this morning," Beck says to the reporter holding the microphone toward him queryingly, "the scans are clean. X-rays are clean. It looks like it could be minor, but with a horse like this you don't want to take your chances."

Damn right you don't, I think. You plop the horse in a stall and let him rest it out until he's better, which is exactly what the vet said. Stall rest. At least a month of it. And after that, we're staring down the long stretch of a New York winter. If Lighter runs by the end of January we'll be lucky.

The jockeys walk into the indoor paddock. Mom is in the silks of the local competition, her bright blue and yellow checkers a marked difference from Jorge's black and white. She sees me and a rueful smile crosses her mouth.

"Don't worry," she mouths to me on her way to Sassy Fran, a big chestnut mare who has been cleaning up among the fillies and mares in California going on two years. I've been watching Mom ride her over Santa Anita's dirt track since the mare's first race, but I know if Dad had offered her the ride on Galaxy she'd have dropped Fran like a hot rock.

Anyone would. It's Galaxy, after all. The colt killer going up against fillies seems a little unfair to her own kind.

"She's got it in the bag," Leo says, appearing next to me, saying it with no boasting in his voice. It's just a fact. Galaxy Collision will win this race, and then we'll put her on a plane for Kentucky. Never to be seen again once she walks into the sales ring at Keeneland, bound for the farm life and raising baby racehorses.

The reporters drift off to their next target, taking their microphones and cameras across the paddock. Beck looks relieved to be back in the safety of what he knows—a Blackbridge boy surrounded by Blackbridge people doing Blackbridge things.

As if Blackbridge still existed.

I want Beck to glance at me, walk his two feet over to me

and smile. Be Beck. But he doesn't do that, and it's a stupid thing to want, considering. He only turns to his dad, and Delaney tilts his head to the side as they talk about Galaxy or Lighter or maybe nothing at all that concerns me.

But I still can't help but feel that it does. You don't just pull up a lame horse in the morning and then snap at the horse's owner and not suffer the consequences. Especially if the owner happens to be someone you were rolling around on a bed with a mere day ago.

I flush at the memory, my skin slicking hot.

God, I am so stupid.

"Riders up!" The paddock judge's booming voice crosses the paddock on a wave of cheers. The Distaff is moments away now, and I watch Dad give Jorge a practiced leg up. The two simply nod at each other, with strategy squared away to *let her do her thing* so many months ago.

Galaxy joins the line of nine other horses, her black mane lifting off her glowing mahogany neck. Jorge puts his feet in the irons and tilts his head up at Izzie as she turns around to tell him something I can't hear.

The area around the paddock empties with a rush of bodies, people shifting to watch the horses wind their way to the track. People who don't want to brave the crush stop in front of television screens mounted on giant poles. It's anticlimactic, but it works in a pinch. Hell, it's even what we're doing because pushing through the crowd right now would take too much time. Delaney stands as though rooted to his spot, Cynthia's arm wrapped around one of his. Olivia looks at her phone, fingers moving rapidly across the shiny face of it with her head bent, lips pursed. Matthew is, inexplicably, still talking to Martina, who has to be watching from

New York. She has to be. Dad and Leo stand shoulder to shoulder, watching the post parade in companionable silence I can't make myself join.

Beck stands off to the side, hands shoved into his dress pants and shoulders slumped forward. He has, of course, cleaned up well. Three-piece suit, gleaming shoes, wild hair immaculately pushed into place. Those aviators are on, blocking out the ruthless California sun and hiding his eyes at the same time. Who knows what he's really looking at.

It could even be me.

I take a deep breath and try to force myself to watch the television screen, where the horses are going through their warm ups. Four minutes to post and Galaxy looks like a freight train, all muscle lines and attention on the job. The camera sweeps across the track, showing us in the saddling paddock because our horse is the favorite. Everyone wants to know what we're doing. I see the image of us and try not to wince when Beck turns his head to me. Maybe looking past me, maybe not. Maybe he's wondering all the same things I am.

This is so stupid. I take a deep breath when the camera glances off to Sassy Fran and Mom, the chestnut trotting down the far turn to the starting gate. Now that we're alone in the paddock, the urge to take the next couple of minutes for myself is overwhelming. Because in two minutes the horses will be in the gate, the gates will open, and then it will be all about Galaxy until we have her back in her stall, cool and clean and eating her head off. Win or lose.

I have two minutes to get this right.

Taking the four steps it takes to get close enough, I come to a tentative step next to Beck's side and hover there. He tilts his head at me, and I know I'm getting the side-eye even through the aviators.

"I didn't mean to bite your head off about Lighter." The words come out in a long rush while I watch his face. Beck opens his mouth and shuts it again, like he doesn't know where to start with my sudden apology. The clock is ticking, quite literally, so I keep going.

"It was my fault," I push on. "I was riding Lighter when he ran out. It's my fault that he's sidelined. I felt guilty and you were right there and—"

"What did you mean to do?" he interrupts, throwing me for a loop.

"What?" I ask, glancing at the monitor. The horses are entering the gate. I see the flash of black and white as Jorge and Galaxy stand behind the three stall, contemplating it as the assistant starters move toward them.

"Juls," he says, sighing like he doesn't want to have to explain this, but will anyway because clearly I need to hear it. "Who knows when he injured himself. You know as well as I do he could have done it at any point, whether or not you were riding him."

"Okay," I say, wondering where this is going. "Point taken."

"Besides, none of what is going on with you and me is about Lighter," he says. "We both know that's not the real problem."

"The real problem," I echo, that flush returning in a sickening flood all along my skin. Suddenly I'm very aware I'm a sweaty mess. The dress Martina picked out for me to wear on this day will be stained and smelly by the time the day is over. I look a little sick with the realization that this is where things are going to end.

The last horse loads.

"They're all in line." The announcer's voice booms tinny and

clear over the grandstand, drifting down to us in the saddling pad-dock while we hear it doubled on the television screen.

Beck tilts his head at me, like maybe he can see the answer if he just changes his perspective.

The bell rings.

"And away they go!"

I jerk my attention away from Beck, back to the television. Ten mares burst out of the starting gate, leaping for position going past the grandstand for the first time. I make myself focus on the race, make myself watch Jorge push Galaxy up to third and settle her on the rail, where she lurks like a big cat on the heels of the front runner.

Next to me, Beck is a solid pillar. He doesn't move a muscle, doesn't even pull his hands from his pockets when the field starts to really move. He looks like he's in another world, staring at the screen because it's what's expected of him when really he'd rather be doing anything else.

It's a feeling I understand all too well.

Jockeys push their fists into manes, crops flicking up and start-ing to come down when they curl into the homestretch. Jorge an-gles Galaxy out into the middle of the track, the big mare starting to roll in earnest. She skips to the front effortlessly, a stream of black, brown, and shining white. Behind her, Mom rubs at Sassy Fran, the chestnut lengthening her stride down the inside rail. It only takes a handful of fleeting seconds for the realization to dawn.

This won't be an easy win. Maybe it won't be a win at all.

Sassy Fran hooks up with Galaxy at the one-eighth pole, her ears tipped back as Mom works hard on her back. Reins are thrown forward, gathered. Crops flick up and down. Jorge's crop comes down on Galaxy's outside three times before he presses the crop along the length of her neck to scrub his fists into her mane, waiting for the mare to light all engines in her classic deep-stretch move to the finish.

But this time Sassy Fran sticks right there, a chestnut burr on Galaxy's side. Mom is a wild woman, all movement and pumping arms. The crowd is a riotous roar, hissing up from the grandstand as people scream at the televisions. It's suddenly impossible for me to tear my gaze away from the big screen. I want to yell, scream, but shock has stolen all of that away as the two horses race down to the finish line and Sassy Fran shoves her impertinent nose in front of our mare's right when it counts.

Galaxy slips off the screen, the rest of the horses tumbling after her before the camera switches perspectives, focusing on the gallop out into the clubhouse turn. Mom is slapping Fran's neck with all she's worth, the grin on her face so visible as the grandstand goes nuts for the local longshot. There are screams of pure joy from men holding winning tickets over their heads, because betting the longshot to win is so much better than playing it safe with the losing favorite.

My breath slips out of my lungs and I squeeze my eyes shut. When I open them again, Dad is shaking Delaney's hand. Cynthia is hugging Olivia, who has her head tucked into the crook of her mother's arm. Matthew is still on the phone, saying words I can't hear. Izzie has gone to collect our mare. That leaves me with Beck, who just shakes his head.

"I think," he says, and stops to swallow, Adam's apple bobbing. "I think I'll head back to New York tonight."

I stare at him, mouth falling open.

"What?" It comes out caustic, harsher than I want, but the way Beck flinches is enough to recognize we both know how wrong this feels.

"Lighter's not running," he says, staying the course. It looks like he wants to say something else, but he stops himself just in time for me to come up with a million words to plant in the void.

This isn't working. It's too serious. It was never anything, July. Never a thing at all.

"And you want to go home," I finish for him. "Because what else is here for you, right?"

He shakes his head. "That's not it."

Which is such a lie.

"But it is, Beck," I say. "That's exactly what it is."

"Hey," he steps up to me, ignoring the looks his family throws at us in confusion as they leave the emptying paddock. There's a horse that needs tending to, but I can't make myself care about that right now. I just tense when I feel Beck close in on me, his fingers drawing across my jaw and his mouth on mine before I can even stop to think.

I kiss him back blindly, finding the lapels of his jacket and gripping onto him like I can anchor him here, keeping him in California until I say it's time to leave. Who cares if Lighter isn't running? Who cares if walking back into the shedrow today will feel like a punch to the gut simply because Lighter won't be out there tomorrow, giving them all hell?

But then this isn't about Lighter. I don't want to think about the real reasons. Neither of us do, apparently.

I pull back just enough to suck in a deep breath, looking up into Beck's aviators which do nothing but show me what I look like right now, when I'd rather look at anything else. Beck's chest rises and falls like he's running a race, and I keep my hands on his jacket because I'm not sure if he'll stay when I let go.

"What is wrong with us?" I ask as his forehead tips into mine, resting there like we can mind meld instead of falling into the treacherous mistake of talking.

"I don't know," he says. "I just know I'm not going to be any good to you if I stay."

I force myself to spit out the obvious. "So that's it? You're going to leave me here."

He pulls a face, lifts away from me. "You know how I am, Juls."

Of course I do. Back in the middle of summer, Beck skipped out on Star's run in the Haskell Invitational to sequester himself inside the city, choosing to brood over the imminent dissolution of Blackbridge and life as he knew it rather than face my questions with his new-found knowledge. It didn't make sense to me at the time, and all I'd seen was Beck being obstinate, pig-headed, all the things rolling up into him acting the way he does.

Now he wants to go do it all over again—and this time it's not even about the world ending. Although, honestly, isn't it? A slip of dread licks at my stomach, and I have to swallow back the bile rising hot up my throat.

"You're going to go back to the city and think until I shake you out of it," I try, going for lighthearted and coming away sounding pained.

He smiles, just a press of lips.

"If I don't do that, I might do something rash and then we'll both regret it."

I suck in a breath, wishing he had a better response than that.

"What does that mean?"

"It means that I make crappy decisions on the fly, okay?"

"And you decided going back to the city is the best way to avoid that?"

"Right now?" He looks at me like there's something he's searching for and can't quite see. Before I can push him again, he bridges the gap, mouth meeting mine in a hard rush. It's so sudden I'm caught under the pressure of it, opening and letting him in before I can even have a half-muddled thought about all the things it can mean.

About how it feels like a goodbye.

I suppose that's exactly what it is. I let go of him, my fingers like claws grasping for something I won't let them touch. If Beck wants to leave, if that's what he needs, I'm not going to try to make him stay.

Not if we're going to regret it.

He lets me go, the kiss breaking off and leaving me gasping after him. Beck takes a step back, and I make myself stand. There's no following him right now. The aviators shield his eyes, mirroring Santa Anita back at me.

"See you on the other side, July."

Then he walks away.

Chapter Seven

I hear the grandstand roaring, and in response pull a piece of carrot out of the baggie by my feet and lift it up for Lighter. The colt lips it out of my fingers and starts crunching. Carrot smell drifts through the air, and I pull out a carrot for myself, gnawing on it as Lighter rests his chin on my shoulder, intensely focused on my snack before I give up and hand him the rest.

"Who do you think won?" I ask, looking up at the colt as Izzie walks out of Galaxy's stall. The filly pops her head over the stall guard and pricks her ears at me, eyeing the treats. I pull out a carrot stick and hand it up to her.

"Since I just watched it on these handy things called phones, I can say with certainty it wasn't us," Izzie says, stepping over my legs and sitting down in the folding lawn chair opposite me. She slumps and spreads her legs out in front of her, frayed hems of her jeans trailing in the dirt. "It was Hot Metal by a mile. Star got up for fourth."

"Mmm," I look up at Lighter, who stretches his neck over my head in an attempt to get at the plastic baggie. He's so unsuccessful, but that doesn't stop him from shoving me around in his quest for carrots. I push his head up, snag a carrot and lift it up for him to snatch up greedily. "Guess Santa Anita was a bust."

"On so many levels," Izzie says, then narrows her eyes at Lighter. "And where's this one's owner?"

"Went back home yesterday," I say, feeding Lighter another carrot.

Izzie just stares openly at me, like she's trying to process this and can't wrap her head around it.

"I know," I say for her. "I'm as surprised as you are."

Izzie snorts at that. "Sure. I'm not the one dating the guy. Something tells me you have the inside track on this one."

A flush rises up my neck and I shift in my spot in the dirt. Izzie's face melts into sympathy, and she shakes her head.

"It's not bad, is it? Juls?"

She almost sounds like one more ounce of crappy news will make her cry. I can hear it in her voice, wavering there, way too soft and unsure for me. Hell, too soft for this business. It doesn't pay off to be soft and sentimental here. Horses still get injured. Owners still leave you in the dirt. Literally, as it happens.

I swallow down the truth.

"Of course not," I say. "You know how Beck is."

Here and gone, like always.

Hoofsteps approach outside the shedrow, and I look up to see Gus leading a sweat-streaked, dirt-splattered, half-drenched Star into the barn. Izzie scrambles to her feet and rushes to meet them, throwing herself into Gus's side and peering up at the colt.

"How is he?" she asks, taking the reins as Gus swaps out the bridle for the colt's leather halter.

"Tired," Gus says, scrubbing a hand against the colt's neck and muttering lilting Spanish to the colt. Star pricks his ears, licks his lips, like he's just happy to be home. Izzie cuts away the rundown bandages around the colt's hind legs before Gus takes the colt back outside for a bath.

"Come on, Juls," he says to me on his way, and it's not like I have much of an excuse to not head out into the world and get my hands dirty.

Or wet. Whatever.

I haul myself up, giving Lighter the last of the carrots, and push the baggie into my pocket as I walk out into the searing California sun. Star stands in the light, his usually glowing coat dimmed with track dust and puckered with dampness. Gus turns on the hose and hands it to me, expecting me to go to work.

So I do, spraying the colt down and then sudsing up a sponge. Star lets out a heaving breath as I start working my way down his body, slinging soapy water over his back, down his haunches, getting it all over the wash pad, my jeans, Gus's arms.

"You aiming at anything in particular?" Gus asks me, and I stick my tongue out at him. He chuckles, rubs one hand over Star's nose as the colt lifts his head high, nearly unreachable for the sponge. Gus takes it from me and presses it over the colt's head until a rivulet of bubbly water gushes down Star's face, making sure every square inch is covered. The colt squeezes his eyes closed, like a toddler in a bath.

Then one last rinse and we're done. I'm scraping the water out of the colt's coat, which is back to a burning dark chocolate glow, when Hot Metal comes back from the track, his body seemingly extra red from the sweat and the sun. The purple champion's blanket over his back glimmers, ruffling as he moves.

"Looks good on him," Gus says charitably.

"Would have looked better on Star."

He just shoots me a smile. "Ever loyal, July."

"Damn straight," I say, flicking the last of the water out of Star's smooth, clean-as-can-be coat. Gus leads the colt off the washing pad as I haul the hose back to the side of the shedrow, straightening it out and looping it into orderly circles so it's ready for the next bath. I'm so focused on it I almost miss Dad's arrival at the barn with the rest of the Delaneys, Beck so obviously absent it's hard for me to even look at them.

Delaney stops to consider the colt as Gus continues to cool him out, hands in the pockets of his trousers as he gives Star an appraising once over. Gus keeps his eyes on the leather lead shank in his hands as Delaney seems to have a silent conversation with himself. I finish with the hose and catch Cynthia's sympathetic smile before she slips over to me.

There's really nowhere to retreat that wouldn't look like I'm obviously running away, so I stand and watch Beck's mom bear down on me. Her lavender dress swirls around her calves, a dark purple fascinator spiked with trembling feathers sitting at a jaunty angle on her head. She looks perfectly prepared to hold an Eclipse Award trophy in front of thousands.

I, on the other hand, have dirt on my butt and sudsy water splashed up my arms. Down deep, she must wonder what her son's doing with a girl like me. But if she does, Cynthia hides it well. Just a testament to good breeding or maybe having been in the horse business nearly all of her life. Maybe Cynthia knows what it's like to have the smell of horses clinging to you. So who is she to judge?

"I was sorry to hear about Lighter," Cynthia says. "I know Beck had such hopes."

Sure he did, I think. *We all did.*

"Lighter will bounce back," I assure her. "Give him a month and he'll be tearing around the track again like none of this even happened."

"I tried convincing Beck to stay for the Classic," Cynthia says, and I feel the real meaning of why she came over to me now. It's not commiseration, it's feeling me out for information. "But you know how he is, July. He gets these wild thoughts and . . ."

She flicks her fingers up at the sky.

Oh, yes. I know this so well. At that moment, Delaney saves me from having to answer when he calls out my dad.

"Rob," he says, and Dad appears in the mouth of the barn. "Change of plans. This one is coming back to Belmont with Lighter. Find a farm for him to cool out on this winter, will you? I want to try my luck with him next year."

We all blink stupidly at him. Star was supposed to be in talks for stud duty, which is basically the polar opposite of racing life. Maybe Delaney's just feeling the sting of leaving the Breeders' Cup empty-handed when we thought we were walking in with three powder kegs. Maybe he can't stand not having a hand in the game, even if it is just one horse with the unfortunate luck of being born in the same year as Hot Metal. Maybe, a little pessimistic voice whispers in the back of my head, the whole stud duty deal fell through without a win in the Classic.

Still, I catch the small smile on Gus's face, the way he reaches out and pats the colt softly on his damp neck. This one we'll get to keep a little longer, which means we're taking at least one thing back with us from California.

"I'll get him a stall," is all Dad says, and disappears back into the shedrow to make it happen.

∾

Sunday means moving out. Lighter and Star on one plane, and Galaxy on another. Horse vans are everywhere, packed into the Santa Anita backside like we're all trying to complete a huge puzzle. It's a long exhale, horses scattering to the wind.

I've been dispatched to the Clockers' Corner for coffee. The hard, black stuff that keeps us all buzzing through the morning. The Corner is less packed, but still plenty active. So I have an opportunity to stand in line and think about how Beck was just *there*, by the rail, watching me jog his horse when it all went to hell.

Out of instinct, I check my phone. No calls, no texts, no messages. I feel deserted, and as I'm staring at it in my hand a throbbing, silent sob rises up my chest before I swallow it back down. Tears spike my eyes, and I know I must look flushed as I wipe at them. Now is really not the time to have a miniature break down, especially since I'm not entirely sure where I stand with Beck.

Although, isn't that enough of a reason?

I order and pay for the coffee, going through mechanical motions when Mom jogs up the stairs, her face lighting up when she sees me.

"July!"

"Hey, Mom."

I leave the line, four coffees in hand. Mom takes two, unburdening me, as we walk into the backside.

"I wanted to see you before you flew back," Mom says, all bright-eyed and bushy-tailed. For her, this has been a successful event. She won a major Breeders' Cup race and got one of her daughters to California, never mind that it wasn't exactly for her. On my end, how do I even begin to describe this disaster?

I think about Belmont, about all the new horses waiting for us. I think about Lighter on stall rest, offering the perfect excuse for Beck to stay away while he broods by himself in the city about things I know I can change if I only find the courage to change them.

A sob rushes up my chest again, and this time it slips out into the open.

"July?" Mom stops in front of me, bringing me up short. "What's wrong?"

"I just—" I try for an explanation but it dies a quick death. There's no *just* explaining this. Mom furrows her eyebrows at me and this is just what I need. My mother, who doesn't even know me—not really—standing in front of me while I need anyone other than her.

But if not her, who? Bri barely has time anymore, Martina is mad at me, Pilar won't come back to the track until she's racing fit, Gus and Izzie don't need to be bothered with my problems, Leo is laughable, and Dad? Right, like that's an option.

"Did I do something?" Mom asks, falling back on the safe bet. "July, if I didn't make you feel welcome here, I'm so sorry. It's been such a whirlwind, and I know I could have tried harder . . ."

"Oh my god," I groan, swiping at my eyes with the back of my hand. The coffee cups are in the way, and I can't believe I'm doing this here, in the backside surrounded by people who have no time for a girl's stupid problems. "Never mind, it's nothing."

"It is something," Mom insists, pushing the two coffee cups against her chest and grabbing my wrist with her free hand as I turn away. "You can talk to me, July. I want you to know that."

"Right," I say, laughing. "What's the point, exactly? You're going back to Del Mar and I'm going back to Belmont. I'll just deal with everything by myself, like I've always done. It's no big deal."

"Of course it is," Mom says, her voice crossing into vehement territory. "You are always a big deal, July. Always. Don't let anyone treat you any differently."

"Especially you, right?"

Mom takes a big breath. "I deserve that," she says. "I know I do, but I also know when someone needs help—especially when that someone is one of my daughters. I may not have been with you the past few years, but I still know you, July. Let me help."

"That's just it," I say. "You can't help. This isn't about you."

"Still," she says, shrugging a shoulder. "You'll feel better if you tell me."

I chew at the insides of my cheeks, wondering how she's managed to maintain even a shred of maternal wisdom. *Talk about it.* Right. Like it's that easy. Talking is my entire problem.

"Beck," I say, blurting his name into the air. Mom just nods, like she expected this.

"He's gone," I continue. "Maybe *gone*, gone."

She clucks her tongue behind her teeth, like she does when she wants more speed out of a horse.

"You didn't talk to him, did you?"

"I don't see what good it would have done," I reply. "Clearly he doesn't know what we are, or he wouldn't have gone back to New

York. He'd still be here if he knew—"

"So why didn't you tell him?" Mom asks, her question pinning me in. For the first time, I see it. The reason staring me straight in the face.

"Because what if he didn't feel the same? He would have ended it. He would have . . ."

Left. He would have left, because that's what people do when they don't have a reason to stay.

Mom lets me go, the absence of her hand on my wrist reminding me of what I'm afraid of.

"Oh, July," she sighs, like she knows somewhere deep down this is her fault. Dad barely gives voice to anything that isn't about the horses, always too little or too late. Mom is barely even *there*. It's a miracle Martina and I can even function, much less have functioning relationships.

Although we don't, actually. I think of Beck in the city, wondering what he does and realizing all over again that's a whole aspect of his life I don't know. He could be anyone, doing anything. I wouldn't know him there even if he walked right up to me. My Beck is track life and horses, sunlight filtering through the trees at Saratoga—a person he only becomes in the summer, when he's with me.

He's someone else entirely when he's not.

It occurs to me we were always so very screwed.

"Listen to me," Mom says, suddenly so insistent I'm taken aback. Since when does she have the right? I suck in a breath through my nose, but she winds her free hand around my shoulders, dragging me into a reluctant hug.

"I want you to know that if you need me, I will drop

everything and come to you," she says, her lips close to my ear as I still hold myself rigid, wondering what sort of promise that is when she's only going back to San Diego, to Del Mar. Of course, I remind myself angrily, I did *tell* her to go back to California. To stop trying so hard, to stop trying to force herself into our lives. So who's the hypocrite here?

Mom pushes back from me, holds me at arm's length. She tucks a loose strand of hair behind my ear so she can see my face better, and I feel tipsy with the care she takes. It's all too overwhelming.

"Will you promise me?" she asks, her dark eyes searching mine.

Sure, Mom, I think, sarcasm laced into each word I can't bring myself to say because she looks so earnest. *That's so likely to happen.*

But instead I nod, like a kid who's happy to let someone else take on their problems. Mom smiles.

"It's all going to be okay, July," she says as we continue our way into the backside, her positivity lapping at me in bright waves, a warmth I want to settle into and believe when I know I shouldn't. Because since when has hope ever gotten me anything?

We walk back into the shedrow, where Gus is holding Lighter while Dad checks out the colt's bruised hoof. Lighter gives us a wild look out of the corner of his eye, the whites showing because the activity has him all riled up.

I hand out the coffees and stop in front of Lighter, who presses his muzzle against my hand, searching for something he's not going to find.

"No treats," I tell him. He rewards me by jerking his head up, snorting right into my face. Gus laughs, and I catch the sly smile on Dad's face as he keeps studying the hoof, like he can tell something's there when the bruise is too deep to see.

"That's enough," Dad announces, putting Lighter's hoof back on solid ground. "Load him up, Gus."

There must be some sort of racing god looking after us today, because Lighter loads right into the van without complaint. Maybe the hoof is bothering him, maybe he wants to put Santa Anita in his rearview as much as the rest of us. Either way, he's blissfully silent in the van, tucking into his hay with ravenous appetite and giving us a white-ringed stare as we shut the doors behind him.

The rig fires up its engine, ready to go home.

Chapter Eight

Autumn slides across Belmont Park with a rustle of leaves, a hint of frost in the air. The heaters are on full blast in the mornings, warming my cold fingers and thawing my cheeks, which have chapped and turned pink from morning breezes.

Belmont's fall meet is finished, the racing circuit skipping to Aqueduct Racetrack as the air turns bitter. Warmer weather calls to the big trainers on Millionaire's Row, their strings shipping south to training centers in South Carolina and Florida, where the horses have huge tracts of green land and endless blue skies. Some of the horses go back to the farm for two solid months, where they get fat on hay and return in January with guns blazing, ready to work. That's where we've sent Star—off to a farm for the worst of the weather until he comes back to us with a spring in his step.

We've always stayed at Belmont during the winter months, shipping to Aqueduct for races when we have to. Some horses would go back to Blackbridge for rest and relaxation, but the farm is empty now, waiting on its own auction. It seems like a waste, or like some hilarious joke. But then I just have to look at Star's empty stall and the reality comes crushing back.

Is it worse to have one lingering reminder of what you had before? Or better, like a happy memory you can always count on to be crystal clear?

Underneath the heaters, Feather walks with her head low, ears flopped to each side of her head. Betty the Goat trails after us, her little tail flickering madly. I've discovered that Feather with Betty is a much different creature than without, like the goat is the security blanket I would love to tie to the filly's rump while we're on the track. Unfortunately that's beyond impossible, so I'm left with a filly who finds skittering leaves caught in the breeze so terrifying it warrants tremors, which disintegrate into full on spins on haunches in efforts to flee.

Now I see why they packed the goat into her stall. Without Betty, Feather would completely fall apart. Talk about shredded Thoroughbred nerves. I'm happy to just get back to the shedrow in one piece when I'm riding her.

Feather and I walk by the office, where Martina stands in the doorway watching the horses cooling out in the row, Betty the Goat the odd man out in the loop of horses walking and walking. I shift in the saddle, sinking my weight back. Feather stops on a dime, and I give her a grateful pat on the base of her neck.

"Getting back to normal around here," Martina observes, her eyes skipping to the horses walking past me in the wide aisle. I nod, knowing exactly what she means. We left Mom in California, so now it's just Dad and us, like we're used to. I find a tentative smile perking up at the corners of my mouth, like maybe this means we won't be at each other's throats anymore.

Maybe I'm forgiven, simply because Mom isn't here to remind Martina of how little I was willing to play the peace maker in her quest to make sure everything stays the same. But then—and here's the kicker—I'm not sorry. If Martina's time alone, managing the Belmont stable while we were all living it up in California, hasn't cooled her down, I'm certainly not going to help.

Martina just nods at me, and I think she's past it. It's water under the bridge.

Then she tips her head toward the office at her back, where Leo is writing out instructions for tomorrow on the whiteboard. "At least as normal as it can get these days with the dude bro still visiting."

"I would take offense to that," Leo says, pondering the board for a moment, like it's suddenly stopped making sense. The board is a long list of which horse does what work, from walking the shed-row to big blow-outs before a race. Usually Dad writes up the instructions every morning, but lately he's had Leo come up with a plan the day before as some backside idea of homework.

I'm trying hard not to be offended by that, too. Dad seems happy playing teacher with Leo, taking his internship so seriously he might as well be the one who gives Leo his final grade and hands him a diploma. Maybe it's just the internship that has Dad pulling Leo under his wing. I hope that's it, otherwise why the hell am I here? And what's going to happen to me when Dad throws caution to the wind and pulls Leo into the barn for good?

"But then," Leo continues, putting the finishing touches on the board, "I remember Martina's bad side being particularly prickly. So I'll remain cool and unaffected by your verbal barbs."

Martina sighs, jutting out one hip and crossing her arms.

"Since when did you become so very wise?"

He smiles, capping his dry-erase marker. "I was always this way. You two routinely fail to notice my natural brilliance."

The urge to roll my eyes is so intense I have to give into it. Leo? Brilliant? That will be the day.

"Can we please send him to another area code?" Martina asks, tipping her chin up toward the ceiling and closing her eyes. "The silence last week was so glorious, and now it's like I'm forced to exist in a cloud of ceaseless yapping and cologne."

"Hey," Leo says, pointing a marker at us. "This scent is my *signature*."

"Oh my god," I groan, shaking my head as Martina lifts one immaculate eyebrow.

"Besides," Leo continues, a small smile showing up on his mouth that he tries in vain to stamp down, like he's trying to hide something—like feelings. "You'll both be thrilled to know Rob is sending me down to Florida this month. Yours truly has been promoted."

"Dad is sending you to Florida," I say flatly, more than dubious as another spike of jealousy threads hot and hard into my heart.

"Palm Meadows, baby," Leo says, winking at me in a way that makes me narrow my eyes at him. Of course this is information I wouldn't know, because it's up there with major life changes like *Mom isn't coming home* and *Leo is staying with us for the duration*. It's one of those big decisions Dad makes like they're simple little things that come up during the course of the day. Then we're all expected to just roll with it.

Would it be so hard to keep me in the loop?

"The internship finishes next week," Leo says, a catlike grin on his lips like he knows he shouldn't be talking about this and can't help himself. "And I've been offered an assistant trainer spot in this very barn."

I suck in a breath, letting it out with a deliberate slowness, because if I don't I'm going to snap at him, and this isn't his fault. Not really.

It's mine. For insisting I've always wanted something other than what I have.

"Congratulations," I say through my teeth, forcing myself to smile. He grins up at me, awash in a happiness that makes me feel hard on the outside, like I'm a stone sitting here in Feather's saddle.

"Thanks, Juls," Leo says, sounding genuine.

"Who are you taking with you to Florida?" I ask, because Leo is now my fount of information. Mr. Assistant Trainer will have these sorts of details. Not me, the kid who's soon to be off to college. My thoughts flit to my Jericho application, which is probably sitting in someone's computer as they sort through individual futures.

Leo shrugs a shoulder, like he can't say for sure when I know he can.

"Leo," Martina snaps at him, obviously finished playing. He ducks his head, as though Martina's wrath really does give him nightmares. "Spill it. Who's going?"

"Most of the young horses," he says, and then points at Feather. "That one included. Wouldn't get too attached to her, Juls."

I find myself smiling hard before I can help it, because hasn't that always been the case? Don't get too attached, because the horses are in and out. None of them are ours, all of them will stay just long enough for you to fall in love with them before they're gone, and they'll leave behind nothing except an empty stall. It's a refrain I've heard repeated like a mantra, all the way up until I went and made one stick.

Kali.

Kali, who is sitting around waiting for me to get back to Woodfield so we can pick up where we left off. Lisa worked with her while I was in California, and I have a few pretty videos on my phone of Kali lunging effortlessly in endless circles. It always looks so easy when Lisa does it, like all it takes is one attempt and Kali absorbs the commands by osmosis.

Now I just have to replicate Lisa's hard work. Piece of cake, right?

I suppose we'll see soon enough.

"What did I say?" Leo asks, and I realize I'm staring at him far too intensely, like he's said something so uncomprehendingly deep that it's taking me a while to digest it. Martina snorts, rolls her eyes over to me and reaches to pat Feather's cool neck.

"She's good, Juls," she tells me, so I nudge Feather away from the open door toward Lighter's stall.

The colt hangs his head over the stall guard, ears flicked back and lower lip dangling in what I know is his attempt to show bored misery. Stall rest is just that—little to no exercise while his foot heals. It's standing in one place, doing nothing while you think about all the things you could do—going forward, plowing into life with a thrilling kind of uncertainty. I look at Lighter's dangling lip and can commiserate, like we're both pent up and waiting to break free.

Only in Lighter's case the last thing we need is an abscess or quarter cracks, which can pull a horse out of training for so much longer than the sentence Lighter has hanging over his head now. I can think of a whole host of things I don't want to see happen to Lighter's feet that are worse than his mysterious bruise, so he's going to rest and walk the shedrow until we know for sure he's perfectly able to go on a jog without pulling up lame.

Of course, the last horse I would want to subject to stall rest is Lighter. He leans into the stall guard, turning his back on the toy I asked Gus to drill into the ceiling so the colt had something to mangle that wasn't the stall guard or even the walls. Lighter has done his fair share of destruction since he came to us, raking his hooves down the walls and gnawing at anything placed in front of him. He's like a toddler who simply can't stop sticking his fingers in the electrical outlets.

Looking at him with his head draped over the stall guard makes my heart hurt.

Then, treacherously, my thoughts tilt toward Beck.

I tilt them quickly in the other direction, but it's too late. Beck slips in and does a few laps in my head. His voice, his face, all of *him* goes careening right to the front of my thoughts and sticks there, making me feel itchy, like I want to move and do something without knowing quite what.

Like call him, I suppose. We haven't done that since he left Santa Anita. I didn't even text him to say we got Lighter home safe and sound. A week has passed since then, and Dad has been the only one keeping in touch through his daily Lighter-based calls. I can't make myself do it.

And neither can Beck, I suppose.

It's as though Manhattan swallowed him up, and I don't know why I keep feeling surprised. He's gone to his corner, and I've gone to mine. We'll lick our wounds and sit here, being stupid in silence.

As if in answer to my thoughts, a familiar Bentley goes slipping past the barn. It kicks up gravel dust in its wake, cruising by like a shark waiting for an opportunity. I narrow my eyes at it, wondering what Matthew Delaney is doing, driving right by us and not stopping, like he has business elsewhere. There is no business elsewhere. This is Belmont. And the only horse he has a stake in is located in our barn, and Star isn't even in the barn. He's in a pasture, eating his head off, which means Matthew Delaney is in the wrong place, at the wrong time.

"I'm going to the kitchen," Martina announces, walking past me and patting Feather on the rump as she pushes her cell phone into the back pocket of her jeans. "Need anything?"

I have absolutely no idea what to say. "Kitchen?" I ask, like the word is foreign to me.

"Yes," Martina says slowly, being her ever wonderful self in the face of my confusion. "You know, coffee and sustenance? I'm hungry, I'm tired of donuts, and Leo won't shut up. I need a break."

I don't say anything, preferring to watch her in confusion.

"Fine," she huffs, raising her hands like my reaction is beyond her. "I won't get you anything."

Then she takes off into Matthew's wake, the dust still drifting in the air. I narrow my eyes at her glossy black hair, which has been pulled out of her trackside ponytail and brushed into a sheen. Mine is the face of suspicion.

"It's cute, really," Izzie says, coming out of Feather's newly clean stall. "Her thinking we don't notice."

"How long has this been going on?" I ask, motioning at Martina's retreating back. She slips between barns, disappearing into the backside. Izzie shrugs, screwing her nose up as she thinks.

"Since we wrapped up Saratoga," she says definitively. "Maybe a little after."

I sigh, shaking my head. "Wonderful."

Izzie laughs. "Delaney boys and Carter girls. The attraction must be on the genetic level."

"Really, Izzie?" I send her a look down Feather's shoulder, and Izzie sends me a bright grin.

"Calling it like I see it, Juls."

Shaking my head, I nudge Feather into a bouncing walk, beating out a hasty retreat past Lighter's stall. The colt perks up at Feather, lifts his head to greet his new neighbor with interest he hasn't shown since it sunk in he won't be track bound in the mornings. Feather lifts into an airy trot, nervous near this new boy, and Lighter stretches out his neck far enough for his flaring nostrils to nearly graze her as we pass.

Feather whisks her tail with a sharp slash, catching Lighter on the chin. The colt tosses his head up and watches us pass with wide eyes, still breathing deeply like he's memorizing Feather's scent.

Which is a little sad for him, I think, because Feather is *so* not interested. I lean over the filly's neck and run my gloved fingers through her orderly mane.

"Good for you," I tell her, making the turn around the short stretch of the shedrow as Lighter slips out of sight. "He's not in your league anyway."

～

Just as they are at Belmont, Tuesdays are dark days at Aqueduct. So with no horses to trailer over to Queens for afternoon races, I get to go to Woodfield instead for my second lesson of the week on Kali.

The damp has dried out of the outdoor arena, and I pull into the parking lot to see Lisa standing in the cushiony dirt. Madeline canters Cricket in a loop off the long wall, the big mare so round and collected I feel a pang of envy spike dangerously close to my heart. I have to tell myself to stop it, push the feeling down and grind it out with the heel of my boot as I get out of my car.

Lisa looks up and waves at me. "Tack up and bring Kali down here, July."

I nod, then duck into the barn's first aisle. Bare lightbulbs cast yellow pools into the space between stalls. Woodfield is mostly quiet save the sounds of horses. That's just the way it is on early afternoons during the week, when most of the people who make the place so loud and bustling are still locked behind school doors. I remember being one of those girls champing at the bit to get out of last period so I could rush to the barn, eager to be done with everything not associated with horses. These days I'm not rushing. And when I do finally get here, Kali is sticking her head into the aisle, watching for me with those dark brown eyes.

I find her looking down the aisle at me, ears pricked, like she knows exactly what time it is right down to the second. Knowing how much horses thrive on routine, she probably does. Back at the track, Kali's days were so predictable most people would have torn out their hair yearning for some adventure. Horses love set feeding times, exercise times, turn out times—the more precise the better.

Today is Tuesday—lesson time. Kali shifts against the stall guard and swiftly pats me down for treats. I pull the baby carrots out of my bag and let her lip them greedily off my palm. She crunches on them as I let myself into her stall, giving her coat a few swipes with a brush. Kali was always fastidiously tidy at the track. Looks like that's holding true for Woodfield, too.

After I tack her up, I lead her down to the outdoor. Kali rises into a prancing jig, blowing happily at the world and shouldering into me every few steps. I shoulder back into her, keeping her from dancing me right into the outdoor's fence.

Once we're inside, Kali pricks her ears at Cricket while I pull down the stirrups and fuss with her girth.

"Picking up any pointers?" I ask the filly, who rotates her ears back to my voice before flicking them toward Cricket as the bigger mare goes trotting by, turning down the center of the arena and leg yielding back to the wall. Madeline keeps her outside rein steady, asking Cricket to *move over, go forward, move over, go forward.* They hit their line and arc into the next turn, Madeline sitting through the trot like she was simply born to do it.

Of course, it's actually years of practice showing. I was there when Madeline started lessons. No one is born knowing how to sit a trot or rock *just so* to a canter. It's drilled in, over time and an increasing sense of obsession. Madeline's had the benefit of both, but then, so have I. The only difference right now is I'm mounting up on a green horse, and Cricket has Madeline putting her head in just the right spot.

Kali strides out eagerly underneath me, the whole concept of the warm up lost on her. We go cruising around the outside of the arena, walking like we have a stiff breeze at our backs. *Go* is one thing Kali certainly has no problem with, which isn't surprising since that's all we ever really wanted her to do for so long. I can only count my blessings she failed so miserably when it came down to turning *go* into *win.*

If she had one competitive bone in her body, Kali simply wouldn't be here.

"That's good, Maddy," Lisa calls out to Madeline, breaking me out of my thoughts because that's when Lisa pins her eyes on me. "July, what have you been up to so far?"

So far? I've made it halfway around the arena. But that's not the answer Lisa is looking for.

"Does thinking count?" I ask, and one corner of Lisa's lips twitch up.

"Maybe," she says slowly. "What have you thought about so far, July?"

God, so many things. Beck, Florida, Leo, Jericho, Feather, *Beck, Beck, Beck*. I have to shove those things away and focus on my horse. Kali snorts at nothing and lifts into an airy trot I know for sure I didn't ask for.

"I'm thinking we're full of go today," I say.

"Which isn't a bad thing," Lisa reminds me, watching us like a hawk as I turn Kali in a twenty-meter circle around her while sitting back, slowly, slowly convincing her to come down to a walk. "Without impulsion," Lisa continues in her trainer voice, loud and carrying, "we won't get collection or suppleness. Everything falls apart. That she's so eager to move is a good thing, July. I'm happy Kali is full of go. We just need to harness it."

"Suggestions?" I ask.

"Transitions," Lisa happily informs me. "And so many half-halts."

"And how do we teach half-halts?" I ask, since Kali blew through them whenever I tried them out on her at Saratoga, simply cocking an ear at me and stumbling all over herself before deciding to ignore that confusing situation all together.

"Keep walking," Lisa says. "We've worked on voice commands on the lunge line, so we'll keep doing that under saddle. You ask her to whoa with your seat, your voice, and when you want her to move forward release the reins and ask her to walk on. Voice and aids together. When she gets it at the walk we'll move on to the trot."

I nod wordlessly and keep turning the circle, letting out a breath I wasn't aware I was even holding when I croon out the *whoa*, sinking down into Kali until I feel her center herself. It's just a shift, weight redirecting from her front end to her hind end as she thinks about coming down to a halt.

That's what I want. That shifting thought. When I have it, I give her rein, letting go of her face and leaning down to pat her on the neck. Kali's exuberant walk reappears, the filly mouthing the bit and relaxing just so until I can ask her to shift again, just a tiny increment I can feel in the muscles along her back, in the way her hind end feels taller. Then relax, let go, *walk*.

Walk, whoa, half-halt, walk. It's a rhythm, and I'm memorizing it on Kali. The filly gets the pattern, starts to collect the second she feels the pressure instead of pushing her weight right into the reins.

"Trot," Lisa says quietly from her spot inside our circle, as if she's just as entranced as I feel.

Tapping my heels against Kali's sides, the filly lifts into an easy *one-two one-two*. I lift with her stride, slow my rise, use my voice.

Whoa.

Kali's nose drops, her neck rounds, the bit jangles just enough to let me know she's stopped trying to chew her way through the metal. A little thrill shoots through me and I let Kali have rein, rewarding her for being so ridiculously smart.

Trot on.

Kali picks up the pace, and I grin as we sweep around the circle, feeling each hoof beat, each breath my filly takes, and it's like the whole world melts away. There is no Belmont Park, no Aqueduct, no Florida waiting for Leo and Feather. There is no Manhattan, no boy locked inside. There's only Kali and her sure hooves finding just the right spot in the dirt, and me, asking and releasing, asking and releasing, until we're one.

Chapter Nine

A good lesson is a cathartic rush, a high that plasters a smile on my face and makes every breath I take feel warm and soft. I might as well be walking on air as I take Kali back up to the barn, the filly's reins in my hands as she floats along next to me with her neck arched, ears swiveling, blowing out theatrical snorts with every few strides.

My filly, the dressage horse. Who would have guessed this was in the cards?

"No terrorizing the outdoor arena today?" Madeline asks from the aisle, where she still has Cricket standing in crossties. I lead Kali right into her stall the way she's used to, clipping the stall guard into place after we're safely inside.

"Technically, there was no one to terrorize in the outdoor except Lisa," I say, taking Kali's bridle off and looping it over my shoulder as I go for her girth. "And you know how Lisa is."

"Unflappable," Madeline replies without hesitation as my phone begins to chime. With Kali's saddle slung over one arm, I dig into the pocket of my jacket until I find the phone. The face glows with messages from Bri, one after the other like a stream of consciousness in gray text bubbles.

It is so ridiculous that I haven't seen you in two months. Don't you ever come to Manhattan? Never mind. I'm making you come to Manhattan.

Dinner.

Tonight.

Then, as I'm standing there pondering the possibilities, another text pops up underneath all the rest.

You know I won't take no for an answer.

Bri is a force of nature on any day, and I already feel myself being driven to the call, my fingers hovering over the little letters to type out my reply.

Then Madeline ducks around Cricket and leans halfway into Kali's stall. "Hey, you applied to Jericho, right?"

I pause halfway through my reply, startled.

Jericho. Right. That was something I actually did and not a highly realistic fever dream in which I typed information into a tedious form, leaving my NYU application to rot in its still open browser. I even have the confirmation e-mail to prove it happened.

"I'm waiting to hear," I tell her, Kali's saddle getting heavier on my arm the longer I stand here. "They promise a response by mid-December."

"That is so great." Madeline grins, letting her weight rest on the stall guard and swinging gently on it.

"Considering I haven't heard back yet, I'm going to defer excitement," I say, pushing my phone back into my pocket. Madeline sighs and swings off the stall guard, the metal clasps squeaking.

"Even so," Madeline says with a shrug. "The second you find

out you're in, you should send in Kali's boarding application. They need to see a video to make sure she's suitable."

I wince at the word *suitable*.

"She's green," I start, because no matter how well we just did today, I'm not sure bringing Kali to Jericho is the best of ideas. The college has school horses I can ride, but if I'm not riding Kali during those classes that just means she'll get shuffled down the list of priorities. Still. If I can at least fold Kali into Jericho, then I know I'll have time to make sure she's still progressing and meeting her marks while I'm juggling the track and homework.

Madeline tilts her head at me. "Kali's a project," she says. "No one expects brilliance yet, July. Get a good video of her performing her transitions and she's got as good a shot as Cricket."

I raise an eyebrow. Cricket, the warmblood wonder mare? Jericho will fall all over themselves to get her into their barn. I guarantee it. A recently off track Thoroughbred is another matter entirely.

"I can help!" Madeline says cheerfully, probably having suspected my less than enthusiastic response. "Just say the word and I will record."

"Today would have been a good one," I say, letting myself out of Kali's stall and ducking under Cricket's crossties on my way to the tack room to deposit the saddle on its post. I hang Kali's bridle up on its hook, straightening the reins just so. "Although knowing me I would've wrecked it while you were there recording."

Madeline huffs, looking at me like she's disappointed.

"You don't give yourself enough credit," she says.

"Maybe," I say as my phone starts to chime again. "I've got a month to iron out the kinks. Think you can record me when I know I'm in?"

Madeline smiles. "You bet."

"Thanks," I say, checking my phone again as Madeline goes back to pampering Cricket and I head back into Kali's stall to tear the galloping boots off her legs.

Well?!

Kali comes over to investigate me as I stand stock still in her stall, phone in hand. She nuzzles my fingers, smears her nose over half of Bri's text. I push her gently away and wipe the phone off on my breeches, then decide I'd better come up with a response before Bri has an aneurysm and blames me for it because of the tardiness of my texts.

Let's do it.

~

When I pop out of Union Square Station, the sky is already sliding toward darkness. Manhattan closes in around me, all dank smells and noise. The park is a flutter of greenery at my back, but that's quickly forgotten in the haze of activity. The city is moving, a constant drone of rushing feet. I take a deep breath of exhaust-tinged air and wonder how I'd be handling all of this now, if only I'd applied to NYU with Bri when I was supposed to.

Because this is where I would be, almost exactly. Bri's dorm is four blocks' worth of walking downtown, where NYU clusters around Washington Square Park. You'd hardly notice it was there for all the activity, but that's just how Manhattan always seems to me. It's a wall of buildings strung through with cars. I think about Kali back on Woodfield's scrap of land and suddenly I'm glad I didn't turn in that application last year with Bri.

I trip over a too-tall curb and have to catch myself before plummeting right onto my face. It's like my body loses all function now that I'm in Manhattan—in Beck's city, no matter how far I am from him. I feel his absence ten-fold, like a weight pressing down on my chest until something has to give.

Hunching my shoulders against a sudden, brisk breeze, I hardly realize it when I run straight into Bri. She's standing at the street corner, and grabs my hand before I can slip around her, yanking me to a halt.

"July!"

I blink my way out of my tunnel vision and laugh, feeling scattered. Bri stands in front of me, her dark hair pulled away from her face into a ponytail. Her skinny jeans end in cute ballet flats, because the chill in the air wouldn't begin to bother Bri's sense of style. Still, she's bundled up in a red plaid jacket, the hand she doesn't have wrapped around mine shoved deep in one pocket.

"Thought you were going to run me over," she tells me, pulling me around the side of her dorm and right past it. It wouldn't be a trip into the city if Bri hadn't already pre-planned for a week ahead of time. I wonder how spontaneous her flurry of texts really was—if she's been plotting this for days.

"I should have noticed this," I say, tugging on the arm of her jacket. "It's blinding."

"You shut your face," she laughs. "It is not."

"I don't know, Bri," I hedge, looking down at my decidedly more sedate navy peacoat. I had decided coming into the city required a shower and change of clothes, since going straight from the barn into Manhattan didn't seem like the best of ideas.

Bri snorts and loops her arm around mine, doing her New

York walk down the street that has me scrambling to catch up. She stops in front of a building called The Cantina and pulls the door wide, hauling me into the warmth of too many bodies pressing close in wait for a table.

"Never fear," she whisper-yells into my ear as she blazes a path through the waiting crowd. "I have Western Civ with the host, and he promised me a table in the back."

The Cantina is jammed with tables. Coats hanging over the back of chairs take up a good portion of the limited space, which is a narrow stretch that dims the further we get from the front window. Voices fill the air, climb up the walls and bounce off the ceiling. The claustrophobic would be in a fetal position by the time Bri squeezes my hand and points to a table wedged into the back corner. She pulls the little note out of the tiny bottle of flowers and holds it out to me.

"'For Bri'," I read. "'Thanks for the save'?"

"He copies my notes," Bri shrugs, pocketing the note and pulling off her coat, hanging it on the back of her chair as I climb carefully into my seat, trying not to nudge into the girl sitting at the table too close to ours. Once I'm sure I'm not going to injure anyone, I sit with a whoosh, suddenly tired—the train ride, the city, the people are all just too much.

"You do take excellent notes," I say, mustering the energy to yank off my coat.

"They are excellent," Bri says, grinning up at the beverage boy. "It's too bad we're starting at different times in the year," she continues. "You won't be able to capitalize on them the same way, but I should have a pretty good archive by the time you start, so there's that."

I open my mouth and shut it again when the waiter glides by, depositing menus on the table.

"This place has the most amazing arepas," Bri continues, and for a second I'm glad. I can just nod and let her bring me up to speed on the finer aspects of Colombian food, or I can do what I know needs to be done.

"I didn't apply to NYU," I say so suddenly Bri stutters to a silent halt, staring at me with wide, shocked eyes.

"It must be because there are way too many people yelling in here," she starts slowly, "but it sounded like you said—"

"I applied to Jericho." I reach for my water, taking a big sip because my mouth just went bone dry. "Last month, actually."

"July," Bri stutters and then stops herself, raising her hands like she can tamp down all the things she wants to say. "That's okay. You still have a few weeks to get in your application."

"That's just it," I lean into the table. "I don't know if this is what I want."

Bri cocks her head at me and sucks in a deep breath. "NYU?"

I look over the heads of the packed restaurant and find the window, where Manhattan is swathed in darkness. "I don't know if this place is me, Bri."

"But it was," Bri says. "It was up until last year and then all of a sudden it's just not?"

I bite my lip, wondering what I should say. NYU looked so attractive up until working with the horses became an obsession rather than a simple job. But then working with the horses had always been an obsession, hadn't it? NYU was a dream, an alternate reality of a life without horses that never would have worked. I'd have gotten here and been gone within a month, back with the horses.

At least now I'm owning up to that.

"Jericho has . . ."

"Horses," Bri sighs, slumping in her chair. "I know exactly what it has, Juls."

"It's not that I'm choosing horses over you," I rush. "That's not what this is. I just can't be here, at the track, and with Kali when I know where I want to be in the end. NYU can't offer me what I want."

Bri nods slowly. "No, I get it," she sighs, shaking her head. "I just wanted to have it all out here, I guess. It's lonely sometimes, and being surrounded by people all the time really just compounds how new it all is."

"It looks like you're doing just fine," I say, thinking of the note on the table. "Well enough to get a reserved table in a packed place like this?"

"That was a favor," Bri shrugs.

"Because you're amazing," I tack on. Bri offers me a ghost of a smile.

"We were going to room together," she says, and I wince. I'm never going to live this down. Bri has the memory of an elephant, no matter how forgiving.

"I'm not going to be that far away," I say. "Look, here I am right now, and it only took an hour."

"Right," Bri sniffs. "Only an hour. It took two months to get you here, and it's not like I'm the only person you have to visit in Manhattan."

"What are you saying?" I ask, the little hairs on the back of my neck rising. I know exactly what she's saying.

"Beck?" she asks simply. "Columbia isn't exactly walking distance from here, but I guess I thought you'd be in town more to see him. You . . . haven't been?"

I shift in my seat, which I know makes me look guilty when I'm not. Bri can sense it like a bloodhound, because her gaze sharpens on me.

"July," she hisses at me.

"What?"

"Tell me what's going on," she demands. "I know I'm not a lawn's walk away anymore, but there are still these things called phones. You can tell me anything, and so far you're not telling me a damn thing. No NYU and now what? No Beck? Is this why you're not applying?"

"No," I shake my head firmly. "Beck doesn't know about NYU either."

"Oh," Bri widens her eyes again. "Shocking."

"It's not . . ." I try, wondering what it really is. Why didn't I tell Beck about Jericho? What was I afraid of? Considering he never wanted me to visit him here, my being at Jericho would have worked out perfectly for him.

I tell myself to stop it.

"I don't know if it even matters," I sigh, remembering that the timestamp on Beck's last text was back when I was in California.

"Do I have to fix something?" Bri asks, leaning into the table, her eyes narrowing at me like she can cut out the truth so she can go into damage control mode. "What else is there, July?"

"Beck left California before the Classic," I say, watching Bri's stony expression on the other side of the table as I go over what happened, from the hotel room on the bed, to Lighter's injury, to Beck's retreat back into Manhattan like it was his Fortress of Solitude and no one could follow.

When I'm done, Bri shakes her head.

"He has been pretty evasive lately," Bri says, reminding me that my maybe boyfriend and my definite best friend chat regularly and say who knows what about me. A flush floods up my skin at the realization.

"He's talking to you?" I blurt out the question when I know the answer. Bri isn't me, so of course he's talking. Beck doesn't know how to shut up, after all, unless it's with me.

Bri waves a hand in the air, which seems like such a common thing for people to do when they're talking about Beck. "He likes to text me conversations he overhears on the subway."

I am somehow not even remotely surprised.

"That's it?"

"Well, we were talking about getting lunch last week but now he won't nail down a day, time *or* place. It's just subway conversations. Is this what he does with you?"

"What he does with me right now is nothing," I grumble. "It's been radio silence."

Bri huffs and scoots her chair back, picking her giant bag off the floor and standing.

"Um, where are you going?" I ask, looking up at her. Bri grabs her coat off the back of her chair and yanks it on, nearly whacking the girl next to us in the head with a swinging coat sleeve.

"*We* are leaving," she tells me.

I stand up automatically. Bri's authoritative, down to business voice tends to have that sort of reaction in me.

"Wait, wait," I tell her as she does up her coat buttons, already spinning to leave. I snag my stuff and follow her, catching her in the middle of the restaurant. "Where are we going?"

"Morningside Heights," Bri says, looking at me like I should know where we're going. My stomach falls like a rock all the way to my feet, and I have to swallow before I can force myself to ask my next question.

"Why?"

But I know why.

"This is ridiculous," Bri tells me. "We both know where Beck lives, July, and I'm not letting you waste a trip into the city without figuring this out."

"How are you going to do that?" I ask, following her out of the restaurant and into the brisk November night.

Bri shoots me a grin. "I have a plan."

∿

Plans and Bri go hand in hand. They always have, because meticulousness is as natural to Bri as breathing. I should just trust in whatever she's cooking up in her head as we ride the subway uptown, sitting on the plastic seats and rocking as the train screams over the rails while my stomach lodges uncomfortably in my throat.

At our stop, I can barely get my shaky legs underneath me to climb up the stairs to the street. Bri leads the way, and I follow her quietly in the dark, my stomach hurting more with every step that takes us closer to our end goal. It's doing little flips by the time we're standing in front of Beck's brownstone, the college's housing for people who can afford the lap of luxury.

I'm not sure how much luxury Beck can afford now that his family has sold off Blackbridge and nearly everything else, but then he does own a horse sitting near the top of the future betting pool for the Kentucky Derby, so maybe I'm deluding myself. Of course Beck lives in a brownstone apartment. Of course he does.

Bri trots up the steps like she's supposed to be there, her bag banging against her side.

"Bri," I hiss at her, grabbing her elbow and dragging her to a stop on the cement steps. "What are you doing? You can't just stroll into a dorm. There are—" I wave my hand in the air, trying to find the right word, which completely escapes me.

"I live in a dorm," Bri reminds me, grabbing my free hand and squeezing it reassuringly, although it does nothing to slow down my wildly thumping heart. "I know how dorms work, Juls."

She leads me the rest of the way up the stairs, and I feel myself floating toward the door rather than actively walking, like I can't believe my feet are moving one in front of the other toward a looming hole of no return.

Beck doesn't want to talk. I know he doesn't want to talk. Since when has forcing him to talk ever amounted to any good? It wasn't like he had great things to say the last time I tried that trick, no matter how much I needed to know.

But that's just it. I needed to know. So I let Bri pull me through the brownstone's chipped green door. It's why I'm letting her lead me right up to the intercom. Before I can stop her, she pushes the top button and waits, hand resting on one jutted hip.

The intercom crackles to life with a buzz, the door unlocking without anyone bothering to ask us for our names.

"Typical," Bri sighs, grabbing my hand and pulling me into the empty foyer.

For a brownstone, it's remarkably utilitarian. The scuffed linoleum floor is pulled up in places, and the walls are dinged and scraped—evidence of too many move-ins and move-outs. I guess it really is a dorm at heart, no matter what it used to be.

Bri pulls me like I'm dead weight toward the stairs, because of course there isn't an elevator. We climb, and by the fifth floor I'm so winded I'm gasping.

"I thought you were more fit than this," Bri says, trailblazing the way to the sixth floor like a woman on a mission, despite the mission not exactly being hers.

"When do I have the time to run several flights of stairs?" I wheeze, pushing myself up to the last landing as Bri stands at the door to Beck's floor. She looks at me like she doesn't buy it.

"I refuse to believe living in this city for a whole two months has made me Wonder Woman," Bri tells me. "Not that I wouldn't appreciate that sort of side effect. Maybe you should rethink Jericho. NYU might turn you into a lean, mean, horseback riding—"

"Okay," I interrupt, my breath coming easier into my lungs while my heart still does an anxious flutter behind my aching ribcage. "That's enough of that."

"Just saying," Bri smiles at me, and hauls open the heavy door.

Two doors greet us. One is marked with a number, and the other must lead to the roof. I stare at the number hammered into the apartment door a little too hard, feeling the pull of the staircase behind me. How easy would it be to go running back down the way we came?

Too easy, I remind myself. That's not why I came all this way, to go running back out the second I get within shouting distance. It's just Beck. The Beck I've known for years. Carefree, ridiculous, adorable Beck.

136

I can do this.

Bri stands there looking at me like she's waiting for something. When I finally blink and look at her I'm met with a sigh.

"Knocking on the door is your job, July," she says. "I got you here, so now it's your turn to take the lead."

"Gee, thanks, best friend," I reply as she sticks her tongue out at me and motions to the door with a flourish. Before I can think much more about it, I step toward the door and rap my knuckles against the solid wood.

It flies inward, revealing a boy I know vaguely from Saratoga. One of Beck's posse of suit-bedecked friends who stood in the saddling paddock, chewing and sucking on their cigars like they knew what they were doing with them. Just the memory of the smell makes me cringe.

I search for the boy's name, sifting through what little Beck has told me about these people before giving up entirely. There are simply too many names, too many possibilities, and I never met any of these people, so how can I begin to label them with their actual given names?

"Whoa, this is not the pizza guy," the boy observes, and I can feel the force of Bri's eyes rolling toward the ceiling behind me.

"Nope," I say, finding my voice as I glance past him into the apartment. There are a few other people—boys mostly, some from the same group I remember at Saratoga. "I didn't come bearing pizza. It's terribly rude, I know."

The boy cocks his head at me, a slow smile spreading over his mouth. "Hey, I know you."

"I bet you do," I say, eyes sliding past him into the apartment again. It's filthy, of course, occupied by boy things. The coffee table is littered with beer bottles. A tattered sofa hosts what looks like an intense video game in progress, boys elbowing each other and laughing maniacally when not staring at the television with scary focus.

Then, out of the kitchen walks Beck, beer in hand. Sunglasses Girl from Saratoga—the only girl Beck ever brought with him that summer, who looked at me like I was someone who should stay well away from the owner's son—is right behind him with her beautiful blond hair fishtail braided over one shoulder like she's cruising through the fashion model shoot that probably is her life.

I tell myself to stop it, even as my mouth goes dry and the urge to run overwhelms me.

Of course, that's when Beck sees me there in the doorway, because how can he not? I'm right here, suddenly in his home, and I really shouldn't be because I'm not invited. I've never been invited.

His mouth drops open. Ridiculously, I lift a hand halfway in a tentative, silent wave.

Sunglasses Girl pulls a face that betrays how much she knows, and a little spike of anger slices up my spine. It doesn't seem fair that Beck could talk to anyone else other than me about, well, *me*.

"Hey," the boy at the door says to Beck. "Doesn't she seem ridiculously familiar?"

"I'd hope so," Beck says, putting his beer down on the coffee table on his way across the room toward us. I watch him walk up to me, wondering exactly what he's thinking right now, with me uninvited and the gulf of silence we created in California trailing in the wake of our silent cell phones. It seems so stupid, but here I am with my heart beating frantically in my chest.

Get a grip, get a grip, get a grip.

It's just Beck.

"Hey," he says once he's right in front of me and I let myself really see him. Light brown hair in its perpetual mess, green eyes dimmed with hooded worry. "What are you doing here?"

He touches my hand, pulls me out into the hall. When he sees Bri he does a double take.

"I insisted," Bri says just as the doorbell buzzes again and the boy leaps to answer it. "Mind if we stick around for pizza?"

"Sure?" It's more of question than an answer, testament to how unexpected this all is. Beck seems to pull himself together and nods. "Yeah. We'll be on the roof."

"Oh, will we?" I ask as Beck opens the other door, presenting the brownstone's immaculate, open roof. Manhattan rises over it in sparkling lights, the occasional screaming siren shattering the soft, perpetual city buzz in the air.

"Unless you want to talk about why you're dropping in out of nowhere in front of everyone," he says, leaning his shoulder into the door as I walk past him, letting that serve as my answer.

"This was Bri's idea," I say, because I don't know where to start.

"I know," he says, letting the door shut behind him with a metallic clang. Now it's just us out here, a hazy dark dome curling over us as the city makes me feel impossibly small. "Kinda figured that."

I frown at him as he walks up to me in the dark. His T-shirt has a ridiculous print of a lion wearing a top hat on it, and for a second I falter.

It's just Beck.

"But I let her drag me all the way up here because you left," I say, mustering what I came here to say. "You left me in California, which is one thing all on its own I'm annoyed about, but then we haven't talked since, which is so much weirder. I don't know what's going on, but I do know I said I'd eventually have to shake you out of it so here I am, shaking you out of it."

He smiles at me, but it's tired, like he knew this was coming and has spent too much time thinking about it.

"Juls, I wish this was easy to say," he says, scrubbing a hand into his hair and pushing it into further disarray. A bit of me cracks away at his words, already anticipating him before he can say anything else. It breaks and crumbles, and I feel the surging need to push past him before he can get another word out.

"Wait," he snags my wrist, pulls me close. "Stop, Juls. Just hear me out, okay?"

"What do I need to wait around for?" I ask. "Some treatise on break ups and moving on as friends? Like that's likely?"

He just shakes his head at me, like he can't believe I went *there*.

"I don't have a treatise," he says, and then stops himself. "Well, maybe I do."

I roll my eyes and steel myself. I came here for a reason, which means I can't avoid the fall out. "Get on with it, then."

"That day in the hotel room," he starts, and I can already feel my face flaming into a hot, embarrassed pink. "Before the post-position draw."

"I remember," I cut in, and he slips his hand from my wrist to my hand, squeezing it like that's a reassurance.

"You were pissed," he says. How astute of him.

"I didn't anticipate getting turned down," I say, deciding to focus on the lion's top hat instead of hazard a look up at Beck. I can't handle that right now, looking into his sparking green eyes and wondering where all of this is going.

"I was honest with you," he says. "I'm a guy, July. Doing *that* with *you* practically haunts me. It's what I wanted and when you decided to push fantasy into reality . . ."

"You threw on the brakes."

"I did."

"So," I hedge, trying to understand and not getting it. Where exactly is the problem here? "Why?"

He looks up at the sky, like he knows he's not making any sense to himself either.

"I don't know, Juls," he sighs. "Maybe because this—you and me—is too new. It's just another change. I feel like I need stable ground right now. Blackbridge is gone, the horses are gone with it, and my family . . ."

He sighs, letting the thought go trailing off into the air between us. Before I can push, he says, "The truth is I don't have any idea where we stand. All I know is you're another change. I thought it would work if there was some distance—you at Belmont, me in the city—but then you pushed, and maybe I panicked. But it doesn't change the fact that I can't deal with this right now, Juls."

My fingers go cold. The breeze kicks up, pushes at me and sinking right through my jacket, helping those icy threads along until I start shivering with it. The need to do something is swallowing me up, but what do I do? What am I supposed to say that is going to make all of this okay?

"I can't bring back Blackbridge," I start, and he huffs a frustrated laugh.

"I know," he says. "It's not Blackbridge—"

"Then what?" I ask, letting my voice rise. "You are not the only one with crap in your life, okay? I've gone through just as much. If you hadn't noticed, not having Blackbridge affects me, too."

"Does it?" he asks, tilting his head at me. "You have a stable full of horses again. You've got—"

"Lighter," I snap. "Whom you haven't come by to see because you're avoiding me, because change is just too damn scary, apparently."

"Hey," he cuts in. "That's not fair."

"Is it not?" I ask. "We were good in Saratoga. We were good in the Outer Banks."

"Neither of which is exactly real life," he says.

No, I think. And that's exactly the problem. I've never really known Beck in real life. He's a Manhattan kid, born and bred, appearing at Barn 27 when he only has a good reason. Lighter used to be his reason. Now it appears I am just as good a reason to keep away, and a laid up colt isn't going to trump that.

Saratoga was ours. And Saratoga is never going to happen again. Not like it used to, anyway. It's time I realize it.

"Fine." I square my shoulders. "You need stable ground? Well, so do I. And I can't do this if you're going to hide out and pretend like I don't exist. The brooding thing? That doesn't work for me."

"Juls—"

"No," I say, foot firmly down. I'm not doing this anymore. "If I'm too much, I'll cut you loose. Congratulations. You don't have to think about it anymore. Go back about your shiny life and I'll see you when you decide to start visiting Lighter again."

"July," he says, insistent now as I take a step backward toward the door. "Come on. That's not what I'm saying."

"But it is," I say, taking another step. "That's exactly what you're saying. You don't know where we stand, but you're not doing anything to figure it out. You just left me in California, and—even worse—I let you. I *let* you, Beck. Like that was a rational thing to do."

"Why did you?"

I laugh, but it sounds scattered, like broken glass clinking against cement. "Could I have stopped you? If it's not smooth sailing then it's not worth doing, right? Easier to just come back here and ignore me. I honestly don't know why I'm so surprised. Everything always meant more to me than it ever did to you, but I fell—"

I snap my mouth shut, a surge of adrenaline spiking as his eyes widen in the dark, filling in the blanks well enough. The city reflects on his irises, like dazzling little flares I have to look away from because I'm saying too much that doesn't need to ever be said. These words aren't for Beck, after all. They're not meant for us.

My eyes squeeze closed, wetness gathering in the corners and threatening to fall treacherously down my face. I'm not doing that. I'm not going to cry. I force myself to look at him and press a smile onto my lips. "And I should just keep my mouth shut," I grind out, more mad at myself now than I am with him, because now is not the time for declarations, even half thought out.

Beck opens his mouth and closes it, like he doesn't know what to say. Fitting. Of course he wouldn't. That would be too hard, right? And it's not like I got all the way to the end. I at least saved myself that embarrassment.

I turn on my heel and slam through the door, not letting myself slow down when I hear Beck say my name. My stomach twists, some part of me wanting to stop and turn, look at him again. But that's a slippery slope, because what on earth could he possibly have to say?

I'm sorry I led you here, July. I'm sorry it meant so much to you, but we can be friends, can't we?

No way in hell am I sticking around for one of Beck's non-apologies. His *I'm sorry, but* refrains were annoying before when it was all about Lighter and whether or not he was worth it, but now it might make me murderous. I'm already down two flights of stairs when I hear the roof door open, the sound of footsteps echoing toward the stairs and down, after me.

The thought of him catching up to me simply so he can tell me the last thing I want to hear makes my breath hitch, so I push myself faster. I'm in the lobby before I can really register where I am, out of the building without thinking where I'm going, running down the steps and hitting the sidewalk before I can grasp my bearings.

I simply move without thinking, instinct taking over. And the instinct simply says *run*.

Chapter Ten

The next day, we go to Aqueduct, which matches my mood: gray, falling apart, and tired. Fog rolls thick over the ground, obscuring any view of the track and the grandstand, which is just fine by me. Aqueduct is a pit of despair, and at least the fog saves me from having to look at it.

We lumber through the gate with Feather suspiciously quiet in the trailer bumping over the gravel behind our truck. I stare out the window, catching glimpses of workers shifting through the mist like ghosts. They look half in and half out of the world, occupied with keeping so busy they can't possibly stop to notice their surroundings. Sometimes one of them looks up, peering at our shiny truck quietly, affording us a pause in their daily grind before going back to cleaning buckets and mucking stalls, getting the midday chores done before horses need to arrive at the receiving barn for the first race.

My phone rings on the seat next to me, and I reach over, silencing it. Izzie glances down at my movement and says, "That's like the fifth call this trip."

"Yup," I reply, unfazed.

I can feel her eyeing me, studying the side of my face with a befuddled quirk of her manicured eyebrows.

"This is a thirty-minute trip, July."

"Oh, I know," I say, tearing my gaze away from the window when Dad turns the truck toward our barn, a whitewashed cinder block affair. The roof is slumped in the middle, slowly caving in after so many years of no one caring enough to fix it.

Typical Aqueduct.

The phone's face is dark, quiet before it suddenly springs to life again and beeps shrilly, informing me that Beck's fifth message has been left on my voice mail.

A message I firmly intend to delete.

Izzie leans over the bench seat, eyes narrowing on the phone.

"Are you ignoring Beck's phone calls?" she asks, voice moving closer to alarm with every word, like she can't believe what she's seeing and needs verbal confirmation from me before she can allow herself to accept it.

"Her phone has been blowing up all day," Leo confirms from the front passenger seat. "Something has to be wrong, because I won't for a second believe July actually became popular while I was gone."

I lean forward and swat at the back of his head, narrowly grazing the shiny, sleek plane of his dark hair before he ducks out of the way, laughing.

"That's enough back there," Dad says to me, like he's policing a bored kid during a cross country road trip instead of a thirty minute drive to Queens. I wrinkle my nose and lean back into my seat, feeling like kicking the back of Leo's seat for good measure.

When we're parked and have Feather out of the trailer, Izzie gives me a good dose of side-eye on the way to the filly's stall. My phone goes off again as Izzie situates the filly in her temporary housing, and when I move to silence the ringer again she straightens quickly and points at me.

"You tell me what's going on," she demands. "Or I'll answer your phone myself the next time it rings."

My fingers pause, cupping the phone as it vibrates and chirps, Beck's impatience suddenly rivaling my own as I consider Izzie thoughtfully. "You wouldn't," I say.

One of those manicured eyebrows rises sky high, and before I know it she's lunging for the phone. A squeak pops out of me as I jump out of her way, Feather throwing her head up and doing a nervous circle in the stall as Izzie stretches for the phone. I leap out of her reach.

I silence the phone and shove it into my back pocket, retreating across the aisle and leaning into the cinder blocks. Safe from Izzie's prying hands, at least. That's something.

"You have been acting like a zombie all day," Izzie accuses me. "You don't have to tell me what's going on, but don't go lumbering around here making it obvious you want someone to ask what's going on and then refuse to talk about it. I'm not playing this game, July."

"I'm not playing a game," I insist, wincing at Izzie's huff.

"Sure," she says, redoing her two-toned ponytail. "Sure you're not, July."

I have no idea what to say to her. She's right, I suppose. I'm advertising something's wrong, but I don't want to talk about it. Not really.

"It's," I try, the words failing to come up my throat and out, because I don't know how to form them. Izzie just sighs, sets her shoulders, and shakes her head at me.

"Look," she says. "It's obvious what's going on. After the Breeders' Cup? I'd say half of Belmont knows what's up at this point. But if you don't want to talk, just block the poor bastard's number while you're around here because otherwise you're going to drive me completely insane."

I find myself ghosting my fingers over my back pocket, Izzie's advice hitting me like little darts. Truth darts, if you will. If I don't want to talk, shut up and get to work. That's what she's saying.

"Okay," I say simply, and pull the phone out of my pocket. Before it can ring again, I block Beck's number.

Just until the end of the day, I tell myself.

Just until I see Feather home safe.

～◦～

Once upon a time, people packed the stands at Aqueduct to see Man o' War and Secretariat. I've seen the photos that prove it, everyone standing shoulder to shoulder in their overcoats and black hats as they wait impatiently for a race to run. Horse racing lives on the shoulders of the greats that came before, and those greats ran at Aqueduct in front of thousands.

Now a new casino took over the grandstand, pumping thousands of dollars into Aqueduct's previously cheap claiming races. How can the owners resist those purses? So many of the horseman here are just trying to get through the harsh New York winter, but when the worst of the trainers run and run their horses in those rich claimers until there is no horse to run anymore, it colors a place.

And right now, it's the only track open in New York. This is what we've got until Belmont opens back up in May. Well, this and Florida.

Izzie walks Feather around the paddock, which is a closed-in oval affair sitting snugly between the outer dirt track and the grandstand—one of The Big A's little quirks. If you want to see the horses before the race, you have to gather at the rail that separates it from the track's apron and look down, like you'd look into an exhibit at the zoo. Covered stalls bend around one long end of the oval, and a white wall with framed silks stretches across the other. Inside the oval are two meager gardens, little mounds of dirt in a sea of rubber pavers, and the most out of place gazebo you'll ever see situated between them. Potted mums provide a pop of yellow here and there, but otherwise it's black and brown and gray.

The people who lean over the railing peer down at us quietly, watching without emotion or studying in a way that makes me feel critiqued. Feather is one of seven maiden fillies in this race—one mile on the outer dirt track—and she's the only one who's never been in a race. She's the wild card, with only her timed works to give these poor souls any inkling of how she's going to do today.

Surprisingly, she's the second favorite. It appears anything can happen at Aqueduct on a nondescript Wednesday.

"This place is a hole," Leo says next to me, standing outside Feather's stall, his eyes on our filly like he's intentionally refusing to look around him. He fiddles with his suit jacket, fastening and unfastening the buttons to keep himself busy. "Did it get worse since I left, or am I just imagining things?"

I cast a look up at the grandstand, which is eerily reminiscent of Belmont's jutting overhang, just not nearly as long or as grand. From here, it doesn't seem so bad.

"They cleaned up the pigeon droppings," I say, shrugging a shoulder. "That's something."

Leo turns to look at me as though he was expecting me to say something else. Then he sighs and closes his eyes. "Whatever. I'll be in Florida soon, and this will all be just some dirty memory."

"Good luck with that," I say, because even if he is going to Florida, when he comes back here to work with us then there's certainly no forgetting Aqueduct.

"Do I hear a tinge of jealousy?" Leo asks, nudging my shoulder with his considerably larger one.

"Hardly," I say, swaying under another one of his nudges. I might as well have said yes, by the way he grins at me. "More like enthusiasm because I'm finally getting you out of the house."

Leo presses a hand to his solid chest. "That hurts me, July. Deeply."

"Good," I reply, shaking my head at his laughter.

"Damn, Juls, I know you're having a bad day with your boy and all, but—"

"I am so not interested in hearing your comments on my personal life," I say, and he just keeps going like I've said nothing at all.

"I just don't think you should make the rest of us suffer because you're having an off day, you know?"

"Thank you for those incredibly wise words," I say as I spot Jorge walking out of the jockeys' room, his torso splashed with the silks of Khalid Sahadi—Feather's owner—bright blue with one single orange chevron diving off his shoulders to meet in a point near his navel. A slip of orange covers his helmet. The effect is nearly blinding, so we're sure to see him plain as day during the race, which I do tend to appreciate.

Khalid Sahadi, however, is about as absent as Beck used to be during these weekday races. By which I mean, totally and completely somewhere else. I know Dad gives him updates every afternoon like he does all his other clients, but for a man who owns nearly half the barn there's been not one sighting. The infamous Sahadi is utterly mysterious.

But that's expected. Few people want to show up to a maiden race at Aqueduct.

Leo is muttering to himself, and it takes me a minute of watching Dad talk with Jorge before I zero in on exactly what he's saying.

"Are you just saying *Florida* over and over?" I ask, shooting him a look out of the corner of my eye.

"Don't judge," Leo says. "I'm a little excited."

The judge calls riders up, and Dad lifts Jorge onto Feather's back like he weighs nothing at all. Feather, though, feels it. She collects herself, and snorts out a breath as they parade past us toward the walkway to the track. Izzie keeps a firm grip on the lead when the filly takes one look at us and decides to spook, leaping forward like a deranged stag. Jorge catches air, reaches to grab mane when Izzie's weight brings the filly back to earth with a jarring thump of hooves on the rubber pavers.

"Unfortunately, I have to take that one with me." Leo shakes his head at our flighty filly, and I smile up at him.

"Welcome to the world of work, Leo," I say as the last filly winds out of the paddock. "Not even Florida can be carefree sunshine all the time."

"True. Can't I just take you down there with me?" His eyes

light up. "I can have an assistant!"

I snort my disagreement, which is better than reaching out and throttling him. Me? His assistant? In what hell have I found myself? "The problem with that plan is that *you* are the assistant. It's your title. *Assistant* trainer."

"Oh come on," he whines. "What is it that you do around here, anyway?"

Such a good question.

"Aside from everything?" I ask, heading for the stands as he falls into step with me. I could make a detailed list of all the things I do for Dad, but then that might only embolden him.

"See, that's perfect," he says, and my hopes are dashed. "That's what I need. A spunky horse girl who does everything for me because she loves it."

"That is remarkably offensive." I step over a small pile of strewn trash as we walk across the apron, because that's how The Big A rolls. Dad and Izzie find a spot by the winner's circle and rest against the fence as the horses go trotting down the middle of the track, getting ready for their warm up.

"It isn't if it's true," Leo dares tell me. I turn and thump him on his stupid, massive shoulder, because I've had it. Unfortunately my hand only glances off his giant muscled hide and I'm left unsatisfied.

"Did anyone ever teach you how to properly talk to people?" I ask. "You're horrible at it."

"Look," he argues as he settles into the fence. "I don't see what the big deal is. I'm taking nearly half the string to Florida—*Florida*—and I'm inviting you to come along. Florida, July. You'd just be doing everything you do up here, but in a considerably better place."

"If you say Florida one more time . . ."

"You'll what?"

I open my mouth and shut it, which Leo takes as a victory because he smiles his annoying, smug grin at me which means he thinks he's got a point. Well, he doesn't. I'm not going anywhere. I have to get Kali ready for her video application to Jericho, Lighter to keep happy while he's stuck in his stall, and who would ever be crazy enough to follow Leo of all people anywhere?

"Think about it, July," Leo says, throwing an arm around my shoulders and whispering like we're co-conspirators. Next to us, Izzie quirks an eyebrow up. I push my elbow into Leo's side and wedge him out of my space.

"Watch the race and shut up, Leo," I advise.

"Does someone need to stand between you two?" Dad asks, throwing us a look over Izzie's head.

"No, sir," is Leo's immediate response. I sigh, because of course he snaps to at any hint that Dad is watching. Leo's new at this. The thing he doesn't get is Dad is always watching. He just chooses not to get involved.

But that's something Leo won't know until he's been around long enough. Even I didn't realize it until recently. I glance over at Dad, who's back to studying the horses as they come up to the gate, which is situated right in front of us for the mile-long distance.

The fillies cluster around the back of the gate, going in one at a time until it's Feather's turn and she digs in. All four legs lock into the earth like deadbolts, and Jorge's urging doesn't have any sort of effect.

"Put gate training back on the to-do list," I mutter to myself as

Izzie winds her hand around mine, squeezing.

The assistant starters surround the filly like ants around a drop of syrup, two of the heavier-set men linking arms behind her butt and half-lifting, half-shoving her into the gate. Feather takes mincing steps forward to stay balanced, and once she's fully inside the starters jump aside, slamming the back doors shut before she can bolt backward.

Two more fillies left. They walk into the gate like princesses, daintily and without drama. The second the last stall door is closed the gates spring open with a thunderous crack, releasing the Thoroughbreds onto the track to do their business.

Race.

All seven jump, and all seven leap at the same time. Feather comes out a bit sideways, her head up and the whites of her eyes showing dramatically even from where I'm standing at the rail. Jorge urges her on, and Feather gets the hint, galloping after the other fillies who are jostling each other for position down the straightaway and into the turn.

"Also we could work on breaking," I say, adding this to my mental list.

"See," Leo whispers to me again. "This is why I need you in Florida."

"Stop talking about Florida!"

"Would both of you shut up," Izzie hisses at us, waving a hand at the race in front of us. I look up at the giant television screen, because the horses are already in the backstretch, completely impossible to see past the inner dirt and turf tracks that wind around the infield like snakes eating their tails. Feather still tracks behind horses, ten lengths from the lead and looking lost with Jorge scrubbing at her to get into the race.

Please get into the race.

By the top of the far turn, Feather seems to get the point. She's moving at a good clip, rushing up on the outside of the pack. The horses spill around the turn and enter the stretch at full run, and I push onto my toes to see. Feather has her lane, Jorge a flurry of blue and orange. His crop is out and swinging, telling the filly that this is it. Move, baby, move.

Behind me, there's a smatter of yelling, a few booming voices screaming for their fillies to get to the wire first. One of them calls for Feather, shouting her name like she's a pet lost in a hurricane. So I join in.

"Come on, Feather!" I scream, leaning into the fence and squeezing Izzie's hand. She bounces up and down, watching as Feather begins a drive that will take her to the front if only there's enough track to get there. We're running out of distance, but Feather is coming. She switches leads and rushes down the leaders, Jorge flailing and Feather's nostrils blowing wide to take in as much air as she can so she can fly.

The wire slides overhead, Feather caught on the outside of a three-filly clump. Fourth, with room for improvement. I let out a breath as the filly goes galloping into the first turn, her head low and Jorge standing in the irons, talking to the second place finisher as they slowly fall back down to manageable speed.

Izzie rushes off to the gap in the rail, groom duty calling. Dad taps at his cell phone, little swooshing noises letting me know he's texting—probably updates to the mysterious Sahadi. Leo crosses his arms and watches the filly trot past us, her bay coat dark with dirt.

"Well?" I ask, in hopes someone is going to answer. Dad looks up.

"Promising," he says, when Feather floats into Izzie's waiting figure. "We'll see what we have next year, after she comes home from Florida."

Leo gives an all-too-ready nod, eager to agree with Dad on anything and everything. I roll my eyes over the fact that Dad has an idiot yes man sliding into one of his assistant trainer slots instead of . . . me.

His daughter.

That thought has me pushing away from the fence and jogging down to the gap, stepping out into the thick dirt to reach Feather just as Jorge leaps off of her.

"Did a good run, this one," he says, slapping the filly's neck before he unbuckles the saddle with professional, quick movements. He gives me a grin and winks. Then he's off the track, headed to the scales.

Feather snorts, breathing hard, as Izzie looks at me as if I've lost my mind standing out here in the dirt with them.

"Here," she says, shoving a bucket into my hands. "Make yourself useful."

So I do.

∾

When we rumble back up to Barn 27, I'm tapping my thumbnail against my silent phone. The little clicking noise fills the truck, hovering over the crunch of gravel as we roll between shedrows. It bothers me that the phone is so silent, which is ridiculous because I'm the one who made it this way. I severed the connection, and now I'm itching to lift the blockade . . . and why? It's not like I was answering any of Beck's calls, listening to any of his messages.

Izzie reaches over quietly and rests her hand on top of mine, dampening the clicks. Leo sighs from the front seat.

"Oh, thank god."

I kick the back of his chair, not that he even feels it or notices, and then slump into my seat. Izzie shakes her head at me.

"Someone is going to need an intervention soon," she tells me, which brings a painful smile to my face. It's funny, because it's only been a day. Less than a day. Of course, it's on the heels of a week of silence and whatever that was at the Breeders' Cup, on top of two months of mostly absence, so this is just the current manifestation of the dark cloud that's hanging over me, insistent and looming.

Then Izzie gasps, and I look up, following her line of sight until I see Pilar standing in the gravel outside Barn 27's mouth like a ray of freaking sunshine. Izzie bounces next to me, making the whole seat shake. Leo twists his head back at us quizzically, a confused question mark practically hanging over his head.

"What is with you?" he asks her as Izzie squeaks.

"She's here!"

He tilts his head at her like a collie, utterly befuddled, especially once Dad parks the truck and we're both out of the cab in mere seconds. It's a footrace to see who can get to her first, and I win, plowing right into Pilar and wrapping my arms around her tight.

She laughs, her wiry arms coming up around my shoulders just as Izzie is the second impact, all three of us clustering like hydrogen atoms bonding fiercely to their wayward oxygen.

"Why didn't you tell me you were coming back today?" I ask, pushing back enough so I won't suffocate in her thick, black curls.

Pilar lifts her cast-free arm and waves it at Izzie and me, an impish grin on her face.

"Just got the doctor's all clear," she says. "Literally an hour ago. So the first thing I did was head straight here."

For jockeys, it's never as simple as breaking your arm and waiting for the cast to come off before you're back on a horse. Pilar needed therapy, weight training, and a whole host of activities to get her back to riding shape. That I had expected. What I hadn't expected was her disappearance from the barn, like if she couldn't ride she just couldn't show up every day, watching everyone do what she couldn't.

"Don't mind us," Leo calls from the truck. "We'll just do, you know, all the work while you three proceed to do nothing."

Izzie waves him off, totally unconcerned as she asks the question we're all thinking.

"You can ride?"

"Absolutely, I can," Pilar says. "But I have crappy timing because my favorite crazy maker is out of commission, huh?"

As if on cue, a hoof striking wood cracks through the relative early evening quiet of the shedrow.

"But not far from making us all crazy, unfortunately," I say over Lighter's ear-piercing scream. It's getting close to evening feed, which has to be the only high point of his life now. He eats and watches the barn activity like he's committing it all to memory, studying us for some nefarious purpose only he could dream up.

Another scrape of hooves on wood sends Feather dancing after Leo backs her off the trailer. The filly whirls her hindquarters around, head up and eyes comically startled at each sound Lighter hammers out of the walls.

"July," Dad says, slamming the trailer door shut with a screech. "Check on the terror and make sure he's not dismantling his stall."

"And if he is?" I ask, surprised for a moment that Dad has finally fallen in with the rest of us by calling Lighter something more fitting like brat, jerkface, mayhem-causing whirlwind colt, or, simply, *terror*. I'm almost in awe. Almost.

Dad just shoos me into the barn, and I go, jogging down to the colt's stall. I'm just in time to witness the vinyl stall webbing fling free of its moorings, hitting the wall with metal bits jangling and sliding down to a heap in the raked dirt. The stall's gate is wide open, probably because a *certain someone* was tied up to the wall, which means Lighter has popped the chain holding him back from the entire racetrack, and what's a little webbing to Lighter?

My mouth falls open, and I don't even have time to react when Lighter goes trotting out into the aisle like he's floating on air, his neck arched and bleach-blond tail drifting behind him like he's on a photo shoot and someone has an industrial fan pointed directly at him.

The colt rolls one dark brown eye at me and hightails it to the other end of the barn, where light spills through the open doorway.

Shit, is all I can think. *Shit, shit, shit. This is not happening.*

"Gus! Loose horse!" I shout, because he has to be somewhere. The tack room, the feed room, somewhere within screaming distance. We're going to need Gus, but in the meantime I run after Lighter, having the presence of mind to come to a skidding halt in the dirt outside the tack room to grab a lead shank before sprinting full flight into the backside.

I arrive into the waning daylight just in time to see Lighter and his stupid, pale tail go carousing off into The Hole. His hooves scatter the gravel, and all I can think about is that bruise and how much we're all going to regret this by the time we catch up to him. The colt favors his bad foot with each step he takes, but it doesn't do anything to slow him down. I push into a run, wondering just how I'm going to chase down Lighter before he finds his way to the gate and then, probably catastrophically, out onto the road.

The road with people driving cars and trucks and . . .

I shove the thought from my head, pushing my burning legs to work harder as I run past Barn 35, Barn 36, watching Lighter skip down the dusty gravel road like this is the most fun ever before a horse transport van rumbles through the gate. The colt throws on the brakes hard enough to send his haunches down, his front end coming up through the force of sheer physics.

This doesn't stop Lighter. Oh, no. Of course not.

He twists around and runs across the grassy lawn between backside rows, heading for the most densely populated part of the backside. For a split second, I'm relieved. Surely someone will be able to catch him if he chooses to go gallivanting toward the training track. There are too many people, too many barns. He'll run into someone.

He has to.

"July!" I hear Gus yell for me, and shoot a quick look over my shoulder as I scramble after Lighter. Gus is gaining on me fast, lead rope in hand. His longer legs put him directly behind me as we chase Lighter past the track cafeteria. I'm heaving for breath, wondering just why it is I don't at all attempt exercise outside of riding, considering chasing Lighter around Belmont has always been a likely end game to all of his plotting, and groan when I see the godforsaken colt slide around the corner of Barn 61.

Just how far is he going to take us?

Gus and I round the corner, and my answer is immediate. People scatter out of the barns, the word out that there's a loose horse in the backside. Lighter pricks his ears up at the activity, like this is a new element to his game he hadn't anticipated but is thrilled about nonetheless, and slides to a rattling stop so he can turn, only finding that we've cut him off.

We're between barns now. The colt stands in the gravel aisle, head up and nostrils flared, his ribcage rising and falling with the exertion. It occurs to me that the colt isn't spooked at all—simply happy to have the exercise we've been keeping from him the past week.

As one, every person flooding the backside around us steps forward, constricting inward toward the colt. Lighter shakes his head and trots an agitated circle, eyeing us for weaknesses. He's not going to find one. I glance over my shoulder at Gus, at the track workers who have formed a line behind us. We're a human fence—one that Lighter's thinking about shattering.

The colt breaks into a wild series of kicks, tossing his head down and flinging it up like he's having a complete meltdown there in front of us. Finally, he slides to a halt and rears, coming down to all fours and standing like he's posing for a painting as we close in on him, Gus sidling up to the colt and clipping the lead shank onto his halter.

I can hear the collective relief—everyone in the crowd is letting out a breath.

"Damn colt," someone grumbles near me. I know there's more colorful language being thrown at Lighter as the crowd tentatively disperses, their job done. I have some choice words for him myself as I let out my own breath, walking up to the colt and putting a hand on his forehead.

"Congratulations," I tell him. "That was easily the worst thing you've accomplished to date."

Lighter gives me one wild, white-ringed look and blows a warm gust of air right into my face. Gus tugs on the shank, the metal chain clinking on the halter, and gives the colt a stern, Spanish lecture on the way back to the barn. Lighter walks merrily along next to him, a swing to each step and ears up, focused, obviously happy just to see some more of his well-seen world.

I hang back, wondering what he's going to be like after three more weeks of rest. If any horse was ever designed for constant movement, it's Lighter. Standing in a stall hours on end is only accepted because we at least take him out to the track each day so he can work out the kinks, no matter what chaos he brings in the process.

Barn 27 appears, and Lighter lowers his head and heaves a snort at it. Gus finally lifts a hand and pats the colt on the neck as they walk up to the dim shedrow, like he usually does after he's silently forgiven Lighter for whatever horrible thing he's done. Maybe he can't help feel for Lighter, too.

I delve into the dark after them, slipping by Dad, who stands just inside the shedrow. His phone is already in hand, a stern expression cut across his mouth, and I know just who he's talking to.

Chapter Eleven

Our vet, Dr. Abbott, comes out in the morning, after the barn has calmed down from morning works. Pilar and I lean against the wall, watching Gus hold Lighter still as Dr. Abbott tries to find the mystery spot no one has quite been able to find. She crouches by Lighter's hoof and glares at the x-ray while Dad stands by her shoulder, watching the black and white images with furrowed brows, like he's trying just as hard as Dr. Abbott to find some physical proof that Lighter's spin around the backside yesterday did more damage.

"How are we supposed to see if he'd damaged an injury no one can even find?" I ask into the air. Pilar snorts and shakes her head.

"Horses are mysteries, July," she tells me. "It's all part of how this sport drives us all a little crazy."

Truer words were never spoken. I shoot her a smile.

"I've missed you, you know that?"

"I know," she says, shrugging one shoulder like being missed is all in a day's work. "If it's any consolation, I missed being here."

"Obviously, it hasn't been the same without you," I say,

motioning to Lighter like what is happening here perfectly encapsulates everything that has happened in her absence. She considers the colt quietly for a moment, and then looks at me.

"And where is his owner?" she asks, which immediately drives a pink shade of rage onto my cheeks. "Usually he's here for these things."

"It's fall semester," I say, my cheeks feeling warmer, so I might as well be broadcasting how pathetically I'm lying through my teeth. "Beck is stuck in the city doing Columbia things."

"July." Pilar rolls her eyes. "Izzie told me."

I suck in a breath. "Izzie is a traitor."

She laughs. "Not that Izzie knows much outside of how horrible it's been to be around you the past couple of days. Something about rage smashing your way through Aqueduct?"

"Hardly," I scoff. "I don't rage smash. I don't have the upper body strength for that."

Pilar laughs in that full-bodied way which makes a little bit of me unwind. It's a reminder this isn't the end of the world. Beck is just a boy, and what were boys to me before this summer, when Beck suddenly became something a little more than the owner's son who never knew when to shut up?

My phone vibrates in my back pocket, and I reach back to slide it into my hand. I still haven't unblocked Beck; still don't really want to see all the messages he's left me. I tentatively glance at the face and find little text bubbles from Bri, screenshots of her conversations with Beck neatly contained within.

Make it stop, she says below the texts I don't want to read. *You owe me for leaving me alone with those people.*

I wince, because yeah, I really did do that, didn't I?

That's the fall out of running away. There are always casualties, and I left Bri in that brownstone like I'd forgotten she was even there. Who am I kidding? Of course I'd forgotten she was there. I was too busy sprinting toward the subway station in my thoughtless need to not hear anything else Beck had to say.

I'm sorry, I'm sorry, I'm sorry I type. *But no go.*

JULY, is the instant response. *SAVE ME FROM THIS TORTURE. YOU OWE ME.*

I stuff my phone into my back pocket as Pilar looks at me with eyebrow raised. The phone keeps vibrating and I cross my arms over my chest, trying to pretend it's not Bri sending more caps locked rage my way.

Dr. Abbott sighs at our feet, shaking her head and drawing my attention away from my phone.

"There's no outward sign he exacerbated the problem," she says, straightening and patting Lighter on the neck in reward for being patient enough to stand still for a few minutes. "Also still no obvious sign anything is wrong at all."

"The mysterious horse becomes more mysterious yet," Pilar whispers to me, and I nudge her in the side, listening.

"What do you suggest?" Dad asks. "He didn't sore up from his adventure yesterday, but since we can't even see the original injury . . ."

"Caution, Rob," Dr. Abbott says, rubbing her back and popping her neck after holding herself in one position so long, crouched at the feet of a stir-crazy Thoroughbred. "It's all I can really tell you."

Dad rocks back on his heels, like Dr. Abbott's advice is the last thing he needs to hear. Honestly, it really is. We already know we have to be cautious. That's why Lighter's on stall rest. This is just one more unseen thing we need to take into account, one more thing to be unsure of. It's like walking into a haunted house and experiencing nothing—it still leaves you spooked.

Dr. Abbott collects her equipment while Dad looks at Lighter as if he can personally see through the colt's skin, all the way through muscles and into his bones. I know what he's thinking because we're all thinking it—something is there, but not there. And if we can find it we can fix it, make Lighter whole and sound again.

But that's not how the real world works. Sometimes things break and you don't know why. Even worse? Sometimes there's no way to fix them. Sometimes you just have to sit and wait.

Finally Dad shoots a look over at me. "Juls, want to break the news to Beck that I'm sending Lighter to Florida?"

I gape at him. "Why?"

He tilts his head at me. "Why am I sending Lighter to Florida or why am I asking you to call Beck?"

"Can't it be both?" I ask, while Pilar shakes her head, hiding her smile behind one gloved hand. "You always call Beck about Lighter, who is fine where he is."

"Breaking out of his stall is not fine, Juls," Dad tells me. He rubs at Lighter's forehead, the colt eyeing him suspiciously and pawing at the dirt floor. Gus tugs on the shank, reading the colt's intentions before he even gets to the part where he snakes out his head and tries to take a bite out of Dad's arm. Neither will let that happen.

Dad takes a step back and sighs, like this definitely wasn't what he wanted. Then he pins his eyes on me.

"And I hear you've blocked Beck's number."

I open and then slowly shut my mouth. Why did I ever think

that was privileged information? Of course everyone knows. The whole Belmont backside probably knew the second I hit the block button at Aqueduct, that's how fast gossip slithers through the barns.

Dad tells Gus to take care of Lighter, which is useless because it's all Gus ever does, and heads to the office to make his calls. I leap after him, leaving Pilar and trotting after him as he disappears into his office. Martina is busy making a third pot of coffee, a sheaf of papers in one hand and a pen pinched between her teeth.

"Who told you I blocked Beck's number?" I demand, falling onto the ratty sofa and rising a plume of dust. Dad barely affords me a glance as he scrolls through the contacts on his cell phone.

"Does *everyone* count?" Martina asks, and I throw a glare at her.

"And who told you?"

"Voices carry, July," she says simply. "If you want secrets to remain secrets, maybe don't broadcast them down the shedrow."

"Thanks for that sage advice, Martina," I grumble. "I'll make sure to remind you of that the next time Matthew Delaney swings by looking to take you to 'lunch'."

I feel like my air quotes around *lunch* are not appreciated. Martina glares at me, pen still jutting out from her beautifully painted lips, like she's got somewhere to be soon and had to apply fresh makeup for the grand event of Matthew arriving to whisk her off to wherever they go for a full two hours on dark days.

"That is not your business," she snarls, pulling the pen from her mouth.

"And yet it happens all the time," I say. "In broad daylight, no less."

"I am updating him on Star," Martina says, waving the pen in the air. "And he is going through an intensely stressful time, so he just needs a friend who understands—"

"If by *friend who understands* you mean casual hook up wherever convenient," I break in, knowing how right I am and not even stopping to consider how many ways Martina can kill me in my sleep.

"July," Dad says over Martina's infuriated growl. I swing my attention back to him.

"It's true," I state, not sure what I'm expecting of his pointed look from his desk, phone in hand, Beck's number already merrily dialing away on speaker. The digital ringing litters the air, making my pulse spike.

"As disturbing as I find this conversation," Dad says, "I can safely say both of you are incredibly bad at hiding secrets. Let it go. Both of you."

That's when the line picks up, Beck's voice filling the room with a tired, "Hey, Rob. What's the news?"

"Nothing," Dad says, leaning over the phone so his voice comes out clear. "Unfortunately. I'd like to say we found something so we know what we're dealing with, but we're still flying in the dark here."

There's a muffled silence on the other end, like Beck has to take a moment to digest this.

"The good news is Lighter's standing on all four hooves and didn't stiffen up overnight," Dad continues over Beck's silence. "I say the longer the rest, the better he'll come out of it in the long run."

"Sounds good to me," Beck says. "Whatever's best for the

horse, you know?"

Dad smiles a little, just a quirk of his lips. I wonder how long it's been since he's had an owner like Beck—just eager to do right by the horse, no matter what. Beck must seem like such an innocent anomaly in an industry of owners who so often don't seem to care.

"I'll tell you what," Dad says, looking up at me. Adrenaline slides into my system like a shower of sparks, because I really have no idea what the next words out of his mouth will be. "I've got nearly half the string shipping down to Florida this week. I'll put Lighter on the rig with them and we'll reassess at the end of December."

"Gus will go down with him?" Beck asks, because Gus and Lighter are synonymous. There is no one who handles the colt better, and I'm happy Beck recognizes as much.

"Of course," Dad says. "My assistant, Leo Reyes, will be in charge of the operation down there, and I have complete—"

"Leo, huh?"

There's a seed of doubt in his voice. I hear it just as clearly as Dad, who wipes a hand over his face and looks at me again. I tilt my head at him, wondering what's going through his head.

"Juls, too," he says, and I immediately stand up, mouthing *no*.

There is no way. Hell would have to freeze over first. No way am I jumping on a rig with Lighter and Leo for freaking *Florida*.

"Oh," Beck says, his voice bringing my ramping tirade to a shuddering halt. I wonder what he's thinking through that *oh*. Like *oh*, July's leaving. *Oh*, July's not returning my phone calls and she's abandoning New York for Florida. He can disappear into Manhattan, and I get to jump on a van to another state and think that's a totally rational way to resolve a problem.

A tiny voice in the back of my head reminds me I've already taken steps to resolve this problem, and I failed. Gloriously. I shut that voice up, anger engulfing it, closing over its head.

"I see," Beck says, voice somewhere between a sigh and acceptance. I want to snag the phone and say that he sees absolutely nothing. That is half the problem. Instead I stand in the middle of the office, vibrating with the need to interrupt and telling myself at the same time that I can't. There's no way it would end well, because what am I supposed to say?

No, I don't want to go to Florida? My dad is a crazy person who just sacrificed me to the racing gods? Take your horse and go to a different barn of sane, rational people?

All of that would be the truth. And yet I can't say it.

Which is my problem.

"Great," Dad says, forcing peppiness into his voice like this is all the approval he needs. "We'll ship him out tomorrow morning with the rest. Leo reports to me daily, but I'll have him send you updates since he'll be closer to the action, so to speak. If you have questions, don't hesitate to call me."

"Yeah," Beck says, sounding distracted. "Sure. Will do."

"You have a good day now, Beckett."

"You too, Rob."

And then that's it. The line cuts off, and Dad turns off the speaker and I yell, "Are you kidding me?"

Dad drops the phone onto the top of his desk and leans back into his chair. "The colt is better off in—"

"I am *not* talking about Lighter," I seethe. "I'm talking about just cavalierly telling me I'm going to Florida."

"It's not that I haven't noticed Leo isn't completely one

hundred percent yet," Dad says. "I need you down there to make sure things run smoothly."

Oh, that's rich. I'll be Dad's right hand man after all, not his own damn assistant?

"Leo's one of your assistants," I say. "Not me. Maybe you should try making sure he's all good before throwing half a string at him and putting them in Florida without supervision."

"July," he sighs, "please don't misunderstand me. I'm sending you to Florida with him to be his supervision. You're better than most assistants I've ever had, and Leo needs the experience of managing a string. You're the guidance."

"That is such bull," I say.

Martina coughs from the sofa, and I look over at her as she twirls her pen in her fingers. "I have to say I actually agree with July on this one."

I motion to Martina. "See?" I say. "Even Martina recognizes how crazy this is."

"And the way you say that instantly makes me think sending you to Florida is the best idea ever," Martina says, smiling at Dad. "Send her to the Sunshine State, Dad. Great plan."

"I'm going," Pilar's voice pipes up from the doorway. I spin around and look at her, surprised. She shrugs a shoulder. "Voices carry, remember?"

Martina smiles and gives her a thumbs up from the sofa.

"You're kidding," I say, then spin back to Dad. "You recruited her, too?"

"I volunteered," Pilar says before Dad can get a word in. "Honestly, Juls, Palm Meadows sounds like several worlds better than Aqueduct in winter."

I huff, falling into the chair across from Dad's desk. I'm outnumbered and overruled. What's worse, having Pilar in Florida suddenly makes the whole thought bearable. Like now I don't even have a reason to say no.

Except for Kali and Jericho.

"I need to keep working on Kali," I say, directing the words at Dad without looking at him. I can't exactly make myself meet anyone's eyes when I let this news loose, which I have to now. It's way past due. "If I'm accepted to Jericho, the only way they'll accept her to board is if they see video beforehand."

Dad doesn't say anything at first, and when I finally screw up enough courage to look up I see cool calm directed right at me, like he's known this whole time.

Of course, if anyone in this world could just know all my secrets without seeming to try, it would be him.

"What happened to NYU, Juls?"

I sigh and slump in my chair. "I didn't apply," I say. "I guess you could say I'm embracing the horse bug."

Martina flops into the sofa cushions. "God help us all, another assistant. I can see it now. First Leo, now July."

"I don't know that I want . . ." I trail off, waving a hand at the office. "This. But I do know NYU isn't going to help me figure it out any time soon. I just know that I can't work on Kali when I'm in Florida, and I need Kali at Jericho if I'm accepted."

Dad taps his finger on his phone, watching me studiously.

"This is simple, July," he says.

"Is it?" I ask. "Because I'm thinking it's one more reason to stay here."

"But you're not staying here," Dad says, picking up his phone and scrolling through the contents. "And if you need Kali, she'll go with you."

Then he taps a number on his phone and makes the call.

∼

Florida.

I stand at the foot of my bed. Two suitcases are spread open across the floor and a heap of clothes is piled up on the comforter as I try to organize. Socks, shirts, jeans, breeches, more jeans . . . shorts?

What do you wear in Florida during November? I still can't believe this is happening. I hold the shorts in my hands and ponder aloud when I last bared my deathly white legs to the world.

"It's not going to happen," Martina says next to me, prying the shorts out of my fingers and pointing me at the pile. "Do what you're good at and organize your riding clothes. Leave the non-riding garments to me."

I give her a suspicious look as she tosses the shorts in the general direction of my exploding closet. Shoes tumble out of it, scattering across the hardwood as if they're trying to escape the mayhem. Martina stares at it like she's composing herself before she dives in.

"Why are you even helping?" I ask, still confused about her purpose here. It's not like Martina is so dedicated to making sure I look presentable when she's not around that she'll overlook my airing her supposed secrets to the world.

"Rest assured, I ask myself this all the time," Martina sighs, shoving her way into the closet and pushing through the clothes, glaring at my collection like everything there disgusts her even

173

though she is responsible for my owning more than half of it. She pulls out a few dresses, on the off chance there's a race day that requires such a thing, and then starts to mercilessly go through my nicer tops.

"Honestly," I tell her, sitting down next to the pile, a pair of socks rolling into my lap. I pick it up and cradle it in my hands, squeeze it like it's a stress-relieving ball. "I kinda told everyone you were—"

"I know what you were telling everyone," Martina cuts me off, giving me a glare over her shoulder before going back to her inspection of my things. Her perfectly ironed, glossy black hair tumbles between her tense shoulders, which have to be that stiff because of me. I'm just on a roll these days.

"I'm sorry?" I test out the words, which come out like a question. Martina snorts.

"Try that again, Juls."

"I really am," I say again. "Sorry, I mean. It's not any of my business where you go with Matthew, or what you do with Matthew. It's just . . . surprising?"

Martina tosses a few tops on the floor and laughs. "Keep digging your grave, July. You're doing beautifully."

"Seriously, Martina," I sigh, squeezing the socks a little harder. "I shouldn't have said it. I'm a jerk."

"Yes, you are," Martina agrees, turning from the closet and settling on the floor by the suitcases, beginning her quest to perfectly fold every garment and pack it into the suitcases with that magical way she has. Packing is truly Martina's greatest talent.

I would never tell her as much. Not if I want to keep my head firmly on my shoulders, anyway.

For a minute, I watch her pack my suitcases with scary, swift efficiency while I sit on the bed like a lump, socks clamped in my fingers.

Martina notices my inability to move. "Are you going to help, or are you going to keep staring at me like I've suddenly sprouted snakes for hair?" she asks, still working her way through the clothes.

"I guess I just don't get it? You and Matthew didn't end well the first time . . ." I trail off when she looks up at me, huffing.

"July, honestly," she growls. "Don't you remember your earlier speech about it not being your business?"

"I do." I nod, forcing myself to put down the socks before my short nails rip holes right through the material. "I guess I just want to know how you got over it. You and Matthew haven't traded kind words in years, and now you're just . . . what? Okay?"

Martina shrugs a shoulder. "I don't know that I have. I'm just . . . interested in maybe seeing if I can."

"Despite everything," I say, unconvinced.

"Yes. Besides, this is really about Beck," she sighs, resting her elbows on her knees and looking up at me like this conversation bores her already. "Right?"

"Am I that obvious?" I ask, even though I already know that answer.

"July, you *suck*," Martina says helpfully, going back to her packing. "I give you credit for that Jericho news, but with Beck? Please. You're about as transparent as a window."

I'm suddenly compelled to check my phone, hit the unblock button. Just to see. I grit my teeth and press down on the impulse. "Good to know."

"To answer your question," Martina continues, oblivious to

my jitteriness. "I know nothing. Matthew doesn't live with Beck. Matthew has a full life outside of Beck. It's something I recommend for you, actually."

"That is not fair," I say, stung. It's also not true. I've been living my life just fine without Beck in it, even when we were definitely, without question—maybe?—together. I frown. Deeply.

"I haven't heard anything," Martina tells me. "Even if I had, what good would it do you? You're still the one that has to man up and unblock the poor boy's number. You're not going to fix this until you start acting like an adult."

"That's hilarious, since I'm being sent to Florida on the basis that I can act like an adult better than other people who will remain nameless," I mutter, and Martina clucks her tongue behind her teeth and points at me.

"Delicious irony, right?" she grins, truly enjoying this. I glower at her. "Don't take all of this out on Leo," she adds. "He's a pain in the ass, but once he's got his feet underneath him down there we can just hope that's where he stays and we'll never have to deal with him again. Think of yourself as the kind soul who's releasing him back into the wild."

I sigh, falling back into the pile of clothes and staring at the ceiling. Sometimes, I wish Martina wasn't quite so right. It's unnatural when she hits the nail on the head so perfectly. Sometimes I feel like that should be impossible, given how fundamentally different we are. How on earth is she always the one who knows what to say?

Reaching out, I grope for my cell phone and unlock it. The phone chirps at me, willing and ready to execute my every whim. I scroll to Beck's number, my fingers hovering over the red block button. There's an itchy feeling crawling down my spine, like anxiety come alive to march down my bones. It's just a simple tap against a screen. I can do this. I can face what he has to stay to me—all the piled up texts and voice mails—and I can even respond if I want to. I just have to open my mouth.

I just have to hit the damned button.

Letting out a huge breath, I toss the phone back onto the bed.

"Chicken," Martina sing-songs from the floor as she folds.

And, again, she's so very right.

Chapter Twelve

Florida is green. It's all sprays of palm fronds and suburban sprawl curling out into the country. It may be my imagination, but it gets more beautiful and emerald green the further we drive. Big, blue sky curves over us, puffy white clouds more cheerful still. We've been in the state all of a few hours, and Leo has been smiling nonstop the entire time, which is an insane feat considering we've driven all the way from New York as we made our way with our precious haul to Palm Meadows.

Smiles. More smiles.

Pilar sits up in the passenger seat with her window down, taking deep breaths every few minutes with theatrical, awed sighs.

"This is wonderful," she croons, pushing her wind-torn hair back into an orderly ponytail.

"Is that the third sigh or fourth?" I ask no one in particular.

"How can you possibly be counting?" Leo asks, looking at me in the rearview mirror. "She's inspired, July. Because it's—"

"Florida," I sigh, like I've caught their enthusiasm, pressing my hand to my chest before waving at the window from my spot in the backseat. "Yes, I know. I see it. It's wildly beautiful and I appreciate that."

"She doesn't appreciate it," Leo mutters to Pilar, who laughs.

"She'll get there," Pilar assures him. "It always takes some time for July to warm up to anything new."

"That is definitely not true," I say, leaning over the center console. Pilar gives me a knowing stare and I sigh, falling back into my seat.

"Fine. I give up. I'm a curmudgeon."

"The first step is admitting you have a problem," Leo tells me sagely, because he's a jackass.

"Is the second step telling you to kindly go screw yourself?"

Leo whistles between his teeth. "Definitely not time for that intervention, then."

I roll my eyes, just as they catch on plank fences and turned out horses. Beautiful barns cluster in the distance, a jumping arena and a flat work arena glistening with white sand nearby.

An equestrian center, right across the way from Palm Meadows. How did I not know about this? Then I kick myself. We're practically right next door to Wellington, land of Florida's equestrian centers. Of course there would be a dressage arena within shouting distance of Palm Meadows. And of course I'm stabling Kali with the racehorses.

Forethought. I don't have it.

Pilar bounces in her seat when Leo turns into Palm Meadows' main entrance.

It is, of course, surrounded with palm trees. There is also quite the meadow out beyond the security gate. Well named, this training center.

Behind us, the rigs holding our fleet turn into the drive. Leo goes through the motions with security, and then we're trucking along into the center, heading through row after row of neat, rectangular barns. Every barn is white with a green roof, cute matching shutters flanking every window. Neatly trimmed hedges run along the barns, young trees planted every few feet for the promise of future shade. Between shedrows, I can just make out glimpses of the sprawling track beyond. It's empty, which makes sense given it's mid-afternoon.

Leo pulls up next to our barn, where Dad has rented stalls. Our horses will have a great view of the field, where—I squint—it looks like a series of round pens are set up for turn out. Maybe—just maybe—Lighter won't go completely mad here after all.

I unfold myself out of the backseat and stretch away my cramped muscles. The rigs squeal to a halt, brakes hissing. Gus and Izzie, who arrived early to help prepare the stalls and set up, appear at the rigs like they can't contain themselves. Really, who could? I'm already moving up to them, waiting for the ramps to lower so we can start moving in.

Between the five of us, it doesn't take long to move our horses into their new digs. The only two who give us any trouble are predictable about it. Feather refuses to move until Betty takes the initiative, hopping her little goat legs down the plywood covering the metal ramp and bleating the whole way. Then Feather goes rushing after her, eyes wild at the thought of being left behind.

"Co-dependent to a fault," I say to her, leading her down the ramp a little faster than I'd like because the filly is so intent on keeping up with her companion. "At least we know your kryptonite."

Feather snorts at the ground, dust billowing up around her legs as she hustles me closer to Betty. Behind me, I hear the beginnings of Gus's argument with Lighter. The colt lets out an ear-piercing whinny right before the knocking starts, the rig shivering gently on its many tires as Lighter lets his opinions be known.

I slide the filly into her stall—a white cinder block affair topped off with gray metal bars. The whole barn is set up like a cubical grid, the roof arching off the ground like a pavilion, leaving the stalls open and airy. Sun pours across the aisle, bright swaths of it painting the ground in huge, happy checkers. Feather surveys the hay net hanging outside of her stall, and I work on pulling off her shipping bandages while Betty explores the bedding, flicking her tiny tail and totally oblivious to Feather's intense need to keep an eye on her. The filly cranes her neck around, sniffing the goat's side like she has to reassure herself this is really Betty. Betty is here, is okay, and is not going to leave any time soon.

God forbid we ever lose Betty. Feather would be inconsolable.

By the time I'm done with Feather, Lighter finally goes trucking by with Gus digging in his heels to keep the colt at least somewhat grounded. Lighter coils up behind Gus's hold on his lead, ears swiveling and breaths coming in repeating, even rumbles. I duck inside the door of Feather's stall as they go by, Gus muscling the colt into his assigned spot. Out of curiosity, I give Feather's metal grate door a good shake, thinking it's better than the stall guard that Lighter decided to do away with back at Belmont.

"Where's this one going?" Leo asks, drawing my attention from my stall door inspection as he walks down the aisle with Maggie. My mare is taking huge, huffing breaths, her ears pricked and her body nearly as bouncy as Lighter's. Clearly everyone's loving the change of scenery.

"Next to Lighter," I say. "She'll keep him in line."

Leo gives me a look. "Sure," he says, sounding like he doesn't believe it. "Wishful thinking, but okay. What's happening with that other filly?"

"Kali," I say, slipping out of Feather's stall. Leo shrugs a shoulder.

"Right," he sighs, walking past me. "The dressage horse."

I bite down gently on the insides of my cheeks, telling myself not to rise to the bait. It doesn't help matters that Dad had to pull strings to get Kali a stall, and Leo knows that. He knows exactly how against the rules this is, but I've already let everyone know that Kali is my responsibility. I'm her groom, I'm her rider, I'm her everything.

But of course Leo would still find it problematic. Kali is taking up a stall that could have held a real, money-making racehorse. Never you mind that all the horses Dad wanted to send to Florida made it on the rig. These are the young prospects, the horses that need a change of scenery, and the horses that don't fit any of the Aqueduct races.

And they're all here, no matter Kali's involvement.

I jog back out to the rig, entering its dim interior to find Kali standing patiently at the far end. She flicks her ears forward at the sight of me and shifts in her restraints, so maybe she's not so patient after all.

"Sorry you had to be last," I tell her, untying her lead and walking her forward out of the rig's knock-down stall. She follows me, gently placing one foot in front of the other like she's not entirely sure about the floor. Outside, she loses all of that careful footing and clomps down to the gravel, a hop to her step once she sees that her travel—for the time being—is over.

Once she's in her stall on the other side of Maggie, closest to the office and the tack room, I go back to unload her equipment. Izzie and Pilar are busy organizing the tack room when I arrive, hauling Kali's trunk into the corner and pushing it open, happy to see nothing has shifted. Her new saddle gleams up at me, her bridle perfectly luminous since the last time I cleaned it. Not that it's ever gotten too terribly dirty in the first place. It's only a few weeks old.

"Oooh," Izzie whistles, looking into the trunk. "Our Kali is suddenly all fancy."

"Not too fancy," I say, closing the trunk's lid. "She's here instead of that equestrian center across the street."

"What's stopping you from just walking her over there?" Pilar asks, squinting at the little bottles of medications she's organizing in the cabinet.

"Money, time, the fact I didn't even know about it because I was given a day to prepare for this?"

Izzie shrugs a shoulder. "Good news is there's plenty of flat land around here, and you don't need jumps to train. The track is plenty huge and dead quiet in the afternoon."

I nod, letting Izzie's optimism rub off on me. She's right, after all. I don't need a perfectly graded arena to teach Kali how to *not* be a racehorse. I was doing just fine in that regard at Saratoga, out in Blackbridge's galloping fields. Kali has a paid up stall right outside, and that's good enough. I can work with this.

I'll just train racehorses in the morning, and on the days we're not going to Gulfstream Park to race I'll take Kali out in the afternoon. In the meantime, there are the turnout pens. This will work. It will.

I let out a breath and nod.

"You're right," I say. "It's going to be fine. Great, even."

Pilar puts the last of the medications on the shelf and knocks down the box. "Of course it will be fine," she says. "Just look at this place. It's like the cleanest training facility I've ever seen. Who needs an equestrian center full of warmbloods when you have this?"

"Seriously," Izzie agrees, nodding as she hangs bridles up on the wall, labeling them as she goes.

"And when you and Kali are ready to make the video," Pilar continues, pulling out her cell phone and waving it in the air, "I'll be ready."

My chest fills up with gratitude, and the smile that pulls on my lips is the real, genuine kind. Maybe this will, really and truly, work. At the very least, I've got Pilar and Izzie here with me, ready to help if I have to ask.

"Thanks," I say. "Now I just have to focus on training her up to it."

Like that will be super easy. Sure, I'll just put an ex-racehorse on a track and start teaching her dressage. This shouldn't be confusing for Kali at all. I tell myself to cut the sarcasm; that it *can* work. I just have to look at this optimistically. Clearly I need to hang out in Izzie's healthy glow of positivity more.

"Done," Izzie proclaims, labeling the last bridle and backing away to look at her work, hands resting on her hips. "Now we just have to keep it this way."

I cast a look around the ultra-clean, intensely organized room, knowing this isn't going to last. That's the case with backsides. Organized chaos is the name of the game.

"Then I think it's time to check out the dorms," I say. Izzie whoops, jogging out of the room as Pilar shakes her head, laughing.

"She would be excited about that," she says, and I raise an eyebrow at her.

"Spill," I say, trailing after her and flicking off the tack room light.

"You and I are rooming together," Pilar says, giving me a knowing look. "Leo is on his own in the pavilion. Who do you think Izzie is rooming with?"

"Gus." I nod. "On again?"

"If they're not," Pilar says, laughing, "they will be soon."

"How do they keep these things so quiet?" I ask, amazed. Honestly, the two of them are like the most understated couple in the history of ever. You'd never know they were in a relationship, whether they're currently in a relationship, whether they'd rather slice onions in an unventilated kitchen than talk to each other—it's astonishing.

"Looking for lessons?" Pilar asks, shooting me a half smile that says plenty. I lunge at her, sending her laughing out of the shedrow.

~

Palm Meadows in the morning glows a certain shade of red. The palm trees look like they are on fire with sun, like shifting starbursts in front of a slowly lightening sky. The whole track looks like a river of fire, horses in different stages of go as they make their circuits around the track, their riders like bobbing puppets on their backs, shifting with their movement.

That's a training oval—movement.

I lead Maggie out into the warm, Florida air. The mare lifts her nose into the soft breeze and breathes deeply, unconcerned with me as I pull on her cinch one last time to make sure it's tight enough. Then I gather her reins at the base of her neck and shove my booted foot in the stirrup, launching myself into her heavy Western saddle. Maggie shifts underneath my weight, but otherwise stands firmly on four legs, mouthing the bit as she searches for my hands.

Further down the shedrow, Leo gives Pilar a leg up onto a lanky bay two-year-old filly named Kickabit. Like Palm Meadows, Kickabit is well-named—her owners must have a comedic streak. Her tendency to send her hind legs sailing up past her butt is impressive, and Maggie already has her ears swept back the second she realizes who she's ponying to the track first thing on this beautiful morning.

"Thought you were getting a taste of the easy life, huh?" I lean over the saddle's pommel, patting Maggie's patchwork neck as my mare mouths the bit again, working up a gentle froth over the edges of her lips.

"Ready?" Pilar asks me as Leo leads Kickabit up to us, the filly already a huffing mass of energy. The second they get close enough, the filly swings her rump toward Maggie, who deftly moves aside. Thwarted, Kickabit twitches, still amped up with the need to kick and nothing to kick at. Leo hands her over to me, a grimace on his face.

"Watch her," he says.

"Clearly," I say, clipping my line onto the filly's bridle and nudging Maggie into her. Maggie, for the most part, is all pinned ears. Clearly she feels this is a filly who hasn't learned her place yet, which is definitely further down the pecking order than Kickabit is willing to accept.

We head off, walking down the dirt bridle path to the training track. That's another thing about Palm Meadows—there's barely a scrap of pavement to be found. Everything is either lush green grass or cushy, tended dirt. Pavement around here is for wash stalls or maybe to jog a horse over to make sure it's completely sound before heading to the track.

So, basically, we're all natural here.

"Can I just live here?" Pilar asks, who's definitely absorbing the same scenery I am, just in a far different way.

"You stop talking right now," I say half-jokingly, because the thought of Pilar leaving our barn makes me want to curl up into the fetal position and never leave it.

"It's not exactly leaving your dad's barn if he has a string down here, right?" Pilar asks, winking at me because she knows exactly what I'm thinking.

"Not exactly," I hesitantly agree. Pilar started out at our barn, but that doesn't mean she's staying forever. She pretty much decided that when she started race riding. "When was your fifth win?"

Apprentice jockeys lose their bug a year after the date of their fifth win, so the clock is ticking. Next year Pilar will be a journeyman jock, and they don't call them *journeyman* for nothing. Soon she'll be gone, and I'll be so happy for her. But I'll want her back with us all the while. I'm going to have to deal with this unsettling fact that nothing stays the same. Nothing ever has, Pilar included.

"Saratoga," she says, giving me a knowing look. "I can't say breaking my arm immediately after was the best move for me, career-wise. I'll need an extension on my bug."

"We'll get you back on something soon," I tell her. "I'm sure Dad is plotting as we speak."

187

"That's just it, though," Pilar says. "It's why I came down here to begin with. I need to build back up to it, get my nerves back."

"Nerves?" I ask, surprise clear in my voice. "Since when have you had anything less than nerves of steel?"

"Since I fell off in a race," Pilar says, shaking her head. "It's ridiculous, but I don't want to be afraid out there. The second I feel fear, I'm done. I'll have to quit, and I can't quit."

"So you won't," I say, attempting cheery optimism like Izzie and only managing to sound unsure.

Pilar rubs a hand on her worn jeans, Kickabit finally settling down underneath her. The filly has run out of hijinks on the way to the track, too busy looking around to get invested in making my mare's life a living hell. That's a good sign; almost an indication she's looking forward to working.

"Right," Pilar agrees. "I won't. So here I am. I figured Lighter is going to Florida, so I had better follow him. If I can climb up on him and only feel exhilaration then I know I'll be fine."

"Hate to break it to you, but I don't know when we'll get him back on the track," I say, threading Maggie through the gap onto the L-shaped training track, Kickabit following right after. We turn toward the outside rail and pick up a trot, working methodically down the dirt.

Palm Meadows comes with two tracks—the oval for gallops and fast works, and the L, which runs alongside the oval's backstretch and borders the property like a big brown moat. The L is for jogging horses, who might at most pick up the accidental canter every few strides. Once Lighter comes back from his foot injury, this is where we'll put him to see how he goes.

A small part of me sees the sense in all of this now. Lighter coming back on Belmont's crowded training track could be a recipe for disaster. With a thick-headed, speed-addicted colt like ours, the L is a perfect baby step. We're all going the same speed here, like a paddling pool full of splashing kids.

God help me, I think this is a *good* idea.

"Once Lighter is headed to the track," Pilar says, her mouth set as she lifts herself in the irons, "I want on him. No one else gets to ride him except me."

"I'll make sure to relay the message," I say, reaching out to the clasp keeping me tethered to Kickabit's bridle.

I let her go, and push Maggie into a canter to keep up.

∽

It's late in the morning when I'm finished with works, which gives me a tight window to put away Maggie and get Kali ready for her first adventure on the racetrack since Saratoga.

Part of me thinks this might be the worst idea ever. Taking a newly retired racehorse back on the track to perform walk-trot transitions just doesn't seem like the clearest of plans, but this is what I have. The L track is waiting for me, and Kali needs to be ridden.

"Need an audience?" Izzie asks, leaning against the metal door as I groom Kali in her stall. The filly has her face pressed against the bars, her nostrils flaring as she breathes against Izzie's hand. Izzie has always loved Kali, and their relationship looks like it's blossomed again now that Kali's back with the racers.

She must be so confused.

"I need an audience like I need a hole in my head," I say, and Izzie laughs.

"Then I'll need to rally the troops," she says, grinning at me as she rubs Kali's nose. "Maybe I can even convince Leo to come watch."

"Leo?" I ask. "Of the *Kali's taking up valuable space I didn't pay for* opinion?"

Izzie shrugs. "I caught him giving her a piece of carrot while you were coming back from the track," she says. "I think he's just saying these things to get under your skin."

"Of course he is," I sigh. "That's what he's done since forever ago."

Izzie makes a face at me and steps back when I let myself out of Kali's stall so I can get her tack.

The tack room, expectedly, is already a wreck. Gus is tidying, but Pilar and I are hurricanes when we're coming in and out during morning works. I give Gus an apologetic smile. He rolls his eyes at me and continues sorting through the tangled ball of bandages as I step around him and pick up Kali's saddle, throwing her bridle over my shoulder. Then I scurry out of there before he decides to accost me for my hand in this disaster.

Once I've got Kali tacked up, I lead her out of her stall and motion for Izzie to come along. She jumps after me, popping her head into the office to grab Pilar on the way. I sigh when I notice Leo trailing after them, a cup of steaming coffee in his hand and a look of perplexed curiosity etched across his face.

This has to go well, or I'm never going to hear the end of it.

"Need a leg up?" Leo asks as I stop Kali in the yard between barns, checking her girth and pulling down her stirrups.

I twist halfway to give him a cursory inspection. Is he being serious?

"I thought you weren't having anything to do with this," I say.

"Doesn't mean I can't enjoy the show," he says. "I'll throw in legging you up as a bonus."

"You make that sound like it's a bonus for me," I say, rolling my eyes as I gather the reins at the base of Kali's neck and mount up on my own.

"It's not meant to be," he grins up at me, waggling his eyebrows. I stare at him for a beat and then lean down, Kali bobbing her head with my movements.

"Is sexual harassment something you'd like me to report to my father, aka your boss? Because I'm feeling charitable right now in that I'm not calling him immediately."

I smile at the way his face morphs into trepidation and then flat, like I've wiped away all the joy he gets in giving me a hard time. Maybe working with Leo is something I can come to appreciate.

"Touché, July," he says, then motions to the L-track. "Try not to get yourself killed out there. I really don't want to have that conversation with your dad, either."

"I'll try to keep you from that," I say primly, and then get Kali moving. She takes off at an energetic walk, head bobbing and legs working in the way you *want* a dressage horse to walk. It's the working gait we all aim for, and usually have to push and push to achieve. Kali just does it naturally, because the training center wraps around us like a green bubble, full of activity and buzzing with the promise of speed.

I tell myself that Kali may have sucked at running, but she's still very much a racehorse. She's expecting a certain routine, and I'm about to throw her for a loop.

Go easy, I tell myself. *Don't ask for anything you know she can't give.*

It's late in the morning. Most of the racers are long gone, back to their stables for their cool downs and steaming baths. The whole training center is about to fall face first into a collective nap, and here I am on Kali, getting ready to go to work.

Threading Kali through the gap in the rail, I ease her back into a halt and hear the polite golf clap pepper at my back. I glance over my shoulder at Pilar and Izzie, smiles stretching across their faces as Leo stands next to them, eyes on me and mouth on his coffee cup, caught mid-sip.

"Stop," I mouth at them, and all three shake their heads no.

I sigh and lean over Kali's neck, scratching the spot on her withers that always has her leaning into me in relief. She drops her head a little and lets out a breath.

"No speed today, girl," I remind her, which is really just a re-minder to me. *Be on top of this. Don't let her get away from you. Keep her focused on you, and not on the track.*

As if on cue, the last breeze of the day goes thundering around the far curve of the oval. Kali lifts her head to watch, nostrils flaring. I put my legs to her sides, just enough to get her attention back.

"Walk." I say the cue and apply leg, getting the gait like we've practiced. When she's back to striding out like a champ, mouth-ing the bit in search of my hands, I push her up into a trot. Her head shoots up, so I push my elbows back to meet her mouth. No slack in the reins. I drive her into my hands, half-halt her when she quickens down the long stretch of the L, half-halt her again when the first does nothing to get her attention, and when she blows right through that, I sit back in the saddle.

Kali slides right back into a walk, her head still up in the vicinity of my face. Her mane fans off her neck, forelock flipping comically away from her forehead. I can hear her working at the bit. The metal clicks against her teeth—she's agitated, confused about what we're doing out here.

"Just trotting," I whisper to her, and she immediately picks up the gait again because she knows the word. I let her keep going, forcing myself not to rise in the saddle and stand in the stirrups like she's expecting—deep down—and making myself rise and fall to the trot.

Up, down, up, down. I feel out of place with each rise, rocky with each slip against the saddle. Kali's head is still up by my face, her legs working faster, faster, nearly running away by the time we curve into the short end of the L. I slow my rise, trying to drive home the lesson we had with Lisa before we left, and Kali decides the proper reaction to this is to shove her head down and pop her hind legs up.

The force of it shoves me up on to her neck, and when Kali rights herself I slide back onto her withers, uncomfortably perched between her neck and the saddle. My stirrups are gone, clanking against the sides of the saddle. Kali doesn't slow down. In fact she speeds up.

Right into the end of the L.

Crap.

I push myself back into the saddle, toes finding the irons as she picks up the canter all on her lonesome, going headlong at the outer fence with her ears pricked at it. I know she won't go through it, and she hasn't jumped anything in her life, so the only hope I have is to get a hold of her and turn.

Quickly.

First, the outside rein. I find her mouth clamped hard around the bit, but that doesn't matter right now. She can resist the pressure as much as she wants so long as she follows the inside rein, which I put enough pressure on to slam the point home.

Turn, Kali.

The filly bobs her head down, coiling herself into my hands, and like it's nothing at all she pivots to the inside and follows my lead. Two, three strides and we're rollicking down the opposite railing, heading back the way we came. I take that moment to sit back, the direction completely impossible to ignore: *trot, Kali.*

She drops back, lowers her head to snort at her knees, and works up the rail like she means business. That's because her head is still on speed, on the work of developing stamina and fitness like we used to do before it was all about balance, about coming back to me and going forward without her whole weight in my hands.

I can feel all of her pressed along the reins, her entire weight leveraging up my arms and across my shoulders. This is what she thinks I want, and it occurs to me how easy it was when I had the reins bridged and pressed into her withers.

Now? Not so much.

I throw in another half-halt, give her a firm *whoa*. Her head comes up, ears flicking back as she nearly trips over her feet trying to figure out what that was supposed to mean.

"Remember?" I grunt, half-halting her again until her stride shortens and she slows into the rise I set. "There, not so hard, right?"

Kali snorts again, right on cue. Like she's saying *fine, be confusing*. I pat her neck and croon to her.

"Good girl."

Her ears flick back to listen, her mouth loosening around the bit, before she focuses forward on our audience clustered at the end of the L. Pilar and Izzie start up their polite golf clap as we turn along the short side of the track, and Leo just shakes his head at me as we churn up dirt on our way into our next long loop down the rail.

Chapter Thirteen

When my phone's alarm goes off, I roll over on my thin mattress and smack at it because I'm too exhausted to look at where I'm aiming my hand. That doesn't accomplish anything, and the happy song keeps belting out at maximum volume, forcing me up on my elbows so I can find and silence it.

Sweet, sweet quiet descends on the room like a blanket.

"July," Pilar whispers, and I take it back. Pilar is already getting ready for the day on her side of the room, pulling on her boots by the door and rolling her jeans over them. She's doing everything in the dark, because here I am still completely dead to the world.

I assume this is how things would have been if I'd gone to NYU with Bri. Instead here I am in Florida, doing the same things with Pilar. What a wonderful world we live in.

"What?" I ask, reaching to the lamp and turning it on, revealing our cinder block bunker. It's more like a utilitarian hotel room—two beds, two bedside tables, a tiny bathroom and an equally small refrigerator and microwave. It's just enough to live on, which is way more than most backside workers ever see at a track. Those are hovels without running water. This is paradise in comparison.

Pilar turns on her light, revealing her mass of dark hair still in chaos around her head.

"Are you thinking about getting up already or am I going without you?"

"I'm going," I sigh, shoving the covers off and rubbing at my eyes. "What are you so excited about? It's too early to be this on."

She grins at me. "Leo told me yesterday that Lighter's shedrowing this morning."

I stop mid-eye rub. "Oh, god. It's December."

"Yup," Pilar replies brightly. "Time to see what we've got."

So far, Lighter's experience at Palm Meadows has been stall rest followed by more stall rest. The metal grate across his stall is bent in a few places, but otherwise holding. The vet's been out each week to search and only find nothing. This week, Gus took him for a trot down the dirt swath between barns and he held up. He strained for more. That's Lighter for you, after all. If it's not full out it's not worth doing.

He's been walking the shedrow with Gus every day after, and today it's time to throw a rider on his back to see what's up.

"Okay, okay," I grumble, finding yesterday's jeans. Martina would be horrified right now if she saw the state of this room, the state of all her careful packing. But there's no time to care about this. I wash the sleep off my face and pull on my semi-dirty work clothes, finding my boots by the door. Then we're out into the cool, December morning.

Pilar mostly skips down the stairs of the dorm, pulling her hair back into a tightly controlled ponytail as she goes. I follow close behind her, headed for the barns on the other side of the training oval. They're already lit up, movement shifting through the aisles. Grooms have arrived to start the day's chores, and we're right on their heels.

It's odd how easy it is to adjust. You'd think I would know by now—first hand—how simple it is sometimes, but even still it surprises me. Palm Meadows has slipped into routine after a few weeks of doing what we always do, just underneath the big blue sky of Florida instead of New York's increasing dull gray haze.

And it feels good. It does. To be here, in a place that isn't dictated by what *isn't* here with me. I like that, deep down. I guess I have to thank Florida for that much.

When we arrive at our barn, Leo is standing outside Lighter's stall, watching Gus tack up the colt with measured movements. Lighter shifts on his feet, presses his muzzle against the bars and blows at us like he's chastising us for being late. He could just as well be saying *How dare you? On my big day?*

Leo sips at his coffee, not bothering to tell me if there's any more left in the pot. I find out for myself, pouring a cup and returning to find Gus locked in a battle of wills with Lighter over the bridle. For as much as Lighter wants to work, he likes fighting with Gus more, I swear.

"Think he's got work on the mind, or play?" Leo asks no one in particular.

"Lighter doesn't understand the difference," I answer, and Leo's lips do a little twist, as though he's not too thrilled with my response. Gus gets the halter on over Lighter's bridle, the chain shank in place over his nose for extra leverage.

"Moment of truth," Gus says, and nods to Leo, who opens the

door. Lighter goes careening out of it, Gus a mere side note in his quest for open air. There's an impressive string of Spanish curses, followed by a battle of wills as Gus slowly gets Lighter back under control and walking like a proper horse instead of a blond hurricane.

Pilar lets out a breath and I raise an eyebrow.

"You're the one who insisted you be the first one to ride him," I remind her, and she nods sharply.

"I know. This is nothing, July. Just antics."

Lighter bounces on his front feet and then rears, forcing Gus to lift the lead shank away from the colt's slashing hooves. As soon as Lighter places himself firmly back on the ground, Gus hustles him into another bobbing, too-fast walk. Keeping his mind on the task right now will at least keep all of his hooves on the earth.

"Let's jog him," Leo calls, pulling out his cell phone and swiping it to the video function, holding it up so Lighter is fully in frame. I stand next to him, craning my neck to look over his elbow, which means I have to push onto my toes and keep my balance by gripping onto Leo's stupidly muscular arm.

"Didn't think you were this forward," Leo says to me. I scoff.

"Keep talking on video," I tell him. "That works perfectly for me."

Leo glares at me and I smile sweetly back, then fall back on my heels and watch Gus put Lighter through his paces. The colt trots big and happy, like he's thrilled to be going somewhere, even if it is up and down the paved driveway. There's not even the beginning of a hesitation. His stride is sure, everything gliding in place like it's supposed to as Lighter's hooves clop along like he's a horse in a parade.

"That's good," Leo says, lowering his phone and tapping at it. He's sending the video to Dad, who will come back with instructions, even though we all know what they're going to be. Pilar is already strapping on her helmet.

When Leo's phone chimes, he nods to Pilar. Dad has spoken.

"Ready to see where we stand?"

She nods. "Definitely."

I take a sip of coffee. "I like how we're pretending this is more than a cruise around the shedrow."

Pilar shakes her head at me as she walks up to Lighter, who is watching us like he finds our attention on him fascinating. Probably he's coming up with ways to keep our attention, like the true drama queen he is.

"Be careful," I say, like an afterthought. Pilar offers me a smile, because we both know what this means to her, even if it is just taking a pleasure walk around the barn.

Gus gives Pilar a leg up, and she sails up onto Lighter's back. The instant her weight slides into the saddle, Lighter whisks his ears back toward her, assessing the situation. The colt hasn't had a rider on his back for a month, so I won't be at all surprised if he decides today is the day to throw in some explosions on his way around the barn. I can see it on the way his skin twitches. After a while, it's easy to see a horse that's thinking about doing something only they think will be amusing.

Lighter has the look.

The second Gus takes his halter off, Lighter surprises us all by launching into an energetic walk. No hysterics. No white-ringed eyes. He just walks out underneath Pilar like it's his mission in life.

Okay, then. I step back and next to me Leo lets out a relieved breath as he finishes his coffee.

"I'll take it," he says, nudging me with his shoulder. "Today's going to be a good day, Juls."

I don't say anything, because Leo hasn't been around Lighter long enough to know just what the colt is truly capable of. One second is all it takes for the colt to get bored, going from well-mannered to a circus act. As soon as Leo turns back to the office to refresh his coffee, Lighter twitches his tail, ears flicking.

Then he's up in the air.

Typical. Pilar goes up with him, her body moving instinctually and falling back to the earth with the colt. Gus is back at his head, but before he can snag the colt's bridle, Lighter is out of there, taking Pilar with him and not seeming to give much of a damn about what she thinks should be happening.

"Whoa!" I call, lifting my hands out as the colt skitters right past me, taking the path of least resistance in an attempt to dodge around me without getting caught. Only the colt jumps too far to avoid me, throwing his shoulder out as Pilar pulls his head around, sending the full force of that wall of muscle right into Leo as he comes out of the office, coffee cup in hand and his eyes down on his phone.

There's a moment where Leo stands next to me, and then there's just Lighter's body, Pilar keeping all her weight as far back as she can make it, pulling the colt's head around so tightly he's practically turned in on himself. Gus runs past us, grabs Lighter's head like a bulldog, and when the colt's hooves clatter clear I can only see Leo on the ground, his body prone in the dirt. Coffee is spilled down one leg of his jeans, and his cell phone is shattered into crushed bits by his hand. A low moan slips out of his mouth as he raises a hand to his forehead.

Behind me, Gus has Lighter safely in hand. Pilar leaps off of him and dashes up to me as I kneel down by Leo's head and lean over his face.

"Leo." I insist on pushing his stupidly perfect hair off his forehead, checking for injuries.

"That horse," he mutters, cursing as if talking hurts too much, but he's got an angry tirade in him and he's not going to let a little thing like his head bouncing off the ground dissuade him.

"It's been said many times," I tell him, resting back on my heels when he shoves himself onto his elbows and sits up with a jerk. He loses his balance and rolls into me, laughing like it's so hysterical. I sigh and push him back into the dirt. "If you have a concussion, please feel free to ferry yourself to the hospital."

"I'll be fine," he says, looking up at the sky as I stand and brush my jeans off.

"Great," I say, stepping over his legs on my way over to Lighter. Gus and Pilar stand at the colt's head, both looking at me expectantly. Good. We're not nearly done. "Pilar? Want to try again?"

She stares at me steadily and nods.

Lighter goes around the shedrow four times, walking the line between behaving himself and keeping Pilar on her toes with each bounce and shy at nothing. When he's done, Pilar jumps down, letting out a breath as she pulls off her helmet.

"Looks like we all survived," she says, sounding satisfied.

"Speak for yourself," Leo says, still looking at his cell phone like he's lost something irreplaceable.

"How's your head?" I ask, peering up at him. He grimaces, which isn't like him at all, so at least I know something isn't exactly on the up and up.

"Foggy," he admits, rubbing his forehead.

"Not surprised," Gus says, shrugging one massive shoulder like he's been expecting Leo to realize his thick skull isn't impenetrable. "I heard you hit the ground."

"I'll be fine," Leo says, shaking all of us off. "Let's get this morning done. I have to go get a new phone."

Well then. Our priorities are at least straight and narrow.

"Okay," I say, turning on my heel and heading for the tack room, calling behind me, "You heard the man, people. He needs a new phone. Daylight is burning."

"Juls," he calls after me, like he knows what he's said has pissed me off. Good. At least some things remain the same. Leo can still detect when I'm through with him as a person. He follows me into the tack room, broken cell phone still in his hand and his dark eyebrows furrowing close together, like he's not sure why he's following me. He just is, and that thought seems to bother him.

"Hey," he tries again while I gather up my exercise saddle and snag Feather's bridle. The filly has a two-minute lick to get done this morning, and Lighter has taken up way too much of my time. The entire string needs to get moving. Training hours only last so long.

"What?" I ask, focusing on organizing the bridle. Leo stands in the door, totally blocking my path when I turn to head back out into the aisle. "Are you planning on being productive this morning or are you hoping to just get in the way?"

"We're stuck here together," he says, looking at me intently.

"You and me, Juls. And I know this wasn't your choice, but if we're going to keep doing this training thing together you could be less cold to me."

I roll my eyes. I do. I can't help it.

"And you could whine less," I tell him. "Ours is not a perfect world."

Leo scowls at me, shoving his broken phone into the back pocket of his jeans, as if he's readying himself for a fight. I don't like this, and I especially don't like being cornered in the tack room while he accuses me of not caring about his delicate feelings.

Please. There's too much to do, and this is Leo's priority?

"I know why Rob sent you down here," he says, and I tilt my head to the side as if that's going to help me figure him out a little better.

"Please enlighten me," I say, because it hadn't really occurred to me that Dad might *not* have told Leo I was here to supervise. To be the person with my head screwed on straight when Leo is too busy fussing with his hair. "What do you think is happening here?"

"Trust, right?" Leo asks, and I sigh because this is disappointing, like he's just thrown his dart wildly at the board with his eyes closed. "He doesn't trust me, but he trusts you."

"I'm his daughter, Leo," I point out. "I would hope he trusts me."

"And I'm his assistant," Leo says, which puts my teeth on edge because that is the problem. Right there.

"You were an intern two seconds ago." I push past him, popping out into the aisle and making my way to Feather with Leo veering after me.

"And that means you can treat me like shit for the duration? I work here now, July. What I was before doesn't have any bearing on what I am now. You have to deal with it."

That smacks of truth, and I don't much like the tightness it puts in my chest.

"You wanted me here, remember?" I say, letting my voice rise. "You invited me because it sounded like a fun opportunity to have me do all the work, and look how well that's going for you."

"I realize I asked you," Leo says, following me closely down the aisle.

"Do you?" I ask over my shoulder, stopping at Feather's stall and letting myself in, surprising Izzie from her work getting Feather's saddle cloth just so. Her eyes bounce from me to Leo and back as she mouths, "What is happening?"

I sigh. "Leo is having a moment of existential crisis."

Izzie's eyebrow pops up.

"I am not having a crisis," Leo barks from behind me. I spin around as he keeps with his incessantly annoying yapping. "I just think that we need ground rules, or some sort of understanding if we're going to keep existing together in the same shedrow. I don't know where we stand."

"Oh my god," I mutter, because I did not ever think I would hear those words coming out of Leo's mouth. They were bad enough coming out of Beck, but Leo? No. "This again?"

"What?" Leo asks, appearing pained. He rubs at his forehead and Izzie tilts her head at him, concerned by something I won't let myself see. It's just Leo. Just pure, undiluted, frustrating Leo saying ridiculous things, and I don't have to listen. There's nothing to say. There's nowhere to stand. It's just us in a shedrow. How complicated is that? What on earth needs to be clarified about a few people running horses in a circle every day?

Because it's not complicated. At all. This is my life, and I'm not going to let Leo of all people question where he stands in it, because the answer is not at all.

And then Leo's knees give out, his body falling slack as he crashes to the ground at my feet. I don't remember screaming, but I know I did. Just a surprised shriek that has Izzie grabbing my elbow to pull me out of the way when Leo falls, his body hitting the ground with a surprisingly dull sound, like a sack of sand hitting a bale of hay.

Feather jumps and tries to pull away from the wall Izzie has tethered her to, the chain snapping taut and her whole body levering into the air. The saddle cloth slips off her back, and that makes her shy hard into the wall, bouncing off of it with a thick thud of muscle against cinder block. Izzie shushes the filly, pressing her slim body into Feather's hulking shoulder as the filly trembles against the wall.

In front of me, Leo sprawls face up in Feather's bedding and out in the shedrow there are footsteps coming. Izzie pulls her phone from her pocket, her fingers stabbing at its face as she turns toward the filly, trying to do two things at once—call for an ambulance and calm a horse with nerve endings lit up like Christmas. I drop Feather's tack and sink down next to Leo, about to touch him when I stop.

Maybe I shouldn't touch him. Touching him could damage some already fragile, injured part of him, and as he lays there I can't help but think everything is delicate and injured. So I look instead, forcing my hands onto my knees.

His eyes are closed. He's breathing, thankfully. So I settle onto my knees next to him as Gus appears in the stall door, taking in the scene. A surprised curse startles out of him.

"What the hell is this?" he asks, eyes bouncing from me in the bedding next to Leo and then onto Izzie, who barks out our location and what's going on to the tinny voice I can barely hear speaking to her on the other end of the line.

"I don't want to move him," I say, curling my fingers into fists above my knees. Gus squats down on the balls of his feet, hands hovering over Leo's quiet form like he's asking himself the same question. Neither one of us knows what we're doing.

Then Izzie steps away from the filly, her booted feet sinking in the bedding near Leo's head.

"They're coming," is all she says, and then kisses her fingertips and presses them softly to the center of Leo's forehead.

～〜

Hospitals have always felt like a contradiction to me. It's obsessive sterility packed full of coughing, bleeding, bruised and broken people. Then there's the itchy quality to waiting, sitting helpless in a corridor with nothing to do except wear down the minutes and the hours. Hospitals are anxious places, and I can't stand it. It makes me twitchy with the need to get up, pace.

Instead I listen to the silence on the other end of my phone.

"Dad?" I ask into the void as Pilar watches me from her chair, her pointy elbows digging into her dirty jeans, chin cupped in both hands.

There's a scratchy clearing of throat. "I'll come down," he starts to say, which makes me shake my head.

"What? No," I interrupt. "Belmont will practically fall apart if you're not there."

That may or may not be true. With Martina running Barn 27 with an iron fist, I'm not sure anyone would notice Dad was gone.

"July." He makes a frustrated noise, which may or may not be about me. It's probably that I'm talking truths and Leo is stretched out unconscious in a hospital bed, machines recording every brain wave and heartbeat. Already he's sailed through a battery of tests, his body carted this way and that, the doctors stopping only when necessary to update me on the fact that Leo still isn't awake.

Leo might not be awake for a while.

The feeling tears a little hole in my stomach, and it stings. I want Leo to wake up. In the meantime, I want to know what we're doing. I hate sitting here and not knowing. It's a completely worthless feeling that has me standing up and pacing before I can stop myself. I'll wear down this industrial-grade carpet before we're through here.

"I can't let you run a stable alone," Dad tells me, which I scoff at.

"Why was I even here again?" I remind him. "I believe it was to look after Leo. I think that puts me in the perfect position to run the stable until he's recovered."

There's a soft sigh, and I can picture him slumped back in his chair behind his desk, Martina watching with that worry mark appearing between her immaculate eyebrows. No doubt the rumors are already flying out of Barn 27 in soft whispers.

Did you hear about Leo Reyes? That crazy colt ran him down.

"Fine," Dad says, which is so surprising I stutter to a stop in the waiting room. Pilar looks up at me curiously.

"Seriously?" I ask, the word out of my mouth before I can call it back. Great, July. Just give him a reason to take it all back. Good going.

"Do you want this or not?" Dad asks, which startles me into realization.

"I do," I say, slowly lowering myself into a chair across from Pilar. My heart is thumping hard, and I can't believe any of this is happening. Then Dad says something even worse. "Good. If you want this, you can be the one who tells Beck what happened."

That makes my entire body run hot, adrenaline spiking my blood until I feel sick with it.

"Wait," I stammer. "That's—"

"Part of the job," Dad tells me, firm. "It was Leo's responsibility, and now it's yours. While he's out, you're calling owners. You're running works. These are your shots to call now, Juls. I'm just approving the plans."

"Oh," I squeak, my voice tiny. Pathetic. I need to get a grip.

"You still on board?" Dad asks, and I know this is a challenge. It's supposed to either scare me off or scare me straight. Either way, it's working, because I volunteered for this. I argued my way into it. Backing out now isn't possible.

"I'll do it," I say, going for firm and coming out significantly less.

"Good." Dad sounds pleased, like maybe this is exactly what he wanted from the beginning. It's my turn to slump into my seat, rub my fingers against the bridge of my nose to relieve the sudden oncoming headache that is blossoming up like a thundercloud, nerve endings glowing brilliantly as lightning strikes.

Dad keeps talking, but the words dim and disappear altogether when a nice pair of shoes appear on the carpet in front of me. I look up at the doctor they belong to, the white coat hanging down his body like a shroud. *Dr. Aldosari* is embroidered across the left breast. His salt and pepper hair is swept back from his forehead, and I can see a tie and dress shirt peeking out from underneath that coat, like a personality striving to be seen.

"Hold on, Dad," I whisper, and drop the phone onto the seat as I stand up. Pilar does the same, slipping close enough to me so her shoulder presses into my arm.

"I take it that you brought Mr. Reyes in today?" Dr. Aldosari asks me, and I nod.

"We're coworkers," I explain. "We were working with the same horse."

Dr. Aldosari nods, like he knew that already but needed to ask, as though my answers are going on some official record with Leo's name stamped on it. He looks perfectly at ease when Pilar and I are nervous wrecks, frazzled by the thought of the words he's about to release into the air around us. This is so terribly normal for him, I realize, as I feel Pilar's hand slip around mine.

"Mr. Reyes' CT scan shows blood collected over the surface of the brain—what's called a subdural hematoma. We are prepping him for surgery now."

"Surgery?" I squeak, feeling Pilar's hand tighten on my fingers.

"To decompress the brain," Dr. Aldosari confirms, "and to stop any active bleeding. We'll inform you when the surgery is complete. Please know he's in the best of hands."

And that's it. Like a cloud, Dr. Aldosari floats back toward the double doors separating us from Leo, disappearing behind them and leaving us to wait. Pilar collapses into her chair and throws her legs out in front of her, letting her head fall back so she can stare blankly up at the ceiling. I pick up the phone.

"Did you hear that?" I ask Dad, who answers me in a way I should have predicted.

"I'll call Leo's parents," he says. "I'm leaving Beck to you."

Before I can say anything else, the phone goes dead in my ear.

～～

I stare at my phone, Beck's information glowing up from it with the block button firmly in red. This has to be fate winking and smiling at me, like some deranged fairy godmother upending my life just to get me to make a phone call. Of course, how self-centered am I? Leo's the one in surgery, getting a monitor inserted into his head to keep tabs on his swollen brain, while I'm out here having a staring contest with an electronic device the size of my hand.

Pilar is curled up next to me, snoring softly with her riot of curls falling over my arm. We're in hour three of Leo's surgery, and that's three hours too long of pondering what I'm supposed to tell Beck about all of this. Maybe something like *Hi! Your horse kind of ran over our assistant trainer. Happily enough, he's not dead, but he's also kind of in surgery. Sorry I blocked your number for a few weeks!*

This is so definitely not good.

Someone has to tell Beck about this, and it can't come from anyone other than me. If the rumor mill gets to him before I do, I'm screwed. I wouldn't even deserve forgiveness—just complete shunning and definitely a firm *I'm never talking to you again, July.*

I would have it coming.

I tap the block button, and just like that my phone starts to

211

rattle in my hand. Messages, messages, more messages. I wait for them all to slide through my voice mail box, text messages littering across the display too fast to read. For a second, I make myself sit and read the first few texts that show up.

You just ran? What the hell, July? What were you going to say?

Then that bloom of warmth rises up my cheeks and I swipe them away, deleting them. It's not that I don't want to think about the night on the roof, when I came so chaotically close to admitting things to him that I shouldn't. It's that I haven't answered any of these, and here I am, about to tap into that channel of communication with days and days of silence stretching between that rooftop and this waiting room. My heart is in my throat, which feels tight, like it's collapsing.

I take a deep, steadying breath before I tap the call button and lift the phone to my ear with a shaking hand.

Maybe I'm expecting Beck to snatch the phone up on the first ring, but it growls on for what seems like forever, my stomach dropping further and further with each ring until I know I'm destined for the call to kick into voice mail, where I can't leave a message. That's not going to happen. I'm waiting for the little electronic hiccup to take me to the recording when the call suddenly connects, fuzzy and soft with breath.

"July?"

My eyes drop closed and I sink into my chair, wondering if this was a better option next to leaving a message. People still leave messages, right? Obviously Beck did. Multiple times. Not like I have any say in these decisions. Here I am, and Beck is right here with me, however far away.

"Hi," I say, my voice hoarse, scratchy with the complete inability to know what to say.

"You're calling me," he says, bluntly.

"I am."

"Why are you calling me?" he asks, like this is a trick. It's almost funny, since I was never the one playing games. That was always Beck.

Although that's not fair. He's not playing games either. Not this time. I take a steadying breath and try to tell myself to relax, but it's not working. This isn't just Beck. This is more, and maybe it always has been, deep down.

"I'm calling you because Leo can't," I say, making myself stick to the message. This isn't about us right now, and I can't let myself fall into that discussion yet. I'm not ready for it. There's a pause on the other end of the line, and I know he's shifting into another gear, out of what he thought this phone call was going to be about.

Surprises, surprises, I think grimly.

"What's wrong with Leo?" he asks, sounding tired all of a sudden, like if this isn't going to be about us, is this a conversation worth having?

"Lighter ran him down," I say over his long, soft sigh. One more piece of bad news, delivered by me, July Carter. Sorry about that, Beck, but it had to be done. I promised I could do it, and I am.

"What happened?" he asks, sounding resigned.

"We put Pilar up on him when he trotted sound," I say. "Lighter got excited and bolted over Leo. He was fine initially, or so we all thought. Then he just collapsed. The doctor says it's a hematoma, so now he's in surgery."

Beck curses on the other end of the line, his voice muffled. I wince, but don't say a word in Lighter's defense, because there's no point to it. The colt is a lot of things—ditzy, ridiculous, bombastic, flighty, and just shy of unmanageable. He's a racehorse, so those things come with the package. Beck knows this as well as I do.

"He'll be okay?"

"Maybe?" I shrug a shoulder to myself. "It's probably too early to say."

"So your dad suggested you call me?" Beck asks, which isn't exactly what I thought he'd say. Then I realize he's still stuck on the *me* of all of this. Me calling him instead of Dad.

"I don't see what that has to do with any of this," I say. "Normally Leo would give you updates on Lighter, but since he literally can't right now . . ."

"July," he says, "this isn't an update on Lighter."

"It is, actually," I say, stiffening. "When your horse nearly kills someone, you need to know about it. There's insurance to consider. Lighter's a liability—now he's even more of one."

He makes a noise in the back of his throat, like that isn't want he wants to hear, which is too bad. Owning a racehorse isn't always perks like champagne rooms and private flights to watch races with multimillion dollar purses on the line. Most of it is blood and sweat and tears, which he's well-versed in. All I have to do is think about Diver. I know exactly what Beck has seen.

"So what do you suggest I do?" he asks me. "Geld him?"

"I'm sure the insurance adjuster would love that." I shake my head, even though he can't see it. "No, don't geld him."

"Why not?" he asks. "He's a terror, isn't he? Haven't you suggested that to me a trillion times in the past?"

"I have," I admit. "But that was then. He wasn't a favorite for the Juvy then. Gelding him now isn't a sane move anymore."

"So what do you suggest?" he asks, sounding tired. Lighter, I realize, is the very last thing he wants to talk about, but I keep at it like a stubborn mule digging my hooves in.

"If you can afford him, keep him," I say. "If you can't . . ."

"Sell."

"Right."

There's a long pause. It stretches out, blowing up like a balloon to the point where I don't look forward to the moment it pops.

"I can't believe this is what we're talking about," he says, circling back around.

"Believe it," I say. "Your horse is a jerk, and after a month of stall rest he's even more of a jerk. It's something we all should have—"

"I'm not talking about Lighter," he interrupts. "I know Lighter's an asshole. What I can't believe is where we left things. You ran away and then you went off the grid. Then you moved to Florida."

"Florida wasn't exactly my decision," I find myself saying, still stuck on that when it's really the last thing I need to say.

"Does it matter?" Beck laughs. "You still went."

"You made yourself pretty clear, so what is there to talk about?"

"That's an excuse, July."

"It is not," I say through my teeth. "I don't know what to say to you. I still don't."

"That's obvious."

"Is it?" I ask. "I don't see how you have room to talk. You ignored me for a solid week after the Breeders' Cup, and when I forced you to talk to me all I got for the effort was I'm too much. That being with me is somehow impossible, so you're just going to pretend it never happened at all."

"I'm not pretending that it didn't happen," he says.

"That is such bullshit," I growl at him. "You don't want to be with me, so what does it matter where I go? How often I don't talk to you? I'm giving you what you want!"

I don't realize how loud my voice has gotten until Pilar stirs next to me, jerking off my shoulder and automatically lifting a hand to rub at her eyes. She squints at me fuzzily, her whole face a question mark, silently asking me why I'm shouting.

But I'm buzzing, too on edge. Beck is all flabbergasting silence. Just when I'm about to yell at him to talk to me, there's a soft noise on the other end of the line.

"I don't want this," he says, and I cringe.

"Then I'm sorry I called," I say hastily.

"No." He pushes past my apology. "That's not what I mean. I don't want not talking to you. I don't want you not being here. That isn't what I want, Juls. You have to know that."

Honestly, that shocks me down to a speechlessness I wasn't aware I had in me.

But then I remember California, and what he said on his rooftop in Manhattan. It sticks to me fast, refuses to pry free. It's easy to say things you don't mean, but acting on them? That's harder. And Beck has said and acted enough that there's no way to know what's real. What does he really want?

What do I want?

"I don't know," I say, swallowing thickly. "Not really."

He says my name, but it's hazy in the background as movement catches my eye down the hallway. A harried couple cross to the nurse's station, dragging luggage with them. They're familiar, if older than when I last saw them.

Leo's parents.

"I've got to go," I whisper into the phone as Beck says my name again, Leo's parents walking toward me. Pilar is already climbing out of her chair, and my body follows along on instinct.

I hear my name one more time. Beck, his voice more insistent. But I end the call.

Chapter Fourteen

You know the saying about how you only know what you had when it's gone? Okay, it's sappy, but for the most part it's true. Without Leo's presence on the training oval at Palm Meadows, I'm stuck doing two jobs. We're down a rider now, since I'm on Maggie's back every morning watching works. When I'm not on my mare's back, I'm going through the motions of getting through the day while preparing for the next. There are plans strung far into the future for each horse in the barn, but those plans can change with each work, with every step a horse takes. It's a little maddening, with nothing set in stone.

But I knew this going in. I haven't been blind to it, after all. The name of each horse we have is written up on the white board in the office, plans scribbled in different colored markers. Red for gallops, green for jogs, black for breezes, purple for the gate. I tap the black marker against Feather's name, my phone glowing in my hand and Dad talking a mile a minute out of the tinny speaker, his voice fuzzy and hard to follow.

"Wait, wait," I say over his voice. "Five furlongs at the end of the week for Feather isn't going to work. She shied at who knows what this morning and dumped Pilar over the outside rail. We didn't get a full gallop in on her."

"And that's the sort of information I need to know before I make these kind of plans, Juls," Dad says with an exasperated sigh. "Is Pilar okay?"

"Sure," I say. "So is Feather, but that's beside the point. She's not ready for a breeze."

"Then make her ready," Dad orders.

"How am I going to *make* her ready?" I ask, tapping the marker's tip against the whiteboard, still refusing to write down the order. "If she's not ready, she's not doing it."

"It's your job to make horses ready," Dad says, which has me rolling my eyes. Thanks for that bit of obvious information, Dad. "The breeze doesn't have to be end of the week," he continues, "but her race at the end of the month still has to be targetable."

"Fine," I say, putting the black marker down and picking up the red. "Two-minute lick tomorrow. I'll put her with Howl to keep her on business."

"No," Dad says, "that colt is jogging tomorrow."

I groan. Right. Jogging. How can it be this hard to keep twelve horses straight? I scan over the rest of the names on the board, wishing I'd been paying attention a little harder to what each horse was doing up until Leo and Lighter crashed out in the gravel.

"Zaatar?" I ask, my eyes falling onto the filly's name. "She's scheduled for a breeze, but we can push her back to the next day, partner her up with Feather for both the gallop and the breeze."

There's a pause in the air, and then Dad grunts. "It will do."

He doesn't sound too thrilled, but looking over the board I'm not sure who else is going to fit the bill for Feather.

"Don't sound too enthusiastic," I mutter at the phone.

"Juls, this is just how the days go," he says. "Sometimes it's unenthusiastic guesswork."

Great. I frown at the whiteboard, trying to work out the puzzle pieces. The horse names blur over the board, and I rub my eyes, making myself glance away for a moment.

"There's also the matter of Lighter," Dad says, and I swing my attention back to my phone, suddenly very attuned to what my Dad could possibly say about Lighter. Beck hasn't called me back since I hung up on him at the hospital, so there's no doubt he's chosen to talk to Dad about anything Lighter-related. I deserve that. Honestly.

"What about him?"

"Do you feel confident getting him back on the track?" he asks. "He's still trotting sound, right?"

"Trotted sound this morning," I say. "He's out in the round pen right now. Gus is babysitting."

"He needs to get back on the track," Dad says. "Start jogging."

"Did Beck call you?" I ask. Curiosity killed the cat.

Dad huffs a laugh. "Sure," he says. "Told me you advised selling him."

"Amongst many things," I grit out, clenching my fingers around the marker as I look down at Lighter's name on the whiteboard. *Stall rest* is written next to his name like a repetitive mantra, like Leo understood all too well the monotonous horror the colt was going through, stuck in the same situation with no way out. I look at those words and feel just as bad, like I'm the one pacing—

around Florida, around the track, around Beck. I'm turning circles. *We're* turning circles. Beck and I are going around and around, going absolutely nowhere.

I'm going absolutely nowhere. That's when I realize.

Leo hadn't been stuck. He'd done it—made the big change, escaped his dad for New York and Barn 27, only to have me standing there rolling my eyes, telling him no and shutting him down. My skin flames at the thought as I read across the board.

Stall rest, stall rest, stall rest. Then, after all of it, a single question: *Jog?*

That was written under the day Leo's head hit the ground, and I try not to think about that because four days later, Leo still hasn't woken up. I put the red marker down on the lip of the whiteboard and use the side of my hand to brush away the words until there's nothing but a smeared, dusty white next to the colt's name.

There. Blank slate.

"I assume he's not going to sell him," I say.

"Couldn't say," Dad says. "Leo's parents are upset, so if Leo wakes up sooner rather than later, we'll have a better understanding of the fall out."

"You think they'll sue?"

Dad grunts, and I know exactly what he means before he says it. I remember Leo's dad. Hard-nosed, loud, always looking for a corner to cut. There were plenty of suspensions littered around their barn back in the days Leo was always hanging out with us.

"I wouldn't put it past Reyes," Dad says. "Leo's another story."

Yes, I think. Leo *is* another story. An unknown one I've put no effort into knowing since he came back to us. I'd just been irritated at his presence, wedging him back into that old role he'd played before even giving him a chance.

That was shitty of me. Especially since Leo's done little more than be here to draw my ire at him. I just assumed he was the same person, even as he kept showing up, doing everything asked of him and more.

I look at Lighter's name on the board and wonder if I'm in over my head right now. The colt is a ticking bomb, shivering out of his skin, and he's in my barn. I may not be his trainer, but I'm going to call the shots, make the crunch time decision when it counts.

"July," Dad says into the silence, like he's wondering if I hung up.

"I'm here."

"What do you want to do with Lighter?" he asks, putting the question out there. Just at that moment, Pilar shows up in the doorway. I glance over at her, and she gives me a knowing look. For the first time since I came back from the hospital, I know exactly what we need to do.

"I want to put him to work," I say, and pick up the green marker.

∿

The next morning, I show up in the barn with my travel mug of coffee warming my hands. There's a soft nip to the air—December licking across the Florida dreamscape like a tiny, barely perceptible reminder it can get cold here if it wants to. Although, this is nothing to the frost of New York. The exercise riders at Belmont must look like skiers on horseback by now. Here, the warm sun will rise soon enough and scatter away the cold. The barns blaze with light in the darkness, and the first thing I do when I set foot in the aisle is point at Lighter's stall.

"First things first," I say, as Lighter comes up to the stall door and pricks his ears at me, showing me the whites of one eye. "Let's get the troublemaker out of the way."

"Whatever you say, boss," Gus says, walking out of the tack room with Lighter's saddlecloth, his long-sleeved shirt already pushed up his tattooed arms like he's worked himself warm in the morning chill.

"Finally," Izzie says, popping out of Feather's stall and headed into the next, throwing a bucket out into the aisle as she goes. "Maybe giving that one something to do will make him less likely to try to take a piece out of me during feed time."

"Unlikely," I sigh, because it really is. Lighter is Lighter, and this is a fact of life we're all accustomed to now. While Gus is tacking Lighter up, I move down the aisle to Kali and Maggie, who have their heads hanging out of their stalls, checking out the morning activity with curious glints in their eyes.

I give Kali an apologetic pat, since she's worked herself up to quivering. Her petite chestnut body is shoved right up against the stall door, her ears strained forward as she digs one hoof into her bedding, like she's trying to tunnel her way out.

"I'll get to you after works," I promise her, just like every day. Kali pays me no mind, throws her head up and backs into her stall to turn an agitated circle, like what is the point of her being here if she isn't going to run? Never mind she was never even good at it. For the first time, I seriously wonder if Leo is right about bringing Kali here. The track life is clearly getting to her, right when I definitely want her mind on something else.

I duck into the tack room for Maggie's heavy western saddle. By the time I've got her tacked up, Gus is giving Pilar a leg up onto Lighter, who stands still with Izzie holding onto the lead shank. I swing up into the western saddle and let Maggie out of her stall. Gus tosses to me a lead rope on my way up to Lighter. The colt stands underneath Pilar like a statue, ears forward, his whole body at attention as he surveys his surroundings.

"Think you can keep it together for a trot down the L?" I ask the colt, who pays me no mind as I attach my lead to his bridle and Izzie lets him go.

"Guess we'll find out, won't we?" Pilar asks me as we head out for the training tracks. Lighter lifts into an airy walk, all clattering hooves and excited, snorting breaths. Pilar smooths a hand down his shocking blond mane, crooning to him as Maggie swings her ears back, monitoring Lighter like she has all the patience in the world.

She does, of course. She'd have to, with Lighter nudging against her with every other step. The colt presses his mouth against her neck, rubbing froth into her coat. Maggie's ears flatten back, her tail twisting and flicking like a whip around her hindquarters. Lighter, ever dull to social cues, shoves his head over her neck and plants it right in my lap.

"Whatever makes you comfortable," I growl at the colt, who looks up at me with a white-ringed eye. Pilar shakes her head at me and laughs.

"Like old times," she says. "Doesn't seem so long ago we thought this one was the eternal screw up of the barn."

"He's still the eternal screw up," I tell Pilar. "A couple of wins in stakes races doesn't erase everything else."

Pilar sighs at me, and pats the colt's neck again. "Blaming him does no good, July. You know better."

I frown, because I know exactly what she's talking about. It wouldn't make any sense to blame Lighter for landing Leo in the hospital. Lighter did what came naturally, and Leo was just in the wrong place at the wrong time. But that's not really it. I can't help thinking about California, about the injury that started it all. What would have happened had I just not yelled at Beck? Had I not felt like the whole thing was my fault? Would he have stayed?

Probably not, because it was never about Lighter. And what does it matter? It's done now. It's been done for a while.

"You're right," I say, reaching out to undo the lead on the colt's bridle. "Now trot this guy down to the end and back. See if he can make it the whole way without throwing a kink in the works."

"Would it be a ride on Lighter without a few kinks?" Pilar asks, throwing me a knowing smile as she takes off into a ground-eating trot. I push Maggie into a loping canter to keep up, knowing there is no ride on Lighter without a few kinks. And a ride on Lighter when he hasn't been seriously ridden in over a month?

I'm not worried about kinks. I'm thinking more along the line of explosions.

Pilar keeps Lighter to a regular two-beat, her reins bridged and her body steady over the colt's withers. I urge Maggie a little faster as the colt speeds up down the long part of the L, his pale tail whipping up in the air and his head flinging up as he eyes the oval nearby, where horses are galloping and breezing—their bodies streams of color blurring along the rail.

"Shush," Pilar murmurs to him when he bursts into a canter, his whole body trembling when a duo of horses go by blisteringly fast on the oval. She sits a few strides of canter and then throws her weight back, which is meant to tug him back down to a jog. That's the universal *whoa* for racehorses, but because Lighter is *Lighter* these sorts of basic commands can't be easy.

He has to round his body and send his hind legs up into a happy buck. Then another, throwing Pilar onto his neck, where she grabs his mane and tries to ride it out like a champ until the colt jumps like there's an invisible barrier in front of him and throws her off his back, her body rolling over his rump and sailing toward the dirt.

Then he flings his head down and takes off, galloping down the straight-away like he's in a race and this is just a very interesting, oddly-shaped race track.

"Damn it," I curse into Maggie's mane, who's already leaping after the colt. I lean into her, let her have her head as she tears off down the track, her breaths coming in excited grunts as she sprints down the middle of the track with Lighter in her cross-hairs. The colt bends into the L's turn, giving me few precious seconds before he's met with a fence to the chest—because I'm not sure Lighter will see the plastic rail and understand that it means stop.

With my heart in my throat, I yell encouragement to Maggie, who bunches up those massive hindquarter muscles of hers and sends herself up alongside Lighter like a rocket fueled on well-managed rage. The mare has her ears pinned back, her mouth tight on the bit. She sends me as close as she can get to Lighter, who straightens out of the turn and brushes up against her with enough power to send them both off the rail, closer to the middle of the track as the end of the L comes racing up to us.

I transfer the reins to one hand, the mare there at the colt's head, his reins flapping uselessly around his neck. Lighter looks at me wildly, like he knows what I'm about to do and is already thinking up a few wrenches to throw into my plan. I have to get there before he starts solidifying his plans, because we've been here before and I, for one, am not going to let this ridiculous colt get the better of me this time.

The end of the line is coming. The white railing is zooming up on us, and I lean out of the saddle, stretching out. The reins brush against my fingers, and I push myself an extra inch out of the saddle to snag them.

Lighter flings his head into Maggie's side, the reins swinging with them, right into my grasp. I lock down on them like they're a lifeline, yanking them toward me and signaling to Maggie at the same time that we are turning now, damnit. Maggie downshifts like a race car, all whining engine and squealing rubber. Dirt goes flying around her hooves, but she curls around my boot and goes rocketing around to the next long rail. Lighter's hindquarters fling away from us, the centrifugal force of the turn forcing him to keep up or fly right into the short rail.

I feel the whole track watching, as if every exercise rider at Palm Meadows is holding their breath. But then Maggie gallops hard out of the turn and Lighter—because he's letting me, I know—follows. He holds his head high, eyes rolling in their sockets and breath coming raggedly, his whole body held in wild lines of bunching muscle.

"Whoa," I call to Maggie as soon as we hit the turn in the L, tugging her down out of our crazy pace and into a bouncing, energetic trot. The mare lowers her head, letting out an explosive snort, and keeps her ears pinned when Lighter, because he can't help himself, shoves his head into my lap and gives me that look. That *I couldn't help it! Aren't I adorable?* look.

"You are not adorable," I tell him. "Far from it."

Lighter grunts, bumping into Maggie with each stride. I slow her to a walk, and Maggie does it on a dime, chewing on the bit and relaxing enough to lift her ears off the back of her head slightly, keeping tabs on Lighter, but not totally out of her mind with annoyance at the colt. I pat her hard on the shoulder, letting her know how much of a lifesaver she is out here on the track.

Once we're off the track, I look over Lighter, who solidly walks along, no worse for wear. By the time I get back to the shedrow, Pilar is sitting on the ground outside of Lighter's stall, head resting against the wall and her eyes closed. She's thwacking her crop lightly against the ground, shaking her head.

"Hey," I say to her, giving Maggie to Izzie as Gus takes Lighter out on his cool off, because after that joy ride he's going to need it. "Are you okay?"

"Two falls in two days," she says, finally opening her eyes and looking up at me.

"It happens," I say, offering her a tentative smile that she doesn't return.

"It shouldn't be happening," Pilar says, glaring down the length of her crop. "It definitely shouldn't be happening on Lighter. He could have gotten himself injured far worse out there, if he hasn't already."

"He's fine," I say, waving my hand at the colt, who is dancing next to Gus and twisting his head in the air, yanking on Gus's arm like he's ceaselessly testing his patience. Luckily, Gus's patience is limitless. That's why he's Lighter's groom.

"You don't know that he's fine," Pilar says, getting her feet underneath her and standing up. "And I don't think I should be riding him."

"Of course you should be," I tell her. "That's ridiculous. You're his rider."

"Let's be realistic," Pilar says, shaking her head. "I haven't ridden Lighter since Saratoga. My arm hurts all the time, and if anything has a way of pointing out to me that I'm not ready for this, it's a fall off of Lighter. It's Leo in the hospital, which—again—happened because I wasn't in control."

"Pilar," I say, grabbing her hand when she turns toward the tack room, afraid she's about to go peel off her safety vest and pack up. I can't allow it. She's the only other rider in the barn—the best person I have right now—and I can't let her quit on me because Lighter did what he always does. "I have eleven other horses to work this morning. If you're not okay to keep going the rest of the day, I get that. But I need a rider, and that's you."

She pauses there in the aisle, and for the first time I notice that she's been trying not to cry. "I'm sorry, Juls," she croaks. "But I can't."

Then she heads to the tack room, slipping out of sight.

～～

Walking Kali back toward the barn, my whole body is stiff and crying out for a long soak in a tub. Too bad the Palm Meadows dorms only offer showers. I wonder if Leo's empty trainer's apartment has a bathtub, and if it's not too weird to go through his things searching for the key.

Then again, what does it matter? If I don't get another rider out here soon, a long soak in a bathtub isn't going to fix my problems. I need Pilar back on the horses, and I need more help. Stat.

Walking Kali into the shedrow, I leap out of the saddle with my thoughts on everything except her. That's where my mind has been for hours, and it shows. Instead of flowing through transitions, Kali has been all jutting shoulders and craned neck. Just getting her to lower her head was a major accomplishment today, but I pat her shoulder anyway as I lead her back into her stall because this is all my fault. I'm not giving her my complete attention, and I deserve everything she throws at me.

Maybe I can't do this. Four days in and everything is already falling apart.

I'm putting Kali's tack away when my phone starts its merry chime, and I wince. I definitely don't identify phones with good things lately, but I pull it out of my pocket anyway.

Mom.

I stare at it for a minute, wondering what crazy prank is being pulled on me now. Tentatively, I tap the talk button.

"Hi?" I roll my eyes at myself. Quite the opener there, July. Mom laughs, like she can see right through the phone.

"Hi to you, too," she says. "I wanted to check in on you, see how things are going. Dad told me about Leo, and it's just tragic. I can't believe he hasn't woken up yet . . ."

She keeps going, babbling nervously like she does when she's not sure what to say, even though she's calling for a reason.

"I know," I break in. "It's been a little hectic around here."

"Your father seems to think you can handle it," she says, and that irks me because it sounds like she's surprised. Like maybe I can't handle this.

Although, I remind myself, I'm already having my doubts. After I finish grooming Kali, I'm going to have to go barn to barn, looking for riders. And there's nothing more pathetic than to go begging for handouts. Then there's the matter of paying my newly borrowed riders. How on earth does payroll work? Is there a payroll at all?

"I can handle it," I say. "We're just down one trainer, and since Pilar quit we're down a rider, so basically it's just me."

Now I'm babbling, because there's no one else to vent to. Gus and Izzie are off the table, because I can't whine to them about Pilar's need to not be on a horse right now. The only person I can tell is Dad, but instead I have Mom. It doesn't feel right, but I take it anyway.

"Wait, wait," Mom says. "Pilar left?"

"Well, not exactly," I say, glancing in the direction of the dorms. "But I can't say she's getting back on Lighter anytime soon. She bowed out of the rest of works; said her arm hurt too much."

Mom is quiet for a minute, and then I get it.

"I'm not going to ask you to come here," I say.

"I can help, July," she says, calmly, rationally, and it's not helping my resolve. I'm already feeling it crack, because this is too much to do by myself. I realize that now.

Why am I always trying to do everything alone?

"I understand if you don't want me to come down there," Mom continues, "but if it would make things easier for you then I will drop everything here the second you ask. Please know—"

"Come," I say, and then squeeze my eyes shut, because I sound desperate and I hate it. It doesn't feel like me at all. Mom's voice stutters, as if she hadn't expected this from me either, and then she picks up the thread again just as quickly.

"Okay," she says, breathless. "I'll be on the next plane."

My phone starts to beep with another incoming call and I sigh. Wow, suddenly so popular these days.

"I've gotta go," I tell Mom and say a quick goodbye as I switch to the next call. The man's voice on the other end is one I don't recognize.

"July?"

"That's me," I say, sounding harried and at the end of my rope because I am exactly those things.

"This is Emilio Reyes," he says, the slight accent tipping me off. "Leo's father."

"Yes, of course," I say, tensing, because all I can think is *law suit* and Emilio's rough edges when he walked into the hospital, looking annoyed that medical emergencies were things when he had a barn back home he needed to keep running. And the thing about barns? They don't run themselves. "Is there news?"

"Leo's awake," he says gruffly, like his son's progress still isn't up to his impossible standards. "And he's asking for you."

Well, that wasn't exactly expected. I sink into the first of the row of saddles, nodding my head against the phone. Leo's awake, and I'm sure his parents are the last people he was expecting to see, given how he'd traveled across the country to avoid working for his father. Or maybe trying to escape his father.

I think about those words written next to Lighter's name.

Stall rest, stall rest, stall rest. Then I push myself up, headed for the office to root for the car keys.

"I'll be there as soon as I can."

Chapter Fifteen

When I arrive at the edge of Leo's room it takes a solid few seconds of drumming up the courage to look inside, which is absurd because it's just Leo, and I've been invited. I'm still not sure I want to peer into the room, for fear of what I'll find.

I'm not sure I want to see the inevitability of working with horses.

That, of course, is ridiculous of me. I've only done this my entire life, the promise of injury—maybe death—peeking around every corner. But it's so easy to ignore when you're caught up in the love of it. It's easy, right up until it isn't.

Stop it, I hiss at myself. *This isn't about you.*

So I step into the doorway.

The hospital bed is up against the wall, like every hospital bed in the history of man. Leo is reclined against pillows, thin blankets wrinkled over his legs. He looks smaller than normal, and for a minute I feel a little pang of sadness because his ridiculously groomed hair is gone—shaved away for the surgery—that ever-present part of Leo totally and inexplicably gone.

Leo's mother, Rosa, bends carefully over his bedside, scraping the last of the pudding out of a plastic cup. A whole meal sits in front of Leo, and most of it is uneaten. The pudding, however, seems pretty popular.

Leo's dad, Emilio, sits in a chair in the corner, his attention on a laptop because work follows him everywhere. That he even found time to sit at his son's bedside with a racing stable to tend is astonishing, but Emilio must be to the point in his career where assistants do so much for him. The ship can sail itself now, regardless of who's at the helm.

With Emilio, though, I'm not sure that fact matters.

Rosa looks up with that sixth sense mothers have, and smiles at me. Relief floods all over her face, and she's bright with it. Leo follows her gaze, and I shift under their expectant faces, unsure.

"July," Leo says, lifting his hand to crook his fingers at me. It's barely movement, but I get what he means, and make myself take the extra steps to his bed.

"Hi Leo." I sink into the chair next to him, my eyes darting to the machines surrounding him. Monitors display numbers I don't understand, recorded in pixelated lines. I know, fundamentally, that there's a hole in Leo's head. The doctors drilled it four days ago to relieve the pressure on his swollen brain and stop the hematoma. One of those monitors is all brain activity, but I have no idea which one.

"Resting up?" I ask, managing enough pep to sound like none of this bothers me when I think it's pretty clear how much it really does.

A soft laugh escapes Leo's chest with a rattle. "Something like that," he says, and then looks up at Rosa and adds something in Spanish I can't hope to follow. The request seems to surprise her, but she quickly abandons her pudding mission and hands me the cup with a nod. Then she rouses Emilio, who frowns deeply at me like I'm the one requesting that he leave.

At least, that's what I'm assuming is happening. By the time Rosa gets Emilio out the door, Leo lets out a long-held breath.

"Truth?" He looks at me once his parents are out of sight. "They're exhausting."

"They care about you," I say, looking down at the pudding cup in my hand.

"If you attempt to feed me some of that, there will be retribution," he warns me, looking at me out of the corner of his eye. I press out a smile and abandon the pudding on his food tray, lifting my hands to show how I have no intention of playing nurse.

"I thought you knew me better," I softly chide, and he manages a barely-there shrug.

"You never know," he says. "I didn't think my dad would ever abandon his stable to see me through surgery, but here we are. People can surprise you after all."

Then he looks at me hard. "How *is* the stable?"

I take a deep breath, thinking about everything that's happened in the past few hours.

"Good," I try, and even I know that's not close to cutting it. Leo smells the lie despite the hole in his head.

"You're a terrible liar," he says. "What's happening?"

"We put Lighter back to work and he dumped Pilar, who decided she's not up for track work after all, and now I'm down to one rider—me. So now I'm going to rustle up riders, while my mother flies across the country to help because four days is all it takes for me to ruin everything."

It falls out of me in a rush, like a confession. I feel lighter after I've said it, even if Leo is my confidant. He just looks at me, his dark eyes set above deep purple semi-circles like bruises. For a minute, we just stare at each other, and then he bursts into a laugh that sounds like it hurts after he clutches at his side.

"Damn it," he says, gasping for breath. I'm halfway out of my chair and he motions at me to sit down. "No, no, it's just funny. You, the perpetual control freak, convinced you've ruined things after four days. July, if the barn hasn't burned down, nothing is past the brink of no return."

"Says you," I say. "I just had to call in help from California. That's a disaster."

"It's not," Leo says, leaning into his pillows, which are about as white as his pasty skin. "It's how running a barn feels. Everything is barely managed chaos. You know it's true, deep down."

I sigh, slumping into my chair. He's right, to an extent. I've seen my father's barn through thick and thin, always a disorganized wreck and an explosion of personalities clashing. It's nothing new, but this time? This time feels different.

And this is what I may want to do for the rest of my life? The thought scares me now, because if I'm panicking after four days, what will happen over the course of four months? Four years? Four—god help me—decades? Because it's all or nothing in this business. I know that, too. If this scares me, what happens when something larger totally knocks me off the rails?

And I passed up NYU for this? God, what am I *doing*?

"July," Leo says, lolling his head to look at me. I break out of my thoughts, focus on the man in front of me. "I know I'm not the best person to dispense advice to you, but you need to calm down. Accept the help for what it is—help. It's not a defeat, and it's definitely not a sign you're not cut out for this kind of life."

"Mighty perceptive of you," I say, feeling awkward, like he's seeing right into me.

"Yeah," Leo smiles. "I remember our fight before all this shit went down, and last I checked I was in your situation before the aforementioned shit. I've been in your shoes, Juls."

"I was kind of hoping you wouldn't remember," I admit, thinking back on that fight and cringing. "I've been angry with you since you showed up, Leo. Pissed and jealous and wildly out of line."

"You were," he agrees, and I manage to shoot him a tiny glare that he smiles at. "Ah, there you are."

I shift in my seat, crossing my arms. It's amazing when he can still find it in him to be a jackass while he sits in a hospital bed with a hole in his head.

"But you did say something that was right," he says.

"And what was that?" I ask, thinking that I've said a lot of right things, even to him during that fight. I wasn't necessarily wrong about any of it. And neither was he.

"That ours isn't a perfect world," he says. "I've been thinking about that all day."

"Don't fixate too hard," I tell him, and he manages to turn his hand over, lifting his middle finger at me. I smile.

"But then I thought about how we really weren't on the same page," he says. "And I don't think either one of us could be. We were too caught up in our own crap to even see a page at all. I needed to get away from my dad to do what I wanted to do, even if it meant pissing you off. You think you were jealous, Juls? I've always felt that way about you. What you've had your whole life—the barn and your family?" He shakes his head. "I was jealous, too."

I stare at him, wondering how Leo managed to become so damn astute. Was I this blind? Has he been like this the entire time and I just failed to notice? No, I definitely need to give myself more credit. Maybe falling on his head was the best thing Leo could have done for both of us.

"I can't believe I'm about to say this, but you're right. We weren't on the same page," I say. "I was pissed at you for simply being there, when I should have been trying to work with you. I'm sorry about all of it, Leo."

"So am I." He cocks his head at me. "Think we can start over when I get out of here?"

"I think we already are," I allow, and he smiles at me. It's a real, genuine smile that I don't think I've ever seen on his face, not even when we were track brats slinking through Belmont's backside.

"That's good, Juls," he says, sucking in a deep breath and letting it out in a whoosh. He closes his eyes, and just like that he looks so tired. "That's good."

I stand up, tentatively hovering there by his bed. Then he opens his eyes with a pop of eyelids and I jump, caught.

"Hey, Juls," he says, "I know I'm remarkably good looking, but your steady basking is off-putting."

I roll my eyes. "Head trauma victim my ass," I grumble, and he laughs, which is again crackled through with a rattling cough.

"Stop making me laugh," he demands, putting on a pout.

"Guess I just won't visit again," I say, and he shakes his head.

"Don't do that," he whines. "How else am I going to be up to date when I come back to the barn?"

If he comes back, I think, and immediately shut up my subconscious. Leo's got a recovery ahead of him, but he'll be back. He'll probably have his shiny hair grown out by then, too.

"I'll keep you in the loop," I say. "And I'll even visit."

He lets out a relieved sigh. "Good. I don't know how much more I can take of my mom's babying and my dad's glowering silence from the corner. I need someone around who won't treat me with kid gloves, or I won't be ready when I come back."

"Then count on me to crack the whip," I reply, and he smiles again. Genuine.

"Thanks, July."

"No problem," I say, shrugging. "Maybe this will even be fun? I give orders, you follow them. You'll be barn fit in no time."

"Something tells me you live for that scenario," Leo says, but the smile doesn't quit on his face. He's actually looking forward to the long road back to our barn, of all places.

"I really do," I admit, and squeeze his hand before pushing away from the bed. "Rest, Leo."

"Will do," he says as I turn, heading for the door. Just before I reach the doorknob, he clears his throat and I glance at him over my shoulder, see him watching me tiredly from the bed.

"Remember, July," he says. "One day at a time. It's not as bad as you think it is."

I nod. "I'll try to remind myself of that the next time Lighter gets loose."

"Which he will," he says, closing his eyes again, like the probability of this hardly concerns him. "Only a matter of when."

His breathing levels out, and I slip out the door.

~~

"Are you kidding me?"

That's the first thing Martina says as she steps out of the rental, sunglasses perched on the crown of her head. She's wearing shorts even though it's on the cusp of winter, and her long tan legs look ready-made for it. Like they've been waiting for Florida sun all their lives.

She spins around, taking in Palm Meadows with one sweep of her critical eye. "I swear, July, only you would complain about being forced to train horses in paradise."

"What are you doing here?" I ask, blanching at her. Kali and I are making our way back from the sand rings, where my filly rolled until the dust she kicked up enveloped her like a storm. Her coat is filmed over with it, pluming into the air with each shake of her mane. I'm so stunned by my sister's sudden arrival I stop in my tracks. Kali runs into me, and then jumps to the side, snorting at me as dust rains from her body in a fine mist.

"Surprise," Mom says, unfolding herself from the front seat, almost childishly giddy, like surviving a trip from the airport to Palm Meadows with Martina is a landmark event in all of our lives.

Honestly, it probably is. This wouldn't have happened a month ago, so what gives?

"Is the world ending?" I blurt out, and Mom laughs, shooting Martina a querying look over the roof of the car, like she's not too sure about this, either.

"Please," Martina scoffs, catching sight of Izzie moving through the motions of evening feed and waving. Izzie stops halfway into Feather's stall and waves back, tentatively. "I was told you needed another rider, so here I am."

"On racers?" I ask, because I seriously don't think so. Of all the things Martina is capable of on Belmont's backside, she has never once wanted to ride a Thoroughbred at top flight.

This earns me a look. "God no. You're looking at your pony girl and barn manager." Then she points at Mom. "That's your thrill seeker."

Mom smiles at her, and then turns that beaming smile on me. Kali lets out a breath, like she's accepted this when I know she just wants to get back to her stall, dig into her grain while I work the dust out of her coat. But something about that sigh steadies me, tells me that this can work if I just let it.

"Okay," I say, and Martina arches an eyebrow at me. I know she was expecting more of a fight, more questions, before the inevitable giving in. Because what was I going to do? Put her back on a plane? I need her, no matter how suspicious I am that she can help with Mom around.

Even so. Since they got down here together just fine, maybe we'll all get through this without screaming matches and broken feelings. A girl can hope, anyway.

I think about Leo.

One day at a time.

I can do that. I can.

Then Mom shuts the car door, hands on her hips. "Well?" she asks. "Where do we start?"

"With Kali's walk-trot transitions," I say, hustling up Kali and walking her toward her stall. Mom gives me a curious double take as Martina groans. I smile at them, pleased to throw them a curveball. "I need a second set of eyes."

Chapter Sixteen

We start in the morning, which dawns suddenly with Martina turning on all the lights in our little room and rummaging through her suitcases like she's trying to wake the dead. I groan and roll over into the blankets, ducking my head into the dark cocoon of their warmth.

"I knew switching rooms would have horrible consequences," I grumble, wishing I hadn't had the brilliant thought of putting Mom with Pilar in some crazy attempt to get my rider back up on our horses. Mom may not be the most consistent with people, but when it comes to the horses there is no one better. Pilar, of course, isn't a horse. But she wants to live Mom's life—wants it so badly she's a head case on the oval—and who better to show her what's so easily within her reach?

So I offered to switch, and here I am, listening to the drone of Martina's hairdryer yowling through the room.

"Who even takes showers in the morning around here?" I ask myself, voice muffled in my blankets. Only Martina would prepare herself for a day in the barns like she's primping for an office job, as if she still *has* an office job.

Finally, I sit up and glare at her. She turns off the dryer and says, "What?"

"Is this something you're going to do every morning?"

"Is this the kind of gratitude I'm going to receive for putting my life on hold in New York in order to save you from yourself?" she snaps right back.

My, how the loving gestures run out in my family. We haven't even started yet, and here we are, glaring. Still, she is here. She is helping. I repeat the mantra as I kick off the covers and swing my bare feet to the chilly tile floor.

"I'm sorry, was I dragging you away from Matthew?" I ask, holding my hand up to my heart, like I've separated true love. Martina gives me a look and drops her dryer back into her bag, shaking her thick, luminous hair behind her head.

"You only say that because things aren't working out with you and Beck."

I blink at her, and let my hand drop into my lap.

"You really are back with Matt," I say, so stunned my jaw drops a little. All my life, Martina has been so consistently anti-second chances. If life or people wronged her, she was done. Just like that. No do-overs, no make-ups, nothing. Just done. And now she's showing up at Palm Meadows with our mother and getting back together with Matthew, of all people. Where did her loyalty to the cause go?

More importantly, when did Martina become better at getting her life together than my own dismal attempts?

Martina shrugs a shoulder as she pulls all that glossy hair back into a ponytail, then starts hunting for her boots.

"Yes, I am," Martina says. "What happened before was so long ago. We're different people now."

"Are we?" I ask, raising my eyebrows because I still can't get over it so simply. Martina pulls on one boot, not looking at me.

"*We* are," she emphasizes. "You, however, I can't say for sure."

"Thanks a lot," I grumble, standing up and pulling out my track clothes. Martina struggles with her second boot, yanking it on and pushing her jeans down over the leather.

"It's not meant to be an insult," she says, looking up at me. "Just an observation. Sometimes you have to let go of the past before you can take any meaningful step into the future. If anything happened to me this year that was it. All those big changes I made in Saratoga? They added up, and I liked it. Matt was always the hanging thread, the one thing I always regretted not letting us figure out. He tried so hard to make it up to me, and after Saratoga . . . I decided to let him."

She stands up, and I have to adjust my steady, befuddled stare. My big sister seems to have it all so figured out, and it leaves me feeling so very . . . disoriented. Like our roles have been swapped and I'm left gasping for breath, trying to cling to the things that I know.

"So does that mean you're our barn manager forever now?"

"You say that with such heartfelt joy, July."

"I'm serious," I say. "I've . . . liked having you at the barn."

Martina shrugs a shoulder. "We'll see. If you get accepted to Jericho, I may not want to be the only non-college educated person in this family."

"You're forgetting Mom," I say.

Martina shoots me a smile. "Am I?"

Ah, there it is.

"Not so forward thinking now, are we?" I ask, and she just shakes her head.

"We were lucky not to kill each other on the ride up here," she says, opening the door and revealing inky darkness, the barn lights twinkling in the distance. "You're lucky you have such devoted family, July."

Then she steps out into the early morning, leaving me to wonder.

Exactly how lucky am I?

∽

Pilar stays stubbornly grounded. It's not like I can't use another groom, but it's only when I see her mucking out stalls with Izzie that I know how deeply wrong it is that she's not up on the racers, slipping through the morning mist with her face pointed toward the wind.

"You couldn't talk her into it?" I ask Mom as we walk toward the training oval with the last of the group, which has gone quickly enough this morning with Martina playing pony girl on Maggie.

Mom glances back at the barn over her shoulder as we walk away from it, shaking her head like she's disappointed. "That one is as stubborn as good jockeys ought to be. She's going to take more effort than a little talk. I can't work miracles, July."

"Well, no," I concede. "I don't think I was hoping for a miracle."

"Falls and injuries," Mom sighs, leaning down to pat Zaatar, a splotchy gray filly. "They take a toll eventually. Major or not, you always remember them. Pilar just has to get out of her own head."

"I would really love it if she did it sooner rather than later," I sigh, knowing I shouldn't even push it. Pilar's head space is her own, and I have no right to be there, nagging her back onto my horses. She'll climb back on when she's ready, even though I don't believe for a second that her arm hurts and that she can't handle Lighter. No one can really handle Lighter. We're all just clinging to stay on.

Beneath me, Feather snorts at the track, steam billowing out of her nostrils. She's calmer than usual walking down to the track, now that we've discovered that doing so with a companion keeps her nerves in check. So long as that companion is right next to her and not slipping out of her eyesight, Feather is right as rain. She pricks her ears eagerly as a horse gallops calmly out of the mist, rounding the turn closest to the barns and plunging back into the fine white curtain hanging across the dirt.

Today we're finally doing that two-minute lick in company. Once we set foot on the track, Mom is all business, putting Zaatar through the paces with that grim look of determination on her face. No laughing, no chatter—Mom is a professional on the track, and I follow beside her on Feather. By the time we're moving into the gallop, I'm surprised by the smile she shoots me.

"Catch me if you can!" she shouts, and gives Zaatar the go ahead before I can even yell back that this is a two-minute lick, remember? Not a breeze, not a *catch me if you're fast enough.*

But Mom is already gone, leaving Feather shaking her head at my hold on the reins. I push them into her withers, the rubber-lined leather bridged one on top of the other, and let her have at it. The track morphs from a sleepy river of dirt bobbing with horses and riders and becomes a torrent. Feather doesn't like being left behind, and I can feel the gritty determination in her to push back into position alongside Zaatar. Only that gutsy drive she has is edged with panic, like if she can't keep up with the pace she might as well fall apart.

So I urge her up, taking up and giving the reins, chirping at her to get her butt up there with the other filly before Feather falls all to pieces, scattering across the track with the wind.

Feather leaps and plunges, so close to breezing speed that I know there will be some adjustment to the plans tomorrow and the next day. There are races to think about, a whole overarching goal with this horse—with every horse in the barn—and here I'm letting that slip out of my fingers just so I can keep Feather together, keep her right on Mom's side.

Another jump and we're there, Feather heaving and stretching next to Zaatar. Mom turns her head just slightly toward me and yells, "Nice to see you!"

"Thanks a lot!" I yell back, and she laughs, so not like Mom right now that I just shake my head at her and keep Feather even with Zaatar's bobbing nose as we round into the turn, completing the mile faster than I would have liked, and hopefully without consequences.

I stand in the irons, shifting my weight back as Mom and Zaatar hold steady on the rail and slow. Feather gallops out evenly, putting her feet in just the right places, her breath coming in happy, deep huffs. No worse for wear, but I'm still annoyed I had to push her. This wasn't supposed to be a work where she had to play catch up, and I thought that was clear enough.

"That was faster than I wanted," I tell Mom, who sneaks me a side-eye and shakes her head.

"So like your father," she sighs. "Conservative as all get out."

"And he wins races thanks to it," I tell her, annoyance still eating at the edges of my stomach. "You manage to follow his orders just fine when we're at Belmont, so how about you follow them now that we're in Florida? Now that they're basically my orders?"

Mom turns full on to face me, bringing Zaatar down to a jigging walk. "You're right, July," she says, which has me snapping back in on myself.

Surprised, I stutter, "I am?" I fight the urge to roll my eyes at myself.

"You are," Mom says, back to that professionalism. "I was just . . . finding the fun in it, I guess."

"It's not like I don't like fun," I amend, because haven't I been accused of that enough by everyone? Bri, Martina, Beck?

"I should hope not," Mom says, "but you're right. They're your orders now, and I'll follow them."

"Thanks," I say, letting out a breath.

"Speaking of," Mom begins, and I let out the tiniest of groans that she completely ignores. I have a feeling I'm about to fall face first into another treasure trove of motherly advice, and there is so little about this that I like. I briefly consider squeezing Feather into a trot to escape, but where would I go that she can't follow?

Besides, I *invited* her here.

"What are you doing down here, July?" Mom asks. "Giving orders, running a barn . . . I can see all of that for you—I can. Eventually. But now? In Florida?"

"Where and what else would I be doing?" I ask.

"New York," she tells me, like that's obvious. "Going to school."

"I applied to Jericho," I say defensively, and she raises an eyebrow.

"So, my question remains," she says, foregoing any sort of positive response to my answering the second part of her concerns. "Why Florida?"

"Dad asked me," I hedge, and Mom just looks at me like she's waiting for something. The truth, probably, because Dad asking me to go to Florida was just convenient. We both know that by now.

"And because New York," I sigh. Might as well just throw it all out there, because I guess years of not being involved have turned my mother into a bloodhound for these sorts of moments. "It's too close to Beck."

"Did you never talk to him?"

It's supposed to be a question, but it doesn't sound like it. It has that I-understand-exactly-what-you've-done-and-I'm-disappointed feeling to it. Which is so rich coming from her.

"I actually did talk to him," I say through my teeth. "And he basically told me that relationships are too hard for him right now."

Mom sighs deeply through her nose, letting out her breath in a gust. "And then?"

"What do you mean?" I ask, twisting to look at her. Feather tips an ear back, monitoring me for anything she should worry about. I put a hand on her withers in silent reassurance.

"What happened then?" Mom asks. "Afterward?"

"I came here," I say, stammering because I don't know what she wants when I really do, deep down. The messages heaped on top of each other and the phone call that ended . . . how had it ended? Beck never called me back, and I haven't called him.

"No, Juls," Mom says, "there's been more. There's always more."

"You know I called him," I tell her, because she has to know. After what happened with Lighter, someone would have had to call Beck, and that someone had to be me. Lighter is in my care. "After Lighter, I unblocked his number and I called him."

Then I make myself remember the end of that call. The way Beck had said my name before I'd hit the end button, the way he'd said *don't want you not being here. This isn't what I want.*

But how can I ever be sure? How can I be sure after California, after that talk on the rooftop, when it seemed like he wanted the exact opposite?

"We're not on the same page," I say, because I think that's the truth, "and if we don't even know what we want then what are we doing?"

"July," Mom says, shaking her head. "Let me be the first to tell you most people don't know what they really want. Not deep down. And sometimes when they get it . . ." she trails off and shakes her head, taking in another deep breath, "sometimes it winds up not being what they want either. I know. I've been there. But the worst thing you can do is run away. It does no one any good to hide out, avoiding the conversation because you're afraid of what will come out of it."

I focus down on Feather's orderly mane, the way it crests over the line of her neck and hangs in a neat row down her coat. If only my life were so easily kept, like a good rip with a pulling comb will make everything fall into line.

"Beck is important to you, right?" Mom asks when I don't say anything.

"Yes," I say, the word tumbling out of my mouth before I can even remember wanting to say it, like it just appeared and was out there in the air of its own volition. A truth.

"Then what are you going to do about it?" she asks, looking at me expectantly.

I really don't know, but the one thing I can't sidestep is the fact that she's right. She's so right. Beck is important, and I'm letting this slip away. I'm letting it, and the longer I sit here silently the less I know how to fix it.

The less I know how to get it all back.

Chapter Seventeen

The whiteboard in the office is a tangle of orders over smears of eraser marks. I stand in front of it, marker clutched in one hand as I scan across the grid. The orders next to Feather's name are a scribble of black: breeze. Then I skip forward a few days to a shock of red: *maiden*.

Plans have been made for Feather's second race. They're still glowing on my phone—orders from Dad in a short, bulleted list, because he's only ever so detailed when it comes to preparing a horse for a race.

Maiden Special Weight for fillies, says the text, which sent me scrambling for the Gulfstream Park condition book, still splayed open in my hand. It's light, like a racing program, and Feather's intended race is just a slip of words amidst it all, halfway forgotten in the pages between the slew of claiming races and the stakes races that take half a page with their descriptions of nominations and fees, guaranteed purse money to be distributed in precise percentages, and who is allowed what weight.

Luckily, entering a maiden race is easy. All I have to do is show up at the racing secretary's office and say we're running. Piece of cake.

Of course, we have to get through a breeze first. Today.

"You look like you're trying to kill that board with your death glare," a voice says from the doorway which distinctly sounds like Bri. Although that can't possibly be the case because Bri is in New York and . . .

"Hello? July?" the voice that is decidedly Bri-like breaks in again and I shake my concentration away, turning to the door and finding Bri standing there with her hands on her hips and a knowing grin stretching across her pearly teeth.

My mouth falls open, and the condition book slips out of my hand with a flutter of pages to thunk on the dirty floor.

"Surprised, I take it?" Bri asks, eyeing the book before swinging her gaze up to me.

"What are you doing here?" I ask, stretching unseeingly to put the marker on its tray as Bri pushes into the room and pulls me into a firm hug. The marker goes clattering to the floor with the condition book.

"To see you, of course," Bri says into my shoulder and pushes back, looks me up and down like I've changed and grown so much she hardly recognizes me in the weeks I've been gone. "If you recall from high school, it's called winter break. They have those in college, too."

"Which is a relief," I say, her smile infectious enough to put one on my face. "I definitely wouldn't have applied had they not offered breaks."

That's when I notice the outline of someone standing in the doorway. It's suspiciously familiar, making my heart do a little stutter, like it wants to take a wild leap right out of my chest and skitter away at the sight of him.

Beck.

"Not that you applied to NYU," he says, straight-faced as he rests a shoulder against the doorway.

Bri makes a little surprised squeak, like she hadn't anticipated being followed all the way from New York, but I give her a look and she whispers to him, "You were supposed to wait outside."

Beck smiles winningly at her. "And you trusted me to do that, which is adorable."

"How is this even happening?" It takes effort to find my voice, like it got lost with all that air that refuses to come back into my lungs. I'll have to question her about the how of all of this later, because trying to imagine my best friend and maybe ex-boyfriend orchestrating a cross-country trip in secret is mind-breaking.

"I figured I always come up to see you at Saratoga, so what's going a little further?" Bri asks, and I give her a look because that's a huge stretch.

"A little further is a three-hour flight," I tell her. "Try again, Bri."

She sighs and waves a hand at Beck. "Fine, it was this one's idea."

"It was my idea," Beck confirms helpfully. I glare at him, unsure if I'm ready for his upbeat, peppy, annoying self right now. It just doesn't seem right, like I'm waiting for an anvil to fall out of nowhere to deliver reality's swift return.

"So here we are," Bri says, letting out a breath and then looking at me as though she can peer into my soul. "You are okay with this, right?"

"Sure," I say with more cheer than I feel, because Bri is watching me like a hawk and I might as well be trapped in this office with Beck standing in the door. I pick up the condition book and the marker, putting them on the desk, staring at them with more focus than they need.

There's a part of me that wants very badly to pack Bri and Beck on a plane and send them back to New York, but I don't have that power. So here they are. Here they'll stay. Great.

"July—" Izzie skids to a halt behind Beck, mimicking Bri's squeak of surprise almost perfectly. We all turn to stare at her, and I am so thankful for this interruption that I leap for the door, skirting by Beck and popping out into the aisle.

"Right, of course," I say as Izzie looks at me like I've lost my mind when really that's on my ridiculous friends. "Feather is ready."

"Yes," she says, still eyeing the office door where Beck watches us with interest before I pull her down the aisle. Izzie trips over her feet, her ragged-hemmed jeans scuffing through the dirt. "But Zaatar is off on her right fore. Not too bad, but—"

"So I'm going it alone with Feather," I interrupt, which earns me a disapproving frown.

"I was going to say Gus is cold hosing her and I already called the vet, so no need to worry," she tells me, arching an eyebrow. "And then you would say, 'Thank you so much, Izzie! What marvelous work you and Gus do for me, the frazzled racehorse trainer.'"

"You took the words right out of my mouth," I say, even though I want to kick myself.

"Yeah, yeah," Izzie shakes her head at me, and I know I'm forgiven.

Outside, Mom is holding Feather. The filly's goat stands next to her, bleating at nothing and flicking her tiny tail. Martina and Maggie stand nearby, ready to ferry us to the track.

"Sure you don't want to ride?" I ask Mom, who rests a hand on the filly's forehead and casts a knowing look toward the office, where Bri and Beck stand in the shade of the shedrow.

"And leave you to an uncertain fate?" she asks. "I think you'd better take a breather and go riding."

"Truer words were never spoken," I say, because she's definitely right. I'm not ready to face Beck. I also know that nothing is going to wipe my mind of these problems except riding, so I let Mom leg me into the saddle. Martina snags the filly's bridle and with an arched eyebrow at me, she turns Maggie and we head to the track.

Feather lifts into an airy trot right from the get-go. Her little ears flick back and forth, monitoring the area for everything from big cats to the tiniest of field mice. Nothing will be overlooked. She shivers and huffs, making me work to keep her together all the way to the training oval.

Beck and Bri slide from my mind. Just like that. Give me a nervous horse, and all thoughts cease. Only muscle memory is of use to me now, and I ride the bumps and starts. Feather climbs into the air with a leap onto the track, her head up like she's stretching to see something far in the distance.

"Nothing is going to hurt you," I tell the filly, running my hand down her mane. Feather snorts like she doesn't believe me at all, and I ask her to put her head on business. Canter, reins bridged against her withers, pushing her into the loping gait until she's on the edge of a gallop.

Martina lets me go when I push Feather into a flat gallop, her breaths coming like thunder claps and her mane lifting off her neck in a torrent of whipping slaps against lips.

I put her on the rail and we go. Feather explodes forward, taking all of that nervous energy and pouring it into my hands that I keep steady on the rubbery reins. I crouch against her withers, watching the track slide toward us in harrowed lines before disappearing under Feather's hooves. She eyeballs the horses jogging on the L like they are bobbling terrors, a potential disaster lurking in the distance.

"Feather!" I yell her name and she leaps under me, digs her head down until I feel the strain on my arms from holding her up. We hit the turn, and she flips her leads, her breaths even little bursts of exhale and inhale, a rhythm that I follow all the way into the stretch and I finally, finally ask her to run.

A chirp is all it takes. Feather gears up and throws down all of that run I've been developing. I feel it there, like a core of energy at her center. It pours through her, lifts us into the air with that split-second in which we take flight, and pushes us down the track to the finish.

My eyes are watering, and my lips feel stung. When we're well past the finish, I ease Feather from her gallop out and laugh when Martina is there on Maggie to reel us in.

"Did the four furlongs in a hair over 47," Martina reports, reaching out to grab Feather's bridle. The filly swings in toward Maggie, her whole body still shivering from the effort. "That's got to be the bullet for the day."

Bullet means the fastest work at a particular distance at an individual track. Palm Meadows may not be a track, but it counts. This work will go right into the workouts listed underneath Feather's name for her second race, and it will have a little black bullet point next to it.

Fastest.

"Looks like you might be okay at this training thing," Martina says, and I laugh, because being *okay* at something is a pretty high compliment coming from Martina.

"Let's wait and see how well she does when we actually run her," I say.

Martina eyes the filly, who is minding her own business next to Maggie. Perfectly at ease with my mare ferrying her back to the shedrow, as opposed to her hurricane-force anxiety on our way down to the track.

"Seems wise," Martina says. "Bullet works don't erase the fact that she spooked at her own feed bucket this morning."

"I just don't think she was expecting it to be red," I say.

"And yet horses can't see the color red," Martina replies, confounding me for a moment with her knowledge.

"All the more reason to be concerned," I say, recovering as Martina rolls her eyes and I lean over Feather's neck, patting her damp coat. "Don't listen to her, girl. We'll make sure you get the blue bucket next time."

"Although speaking of concerned," Martina says, narrowing her eyes at our onlookers as we approach the shedrow. Beck and Bri stand outside Lighter's stall, the colt basking in the attention. Someone has armed Bri with apple quarters, and she feeds them to the colt. With each swipe of his searching lips against the palm of her hand, Bri's face cringes into a look of half-fear and half-wonderment. Like she has a monster eating out of her hand.

And, really, she does.

"Why are they here?" she asks pointedly, because leave it to

Martina to ask the blunt questions.

"I think I'm about to find out," I say as we halt outside the shedrow and Izzie comes running to collect Feather, her voice all coos of excitement when she hears how well the filly did.

That's when a car backfires, but it might as well have been a cannon shot by the way Feather reacts like she has to fling herself from danger. Her whole body leaves the ground, dragging Martina off of Maggie and tearing Izzie right off the ground. Maggie does a startled wheel, her ears back like she can't seem to find the problem but will not be involved in this catastrophe, *thank you very much.* Martina goes skidding right into the filly's hindquarters, sending Feather into a spin that tosses me to the ground like I've been flung from a mad carnival ride.

My back hits the gravel first, followed by my shoulders. My head hits last with a hard crack, the helmet taking all the punishment while the rest of me skids across the gravel and Feather goes crow-hopping over my legs with Martina and Izzie battling her down to a trembling, sweaty halt.

I stare up at the sky, happy the commotion is over and less happy that I can already feel the pinpricks of pain dancing up my nerves, singing along stretches of skin. The gravel bites into every bit of me that presses into it, and I feel absurd for wanting to ask *How is Feather?*

It's so much easier to focus on the horse than it is to catalog what parts of me are bruised and bleeding.

Then I feel a hand on my shoulder, cupping around my neck. Beck slides across my breathtaking view of that big Florida sky and I gasp, because now I remember where I am. Now I remember who I'm with.

And, absurdly, a sob rushes up my throat.

"Hey," he says, shaking his head. "Juls, are you—"

I bring my hands to my face and feel his hands move to my wrists, like he's trying to move my arms. I feel a tug, and I bolt up no matter how much my back cries out at that idea. Beck lets go, lifts his hands like he's just trying to help, and rests back on his heels.

"Okay?" he asks, watching me carefully. The shedrow seems too quiet, and then I remember Feather and Maggie. Swinging around, I catch sight of Izzie tending to Feather. Martina is on her feet, leading a baleful Maggie up to me, my mare's head down like she knows she bailed and she's so sorry.

I feel an intense need to stand up, and when I do my legs won't hold me and Beck is there, jumping to his feet and grabbing me before I can wilt back to the ground.

"Sit," he says sternly, and I nod, resting my forehead against my knees. "The horses are fine, July. You're the one who took a dive onto hard ground."

"I really did," I say, and then I laugh, because it's kind of hilarious. Or maybe I'm punch drunk. I laugh into my knees until my lungs hurt, because it's so ridiculous, isn't it? It's all so stupid. I, July Carter, am running my father's Florida stable with my mom and my sister. I'm about to saddle my very first horse in my very first race as a trainer. I'm trying to retrain an ex-racehorse on top of it. Then I bit the literal gravel dust and the boy who ran away from me is here, waiting to pick me up.

I don't know what happened to my life. It's so surreal I can't recognize it anymore, so I laugh until my ribs hurt and there are tears in my eyes. When I look up, Beck is watching me like maybe

I hit my head too hard after all.

"Care to share what's so funny?" he asks.

"You," I say, gasping for breath. "You're here."

"Yeah," he says, letting me have a fleeting smile. "Flew all the way and everything."

"Why are you here?" I ask, watching him look down at our feet—my dirty boots and his worn Chucks. Such polar opposites. Then he reaches into the back pocket of his jeans and pulls out an envelope. He unfolds it, and I see the flash of a logo.

A very recognizable logo.

"Your dad called me," he says, holding the letter between us like an offering. "Said he had something for you."

"And you volunteered to play mailman?" I ask, reaching for the letter and hovering my hand over his as he looks me in the eye.

"Yes," he says, like obviously he did. He's here. "No one forced me here, July, and I'd do it all over again if I had to."

I honestly don't know what to say to that.

"Open the letter," he says, pushing toward me, the letter meeting my hand and my fingers curling around it.

It's so easy to rip into the paper. My skin is coated in dust, in horse hair that sticks to me like glue. The letter is already impossibly dirty by the time I unfold it, taking in the first words.

Congratulations, it reads. *You have been accepted to Jericho College.*

There's a roaring in my ears as I read the rest, my eyes always skipping back up to that first line to make sure this is real. *Accepted. Congratulations. Jericho.* Then I suck in a breath when Beck puts his hand on my knee, like he can't help himself.

"Hey, Juls," he says, and I fold the letter back in on itself.

"Hey, Beck," I say back.

"What's the news?" he asks, like he doesn't know damn well.

"The news," I say, setting my boots in the gravel. "Is that I have to get Kali's application video ready or there won't be any stalls left for her at Jericho."

Behind me, Bri lets loose a little cry of delight. Beck grins at me and stands, offering me his hand.

I take it, and he rockets me to my feet.

Chapter Eighteen

Have you ever tried to convince someone to do something they really don't want to do? Incredibly hard, right? Pretty much impossible. Now, have you ever tried to get someone to do something you know they want to do, but won't because of reasons?

Equally as hard. Believe me, I am living this nightmare.

"Here are the facts on the ground," I say, leaning into the picnic table outside the dorms. Pilar sits across the table while Izzie nurses her beer next to me, watching shirtless Gus play volleyball nearby with glazed over eyes, consumed by the show. They are totally hopeless.

I try to ignore the fact that Beck is out there, too. He's equally shirtless, his pale New York body easy to find and hard to tear my gaze from, no matter how many times I tell myself there's a talk coming.

A serious one.

One in which things may not go well. I shove the thought aside and try not to think about the fact that shirtless Beck is gallivanting around mere yards from me. I have a jockey I need on my horse, and Beck has nothing to do with it. Get a grip, July.

"I enter Feather in a maiden special weight that is perfect for her this coming Wednesday. You ride her, because you are here and I need you. Feather breaks her maiden because I have you on her, and everyone wins. Sound like a plan?"

Pilar doesn't look convinced, so I know what's coming.

"I already told you, July," she says. "I'm not ready to get back out there."

"Okay," I say, nodding like I expected this and her rationale is water tight, which it is not. At least, it isn't to me. "My second plan would do all the same as before, but beg you to ride. I am begging, Pilar. See me begging?"

Pilar cracks a smile, but it's wiped away when she says, "And yet it still does nothing to sway me. I've said I won't do it right now, and I would like you to respect my decision."

I slump into the table, lay my hand on it so my forehead has something soft to land on.

"Pilar, you're killing me," I groan into my arms.

"You have your mother," Pilar says, motioning to Mom, who's trotting back to us from the roaring grills with food mounded high on two plates. Bri follows in her wake, struggling to carry a bundle of water bottles.

"Yes," I nod, looking up. "I do have my mother. But—"

"So your begging doesn't mean much when Plan B is living with me currently," she tells me, and I sigh. This whole switching dorm rooms thing has backfired so gloriously I can't even wrap my head around it fully.

"Help me out here?" I ask Izzie, who looks at me like I've

suddenly sprouted another head. It occurs to me that she may have no idea what I'm talking about, given her Gus-watching.

"She'll get back on when she's ready, Juls," she says. "Don't rush things."

But that's not even it. I'm not rushing it at all. Pilar was ready not a week ago. More than that—she was determined. Lighter, with all his blond antics, was a challenge, not an obstacle.

Then Mom sets the plates down between us and Bri deposits the water with a thunk. The whole table shakes, like one big exclamation to *let it drop, already*. Pilar reaches for a hot dog, like she doesn't have to make weight anymore and I guess she doesn't.

Not if she isn't going to ride.

My appetite vanishes, and I push away from the table as Gus and Beck appear—shirts in hand and bodies distractingly shiny. One look from Beck, and I feel frozen to my spot. Of course, that could also be my still aching muscles from this morning's fall. It takes deliberate slowness to stand and straighten.

"I'll be in the barn," I sigh, like poor me. My racehorse needs a rider, and I only have my ridiculously talented mother to fall back on. Such a dire situation. I want to shake myself out of this disappointment that tightens across my chest, especially when Pilar looks like I've kicked her right across the shins.

"July," she starts, but I wave a hand at her.

"No," I say, "you're right. If you're not ready, you aren't. And I won't push you."

Then I look at Mom, who is studying her passing of plates and napkins like it's her job. I touch her wrist and she startles, although we both know she's been waiting for it. She's been waiting for this since she showed up here, knowing it would happen.

"Want to ride Feather?" I ask, and Mom shrugs, like this is no big deal.

"Of course," she says. "I'm at your disposal, July."

Disposal. Like I can just throw her away and she'd be okay with whatever I chose.

"Okay," I nod, and just like that it's done. Contract made. "I'm going to go find some ibuprofen, because this falling off horses thing doesn't seem to agree with me."

"Need any help?" Beck asks, shrugging into his shirt with that swift, boy efficiency. I suck in a breath, immensely aware the entire picnic table behind me has fallen silent as they wait on my answer.

Do I need help to the stable? Do I need help finding and consuming pain killers? Do I just flat out need help? Beck's in particular?

I consider him long enough to feel the itchy stares centered on the back of my head. Beck, to his credit, doesn't even flinch. He just waits, because he knows what my answer is going to be.

"Let's go," I say, which doesn't answer his question, exactly, but it feels right.

It feels like going forward.

Then the thundering applause starts up. I jump, twisting around to witness each and every person clapping enthusiastically, including Mom and Martina. Izzie raises her hands over her lead like she's scored a goal. Pilar lets loose one of those ear-splitting whistles. Gus yells something to the sky in Spanish that I have no hope of understanding, even though I can imagine well enough. Bri just stands there with her hands on her hips, smiling with satisfaction, like her job here is done.

My mouth falls open.

"Think they know something?" Beck leans toward me, edging close enough for me to smell him. All sunshine and sand, cooling sweat and horses. I tell myself not to panic, because it would be so easy to let him lead me all the way back to where we started, to that easy Saratoga life, so ruined by reality.

This is not Saratoga, but it could be something just as good.

Maybe. If we let it. There's that whole talking thing we still have to do, and suddenly I'm eager to get to that part. Anything to escape the ridiculous grins of my friends and family.

"They *think* they know something," I say, shaking my head. Then I grab his arm and spin, leading him across the grassy lawn to the barns and leaving the raucous approval behind.

∽

"You're remarkably spry for someone who ate gravel this morning."

Beck trips over his untied shoelaces—because playing volleyball in Chucks wouldn't make any sense—and nearly brings me down to the grass before he gathers his balance and leaps forward. That nearly takes me down too, because I've decided to keep dragging him toward the barn. So he jumps to grab me, and we're a tilting, wavering mess before I let go, letting him right me.

"We're a hot mess," I say, and the look he gives me is classic smirking Beck.

"*That* I know," he says. "Kinda been living it by myself for the past few weeks while you were in absentia."

That gets my hackles up. Good job, Beck. Thanks a lot.

"That's rich, coming from the guy who *in absentia*-ed his way out of whatever this is," I say, pointing between us. "You left

California, you disappeared into the city, and you decided this whatever-it-is should stop."

"Wait," he says, "when did I say this should stop?"

"Did you casually forget that you said I was too much?"

Beck shakes his head, takes a step closer to me.

"And last I checked you told me you were cutting me loose, then you ran away."

"After you ran from me," I insist, voice rising. "After you said I was too much change."

"This really isn't a contest, Juls," he says, lowering his voice and putting both hands on either side of my head, like he can figure out what's going on in there by touch. "And can we maybe stop shouting?"

I don't move away. He's close—so close I can hear him breathing—and I don't want to move away. I don't want to keep arguing about this, about how we're ridiculous people who don't know how to be together or apart.

Can't we just be us?

He eases closer to me, his warm body filling the space between us until there's almost no space at all. I lift my hands, tentatively put them on his wrists and rest my fingers across his thrumming pulse.

"Okay," I say, just as my forehead meets his. "We can stop shouting."

"Because I did come here," he says. "It was supposed to be my big gesture."

"I recognize your big gesture." I push into him a little, emphasizing my words. "It hasn't gone unnoticed that you're here."

"I should hope not," he says. "Because I'm me, and I'm pretty amazing."

I groan, pulling away and turning for the shedrow. "So you keep telling me."

"It's the basic truth, Juls," he says, following me into the barn office. "I can't just ignore facts as fundamental as that."

"You are remarkably deluded," I tell him, finding the ibuprofen in the tiny desk and cracking open the bottle.

"Well, you love it," he says, dropping into the chair next to the desk as I start choking on the pills, my whole face flaming.

"What?" I ask, managing to force the pills down my throat with several determined swallows. Beck just looks at me, rocking the chair back and forth like he's being casual but is really just a tic. He's nervous, I realize. These are nerves, because he's said a word that means something.

Which is also why my face is flaming red right now.

"You love it," he says, looking down at his hands for a minute, like he's thinking about something. I still stand at the desk, frozen like an idiot statue, waiting for the next words out of his mouth, which spill out like a trickling stream. "You love me."

I open my mouth, but have absolutely no idea how to respond. So I sink down onto the desk, perching on the edge. Once I'm there, I'm still not sure what to do. How to talk about this, how to say anything back. It's like the words won't come, no matter how right he might be.

"I'm just going to keep talking," Beck says, his voice filling the room, brushing up against me. "I realize it's kind of a dick move, claiming that sort of thing. It's just . . . ever since that night, it's been driving me crazy, imagining what you were going to say. But you ran and you hid, which . . . fair, right? I ran and I hid, so touché and all of that. It was just that you were going to say something huge after all the shit that I spewed out at you about fear and change and how justified I was about leaving California, about keeping you at arm's length. You were going to say you fell in love with me, and I knew—right when you left—that I was in love with you, too."

He pauses, taking a breath like he's running a marathon at full sprint. I stare at him like a deer caught in headlights, but I still can't force the damn words out until Beck begins to launch into the second round.

"I know—"

"Pages," I blurt, like I've lost all social grace and can't form coherent thoughts. Beck stops in his tracks, looking at me curiously. I squeeze my eyes shut, willing myself to get it together, and when I open them again Beck is leaning forward, arms on his knees and that look on his face. That intrigued look that he's hit me with so many times since Saratoga, like he's waiting for something.

"When Leo woke up," I say, grinding out the words, "he told me we couldn't be on the same page because we didn't see it. We were too caught up in ourselves to see it, and if we couldn't see it, how could we be on a page at all?"

"And when you dumb that down for the ridiculously slow-witted, that means?" Beck asks, eyebrow quirking.

"I never knew what to say to you." I push off the desk, standing in front of him. "I couldn't tell you what you meant to me, and I let that go on too long. To the point that neither of us knew what we were. I suck at jumping, at taking leaps of faith. And—"

"And I suck at seeing things through," he says, nodding. "So you're saying there's no hope?"

I shake my head.

"No," I say, feeling a lurch in my stomach at the look of

surprise on his face. "Because you're right."

"I am, huh?" he asks, resting into the chair and bringing his hand up, slipping his fingers through mine. "What am I so right about?"

"That I fell in love with you," I say, nudging my knee against his and trying to drown this stupid, fuzzy shyness that makes my skin flush hotter and hotter. I tug on his hand, but Beck is stronger, with his stupid, lazy boy strength. He pulls me into him, and I let myself fall, catching my hand on his shoulder.

"Good," he says, voice husky. "I'm always right, so that comes as no surprise to me."

"Says the person who just detailed how they made many wrong moves," I point out, as he makes a show of rolling his eyes.

"Only to get to the rightness of it," he says, lifting a hand and threading his fingers into the hair at the back of my head. "Which is that I love you."

"Nice to know. I'll make sure to file that away," I say, more breathless the closer he gets to me. My heart is thump-thumping away like a wild thing in my chest, and I clench my fingers on his shoulder, like I'm testing that he's really here. That we're really doing and saying these wonderful things.

"So we're good?" Beck asks, even though it doesn't sound like a question.

"Shut up," I tell him, and he laughs, pulling me into him as I let myself fall, his mouth meeting mine in a swift rush that feels warm and heady and true.

Chapter Nineteen

Four days later, after I insist on packing Bri on a plane so she can spend her hard-earned winter break with her family, we trailer Feather to Gulfstream. She rattles down off the rig, her body like a spring coiling into Izzie's hold, Betty the Goat flouncing down after her with all the air of a rock star expecting the unwashed masses to fall at her split hooves in supplication. Feather takes one look at the backside, which is not unlike any other racetrack's barn area, and decides that this is too much. Her nerves? Shot. Her fortitude? Gone.

Not even Betty the Goat, who is off sampling the grass near a rather famous trainer's barn, can soothe her. Feather bounces once on her front hooves and rears off the ground, coming down with a clack. Izzie rushes to get her moving again. No more rearing, not if we're too busy moving forward.

"Maybe we want to rustle the goat out of the Castellano barn?" Beck asks, pushing his sunglasses up his nose and not making any move to do any goat rustling. "Because I don't think other people will be as fond of her as we so obviously are."

"That sounds like you just volunteered yourself," I say, climbing into the truck to pull out Feather's things. I hear Beck's audible sigh and laugh to myself as I yank on the equipment bag, hauling it backward out of the truck until we both go tumbling to the ground and I have to do some fancy twisting to stay on my feet.

In the dust cloud I've kicked up, I hardly notice the man who's stopped to observe my flailing. By the time I've yanked the bag out of the dirt, he clears his throat.

"This is certainly charming."

I whirl around, focusing on the source of the voice and finding a man in a dark gray suit—unusual for Wednesdays at the races, especially if you compare him to my jeans and T-shirt. Then it hits me, and my stomach drops.

I should have brought a change of clothes.

The man smiles and shoves his hand out at me, and tentatively I take it.

"Khalid Sahadi," he beams at me, his warm brown skin almost glowing in the late morning sun. His near black hair is closely cropped, much like his beard that looks like someone has been paid handsomely to manicure it every day. I gulp down enough air to squeak out my name.

"July Carter."

"I know," he says, squeezing my hand harder before releasing me. "Your father and I have had many discussions about you."

"Many discussions?" I ask, just as Beck pushes Betty the Goat past me, nudging her toward our assigned stall, where Feather is busy freaking out because her goat isn't within direct eyesight. I suck in another healthy breath.

"Of course," Khalid says, putting his hands on his hips and

looking around at the backside like this is his magnificent domain. He takes a deep breath and smiles at me. "Don't you love that smell?"

"Horses?" I ask, bewildered.

"Yes," he says, taking another breath. "Horses."

Then he smiles and reaches for me, directing me under his arm and into the shedrow. I can see Beck down the aisle, pushing Betty the Goat back into Feather's stall. The panicked screaming stops, but I'm unnerved. No one needs to start a race day like this.

No one.

"I was in town for a meeting when your father called about Feather's race, and decided I had to come see. Feather is a home-bred, you know, and I've always had such high hopes for her. Investments can wait for sentimentality, don't you think?"

I'm going to nod. Yes, nodding will do here. Khalid Sahadi looks pleased with this, so probably this is the right move.

"May I?" he asks, whipping a small baggie of baby carrots out of his pocket.

It's frowned upon to let a horse snack before a race, but right now my brain cannot allow myself to form those words.

"Of course," I stammer, and watch as he approaches Feather, who goes to the stall guard like a puppy meeting her beloved owner and puts her nose in his hands, snuffling and woofing the carrots he holds out to her. Izzie stands by and smiles, already taken with Mr. Sahadi and his bag of carrots.

Beck walks up to me, wiping goat smell onto his jeans.

"Is this our mystery owner?" Beck asks, tilting his head. "Looks pretty par for the course, maybe a little more lovey-dovey than the usual—"

"This is a disaster," I hiss at him, pulling out my cell phone and hitting Martina's number, listening to the dial tone drone and drone until she answers with a flippant, "What?"

"Khalid Sahadi is here," I whisper-yell into the phone and the surprised gasp I receive is at least satisfying.

"You are wearing peasant clothes," she helpfully informs me. "I told you not to wear peasant clothes!"

"Thanks a lot for that wisdom," I reply. "It's so helpful now that I am at Gulfstream and smell like goats and horses."

"This is not my fault," Martina says. "I told you this was your first race and you should be presentable for your first race, to which you told me—"

"'It's Wednesday'," I say. "I know what I said, Martina. I know that was a colossal error in judgment. You can be smug about this later and bring me a change of clothes now, please?"

"You are cutting it so short," Martina says, and then hangs up without another word. I think that's good. Beck just looks at me like all of this is beyond his help.

"How long until we need to be at the receiving barn?" he asks.

"Two hours." The time on my phone glows up at me, not at all a subtle reminder that it takes an hour to get from Palm Meadows to Gulfstream Park. I shove it into the back pocket of my jeans as Beck throws an arm around my tense shoulders, pulling me into him until I'm buried against his T-shirt with its jaunty message proclaiming *Go local sports team!*

"The good news," Beck says, "is that we just got here. The universe has thrown you an unexpected curveball, sure, but Betty the Goat is no longer in the Castellano barn and Feather has carrots so she's calmed down. There is a bright side."

"Right." I let out a breath. "Bright side. And what's the bad news?"

"That universes are unpredictable and could keep throwing us setbacks," Beck says, shrugging his shoulder and freezing when I send him a look. "Not that we should worry."

"It's going to be okay," I say, although I know horses. I know racing. If anything is always proven correct time and time again it is that if a horse is involved, what can go wrong usually will. And I won't like it at all.

I look down the aisle at Khalid Sahadi happily feeding Feather, the filly pricking her ears at this man I've never met like he is her entire world, and I hope that baggie never runs empty.

～

When Martina arrives in the shedrow, we're thirty minutes from the receiving barn and I am pacing. Back and forth, back and forth, feeling like an idiot for wanting better clothes. I can't tell if Khalid Sahadi even cares, but I don't want to be that person—that kid who doesn't take the game seriously—when my multimillionaire owner is standing in the paddock next to me.

Not if I'm going to keep playing this game.

Even worse, Feather polished off the carrots.

"It's a little comical," Beck says, watching the filly circle the stall, checking in on Betty the Goat every few turns like she obsessively needs to be reminded that she's not alone.

"What is?" I ask, walking by him.

"That you're both doing the same thing."

That puts a stop to my pacing, but before I can say anything Martina's rental car pulls up outside of the barn and I jump into the parking lot, rushing up to her and throwing my arms around her neck when she produces the garment bag.

"That is not necessary," she tells me, pushing the bag toward me, which I happily take. Pilar climbs out of the passenger seat just as I'm turning for the barn's minuscule office.

"Wait up," she calls, waving a pair of shoes over her head. She rounds the car and deposits them in my arms. "We took forever deciding on this pair, so you will appreciate our time and effort."

"It's immensely appreciated," I reply. "I thought you wouldn't come."

Pilar laughs. "Just because I'm not riding doesn't mean I don't want to be here, July."

"Point taken," I say, as she shoos me into the office.

I shimmy into the dress and pull on the shoes. Hair goes up into a ponytail, because there is absolutely no time to think about that when I hear Feather's hooves hit the side of her stall.

"What's happening?" I ask, bursting back out of the office to see Izzie and Pilar wrestling with Feather. Her bridle needs to go on and Feather is tossing her head all over the place.

"Feather is happening," Beck says dryly. "I can't believe I'm about to say this, but I think Lighter has a gentler touch."

"If you call a wrecking ball gentle," I tell him, and he only smiles at me as Izzie gets the last buckle done on the bridle, letting out a big breath.

"Who wants to lead this one over?" she asks us, and when we all stare at her uncomprehendingly she sighs. "Oh, right, that's my job."

She slips the halter over the bridle while Pilar murmurs nonsensically to the filly, stroking one calm hand down Feather's neck.

We all part ways when Izzie turns Feather toward the shedrow and the explosion starts from the ground up.

I leap back when Feather pulls Izzie into the yard, her big body trembling and her hooves slashing. There's a clatter and a throaty horse scream as woman and horse wrestle each other down to a heaving standstill.

"Whoa," I say, just as Izzie starts to make a move to try to lead her again. "Let's not push it."

"What do you mean?" Izzie asks, twisting over her shoulder to look at me while still giving the filly the evil eye.

"We cannot scratch because of this," Martina helpfully informs me from the shedrow. "Dad would have your head."

"I'm not scratching," I say, turning and going for the filly's equipment, finding my exercise saddle I shoved in there—an insurance policy. "We just need someone on her back. She's better under saddle."

"Marginally better," Martina reminds me, continuing to be the voice of reason. "And can we even do that?"

"Dad got permission," I say, because leave it to my father to have all the bases covered when it comes to the horses. "Just in case."

Martina doesn't look convinced. "Then who's going to ride her? None of us are exactly ready for—"

"I will," Pilar says, taking the saddle from me matter-of-factly, like she was waiting for this to happen. Izzie gapes at her.

"You don't have to do this," I say. "I am completely prepared to change back into those jeans if I have to."

Pilar snorts at that. "And play the trainer at the same time? I don't think so, July. This is my job, and who else is going to do it for you?"

I really don't have an answer for that. Pilar is the best person I have, and we all know it. When I put that saddle in with the rest of the equipment, I figured it would be me on the filly's back, the horse-training, exercise-riding, grooming jack of all trades parading into the paddock on Izzie's lead.

That is so completely unrealistic now. And it always was. Whether or not Khalid Sahadi showed up, I should have known better.

"I don't want to put you in this position," I say, but Pilar waves me off.

"I am choosing this, July," she says, and then looks at Feather with a cool, unreadable expression on her face. "It's time that I stop being scared of something I love."

She puts the saddle on the filly's back, and I jump to help her with the girth. It's ready in no time, and when I lift her onto Feather there's a minute when I don't know what to expect. Fireworks? A roll of thunder? A car horn?

But none of that happens. Pilar only leans over the filly's neck and murmurs, "*Coraje*, Feather. *Coraje*."

Courage.

Then we go.

∿

The filly is a walking picture of perfection under Pilar. When we get to the paddock, Feather gives the row of stalls under the grandstand a white-eyed stare and works the bit between her teeth, her ears tipped back, listening—always listening.

Pilar keeps a light touch on her mouth, letting Izzie lead the way and nudging with her legs when the filly needs a hand. Between the three of them, walking over to the paddock doesn't look like a journey fraught with terror. It's just easy, like they were meant to do it. Of course, I know it's not that simple. It's never that easy with horses. Pilar has her focus on the filly, there with her the whole way, and that is what keeps Feather together, focused, her mind on the job instead of off in the clouds.

Izzie leads the filly into her stall, and Pilar stays on her back, crooning to her and stroking a hand down her neck as I sidle up to them with the filly's tongue tie, working the bit of cloth into her mouth—literally strapping her tongue down so she can breathe better and can't flip her tongue over the bit. The filly eyes me with interest, but otherwise stands still while I tie off the cloth beneath her chin.

"Good girl," Pilar says to the filly, and swings down to the ground when Mom's valet appears with her racing saddle. Time for my heavier exercise saddle to go, replaced with the tiny scrap of leather that looks comical in comparison. I take it from the valet. It weighs only ounces—much like a feather itself.

After the valet and I get the stretchy undergirth buckled up, we pull the overgirth across the top of the saddle, my fingers stumbling on the buckle nervously. I've watched Dad do this hundreds of times, but it isn't as easy as it looks. Feather dances back and forth, and I slip next to her, pulling on the girth until the buckle finally catches and I can jump back just as she thrashes a hind leg in the air, ears tipped back at me like she's saying *you are taking too long back there.*

"Okay, okay, go," I wave at the filly, and Izzie takes her out to do a few circuits of the narrow hallway as we wait. My fingers are trembling and I muster a smile as the valet claps me on the shoulder, gives me that nod like he knows exactly what the problem is and isn't going to try to fix it, and walks back the way he came as Mom appears with the stream of other jockeys, her bright blue and orange silks flashing in the dim saddling area.

"Feather looks good," she says, as though she's surprised, and then raises an eyebrow at my dress. "I thought you said 'it's only Wednesday.'"

"I did say that," I nod. "And then Khalid Sahadi showed up and I rethought my whole process."

Mom laughs. "Khalid is here?"

Of course she's on first name basis with the man. Of course she is.

"July," she says, rolling her eyes at me, "take it from me—Khalid is the last person you need to impress. He's here for the horses."

"Good to know," Martina grumbles from behind me, while Beck stifles a laugh.

"Wonderful," I sigh, plucking at the skirt of the dress. "So all of this was for nothing."

"Not for nothing," Mom says, shaking her head. "July, it's your first time saddling a horse to race. It was always more than just a typical Wednesday at the track. Be proud of yourself. This is an accomplishment."

"Right," I say. "This is an accomplishment worthy of a dress."

"Which I provided," Martina pipes in again. "Never forget, July."

"I don't think you'll ever let me," I tell her, taking a deep breath as the paddock judge motions for riders up. The jockeys are being lifted into the saddles by each trainer like they weigh nothing.

They're just flitting pieces of fluff flying through the air. When Izzie leads Feather up to us, I walk alongside as Mom gathers the reins and lifts a leg for me to cup a hand around.

Then she kicks, and just like that her weight is in my hand and she's in the air. Feather keeps dancing her white-eyed jig, and Mom settles in the saddle despite the fact that my hands are shaking. She smiles down at me.

"Good job, July."

Then they step out into the blinding light, walking into the paddock with its oblong fountain and its clusters of well-dressed owners looking on. I see Khalid talking with a woman in a flowing dress, half-heartedly in the conversation when Feather goes clattering by with Mom in the saddle.

"Time to go play trainer, I think," Beck says next to me when I hesitate. He gives me a nudge in the back for good measure. "Meet you in the stands."

I let out a little, pathetic groan. Beck nudges me again and I stumble out after Feather, picking my way across the paddock to Khalid, who gives me a dazzling smile.

"Look how lovely she is!" he exclaims, motioning to Feather, who's head is somewhere up by Mom's face and is yanking hard on Izzie's arm. One of the outriders has already spotted them, and is cruising like a shark on their outside.

"She is," I say. "Feather is one of the favorites in the barn. Definitely."

"Your father has been telling me how much you've been working with her," Khalid says, his whole face bright and animated. I am starting to see how he's an entrepreneurial phenomenon at talking people into buying whatever he's offering. "I'm impressed, July.

Truly. To take over the stable at this point in your life is a landmark. I'm honored to own the first horse you're saddling by yourself."

"That's kind of you to say," I tell him, trying to diplomatically respond to his enthusiasm. I'm not used to this much gushing. Honestly, I'm only used to Blackbridge and Delaney, who kept his interaction with me mostly down to "where is your father?" That was always an easy question to answer. Today I'm by myself, but at least Khalid seems like an open book.

Then again, we'll see how open he is if Feather doesn't win—which is a distinct possibility. She's certainly no favorite.

"Should we head up to the stands?" I ask him after the last horse has made the circuit around the paddock, heading back under the grandstand en route to the racetrack.

"Of course," he smiles at me and actually offers me his arm. Instead of giving in to the huge temptation to panic, I thread my hand around his elbow and off we go, like debutantes to the ball. When we arrive at our box, Beck is smirking at me.

"Stop," I mouth at him, but it's like he physically can't, so I unwind my arm from Khalid's and stealthily poke Beck in the side as the horses go warming up down the track. Beck jumps and reaches to grab my hand, because we both know that we can't get into a childish poking match in front of Khalid Sahadi, no matter how much my mother claims he doesn't notice anything except the horses.

Half of me thinks she said that just for my benefit, trying to soothe my ruffled feathers like a normal mother. Only my mother isn't normal, no matter how much she's put herself out there for me this past month. Flying out here to help—and staying—is definitely not a place I ever thought we'd be. Add Martina to the mix and I'm truly shocked we've gotten here at all—to Gulfstream with a horse running and my Mom on her, like this is no big deal. Like we do this every day.

I take a big breath as Feather approaches the gate, pricking her ears at the contraption as the rest of the fillies load into line. Feather is the last horse in the field—lucky number seven—so she waits, turning and turning in a circle while the horses are lead and prodded and pushed until they're all in line.

Feather takes one look at the gate and goes right in, presses her butt up against the metal as soon as the back doors close.

"Here's to small miracles," Martina says to herself, her presence calm at my back, so above the fray. I feel Pilar bouncing on her toes nearby, her nervous energy working its way through movement. Beck moves his hand, going from pinning my fingers to weaving his through them, because we're going to be holding on for dear life soon.

Then the gates bang open and the horses start, like a crackling current has snapped across their hindquarters when really it's a surge of adrenaline that pushes them to dig their toes into the dirt. They launch out of the gate, bunching muscle and forelegs shoveling dirt, every single horse down there going from standstill to racing speed in mere half-seconds.

Mom's candy blue and construction orange silks are a shock on the outside—easy to follow. Feather's bay body can get lost in the crowd of horses, but she's right there, pushing down the track with her head down like she has places to be. The horses race past the grandstand and hit the turn, a small bunch on the lead and the rest trailing behind like specks of melting ice off a comet. Feather is one of those specks, racing fifth and Mom sitting steady in the saddle, her body angled over the filly's withers and her hands so very still, like nothing is moving when I know that's all she's doing. Riding racehorses is all about balance, shifting weight, putting yourself in the right position to give the horse room to run. That's what Mom is doing: little movements, tiny adjustments, all soft messages that say *hold, hold.*

Only when they're deep in the turn does every part of Mom's body change the message from *hold* to *go.* Even though it doesn't seem possible, her body gets smaller. She crouches, lowering herself until she's lost against Feather's black mane. She's an afterthought to the filly, who is listening intently, her ears slipping back and her nostrils blown wide. There's a moment where they're hanging mid-air, and Mom flicks her crop up, re-crosses her reins, and goes for it.

Then they're wild. Feather reaches, speeding up when the rest of the field is either running full tilt or throwing in the towel. She passes horses on the outside, taking a path down the middle of the track with the leader still laboring to keep in front with Feather breathing down her neck.

Khalid is yelling next to me, his hands in the air and his whole body leaping up and down. I hear Martina and Pilar yelling their encouragement behind me, and Beck's hold on my hand tightens, his body lifting onto his toes like he needs to stretch to see when really he just wants closer to the action. We all do.

Normally, I'd be yelling along with them. But I'm too busy staring at the filly, cataloging every bit of movement. Every bunch and stride. She's moving, moving, lengthening that big stride of hers like there's no limit to reach. She's going to win. She's going to—

Mom lifts her weight off the filly's neck, and the jarring of it throws my heart into a chaotic thumping. Immediately everything that I can think of that could go wrong goes running through my head, but Feather seems fine. She wants to keep throwing herself at the leader. It's just Mom.

It's just the saddle.

The stretchy girths aren't where they're supposed to be. They've crawled five inches back, sucking closer and closer to the filly's flanks. Mom struggles to stay on and push at the same time, but she has to lift her weight up to compensate for the shift. She's not in the right spot anymore, but Feather still runs like that's the least of her worries. It's just this damn horse in front of her, *thank you very much*. She tips one ear back and flicks the other forward, classically signaling that she has no idea what's going on back there.

Mom throws more crosses, puts the filly to work as the saddle keeps slipping back and the wire looms. The leader leaps for it first, Feather only a shade behind, the saddle still sliding and Mom reaching down to grab mane the second they're past the finish.

"Damn it," I hiss under my breath, watching them go galloping up the first turn with my heart still lodging itself into my throat. It feels hard to breathe, but Mom gets Feather down to a trot and turns her quickly, heading back to the grandstand.

Khalid shakes his head, and I am now painfully aware that I have an owner standing next to me.

"Terrible luck," he says to me. "She looked so good coming down the stretch."

"I . . ." My voice dies out, because I don't know what to say. Is this my fault? Did I not get the right buckle hole? Did I not check to make sure the girth wasn't damaged? What did I not do right?

"It is terrible luck," Beck says, jumping into the silence.

"Good news is Mom stayed on," Martina adds, which I think is an amazing pronouncement coming from her.

"And Feather wanted the distance," Pilar says, watching the filly trot back, poking me in the back because I'm the trainer in this situation, I need to say something constructive because this isn't about the saddle anymore.

This is about the filly.

"More from the looks of it," I say, building off of Pilar, who smiles at me. "*Classic* distance, I think."

That does it. Nothing puts a grin on an owner's face like the promise of reaching the classic races—the Kentucky Oaks, the Kentucky Derby if the cards are played right. Khalid smiles. "Classic?"

I nod, like I'm so terribly sure. "Definitely."

He looks down at the track, where Mom jumps off of Feather and pats her liberally on the neck before pulling off the wretched saddle. Izzie scurries around them, pulling the tongue tie free before taking off for the spray hose further down the rail.

Khalid nods and looks to me. "Perhaps waiting on her maiden win is not the best use of our time."

I swallow my heart back down to where it belongs—thumping normally in my chest. "Going off of her work coming into this race, I think she's ready for a challenge."

The words fall out of me, and I think they're actually right. They're true. Feather needs a challenge to keep her mind out of the clouds. She needs something to keep her working and from going totally crazy. She's a racehorse, this one. Work is what keeps her sane.

"Excellent," Khalid beams at me, then offers his hand for me to shake. "I think we'll be in touch soon. It's been a good day, July

Carter."

"It has," I say, even though my horse didn't win, my Mom almost fell off, and it might all be my fault. The owner is happy, and that? That little fact trumps all the negatives and all the things that didn't go right. In the end, today goes in the column with all the other good days. We're going home with our horse and a little money to show for our effort, however crazy.

I close my hand around his, and we shake.

Chapter Twenty

In the morning, it's back to work as usual. Horses clatter in and out of the shedrow, heading off for the track and coming back blowing. Feather walks, her whole body languid and loose, next to Izzie as Betty the Goat trails in their wake, half-forgotten and loving it. It's only until we've finished with all the horses that I turn my attention on Lighter.

The white board says *gallop*, and Lighter is scraping his hooves down the stall's walls, gouging into them like he's trying to tunnel his way out. Pilar stands in front of his stall with her exercise saddle cradled in her hands, and I stand next to her.

"You ready?" I ask, because I have to give her the out.

She just gives me a look and sniffs. "Don't start, July," she says. "Today I'm riding Lighter, and after that we're going to video you and Kali. No more delaying the inevitable."

"Okay then," I laugh, because just the thought of that video puts my stomach into knots. "Let's get this show on the road."

Gus gets the saddle on Lighter's back with a few quick movements, swift pulls of leather and bulging muscle. Lighter pins his ears and flicks his tail like an angry cat, even though I know he's only excited. He's a bottled explosion, just waiting for the opportunity to take advantage of his time out of his stall—which is no longer his happy place when he has places to run.

Pilar watches stoically when Gus and Lighter crash out of the stall, the colt wheeling around in front of us and snorting like a dragon, all quivering muscles and breathy plumes of air shooting into the morning dim. Gus digs in his heels, shoulders the colt around and pulls him to an insistent halt.

I give Pilar a leg up, and Lighter instantly comes together like he's just been relishing this moment. He's been thinking about it since daybreak, watching the rest of the horses come and go while shaving his hooves down the walls.

"Remember," I say up to Pilar, "he's just a baby."

"Biggest baby there ever was," she says over her shoulder, laughing.

Then they're off, Gus leading the colt down to the oval, where Beck is waiting, leaning into the rail with his coffee mug cradled between his hands. Lighter goes gallivanting onto the track the second Gus releases him, trotting over the dirt with his head arched down and his stride lengthening and lengthening until he cruises right into a gallop, pushing his entire being into the bridle.

Pilar stands in the stirrups, reins bridged against the colt's neck. They rollick down the track, sliding into the mist and vanishing altogether.

"Think she'll stay on him this time?" Beck asks, like it could make for an interesting bet. I cast him a sidelong look, which he smiles at.

"You are never drawing me into another bet again," I say, to which he grunts.

"Right," he says. "I think we have some time to test that theory of yours."

"Do we?" I look over at him, listening to the thuds of hooves in dirt, the calls of exercise riders laughing and talking to each other, keeping track of their positions in the mist.

"Of course," he says, and pulls out his phone, showing me the text that glows up at me. "Your dad says Leo's parents aren't going to sue. Guess he talked them out of it."

I smile, because I knew with Leo back in the waking world there wouldn't be a chance of a lawsuit. Leo isn't his father—not by a long shot—and when he gets out of that hospital bed I'm going to greatly enjoy whipping him back into shape for racetrack life. Besides, Dad's going to need his help, now that I'm bound for Jericho. Aside from that, well, sharing the barn with Leo Reyes doesn't sound like the worst thing in the world anymore.

"So no selling Lighter?" I ask, looking up at Beck.

"No selling Lighter," he confirms. "Besides, I like having him. Keeps you on your toes."

"Well, sadly for you, I will be in college this time next month, so there will be less Lighter in my life."

"You say that now," Beck says, "but when he's winning those Derby preps you'll be changing your tune."

I sigh, because he's right. We both know it. Beck looks at me knowingly.

"Guess you're going to have to make a little room in your life for our lovable, huggable Lighter."

"Guess so," I say, wondering just how I'm going to make all of this work. Kali and Jericho and Belmont Park. The lead up to the

Kentucky Derby is not for the faint of heart. It takes everything. Every little ounce of heart you have, and here I am trying to split it three ways.

Then there's Beck, who throws an arm over my shoulder and brings me close. He smells like coffee and boy, which is oddly appealing. I let myself rest there in it as the track becomes a drone of hooves beyond us.

"Want to hear the good news?" he asks, and I lift my head just enough to look up at him.

"What's that?"

"You're not alone," he says, and I lift my hands to his jaw, pushing myself onto my toes to kiss him.

Then the siren starts to blare.

Loose horse.

"Are you kidding me," I groan, falling back to my heels. The entire track shifts in front of me, the mist lifting just enough to show the outline of a horse galloping around the turn, reins flapping uselessly.

Then the mist pulls away, revealing a solid chestnut barreling around the turn with an outrider in hot pursuit. They go flying by, leaving me breathless with the knowledge that it's not Lighter.

"That was unexpected," Beck says dryly, laughing like the thought that another horse could even cause trouble with Lighter around is absurd. "Do other horses even cause chaos?"

"I think we just saw evidence of it," I say, just as I finally catch sight of Lighter.

The colt gallops around the turn with his head down, pressure in the bridle, his mouth gaping and Pilar balanced over his withers with her eyes focused between his copper ears. I watch him make the turn, completely at ease with the world, and turn into the stretch with a flick of his platinum blond tail.

~~

The shedrows quiet down after the last of the work tab walks off the track and into the maze of barns. Steaming horses walk, stand for baths. Those that are off to the races are long gone. This is the downtime that I take advantage of with Kali, who stands tethered to the ring in the wall of her stall and waits as I go over her tack, position it until it's perfect, tightened to just the right hole.

No slipping girths this time.

"So I was thinking," Mom says, leaning against the wall as I go over the tack, checking to make sure the stirrup buckles are still where I left them.

"About?" I ask distractedly.

"About New York," Mom says, and I still, looking at her over my shoulder as she presses on. "I've enjoyed this, July. I don't know how you feel about this, but being here with you girls, it's been more than I ever thought you'd let me have after everything."

"Well, you've really helped out," I say, turning back to the stirrup and running it up, pushing the leather through the iron. "I couldn't have done this without you. Without everyone, really."

Mom nods, like that reminds her. It's not just her, after all. So much has gone into making Florida a success. Granted, she did fly across the country, dropped everything when I asked, and hasn't said a word about leaving. She's sticking, like she's riding a difficult horse on a bad day, and she's riding through it.

I give her credit for that. I do.

293

"I know that things in New York . . ." she says, sighing like she's not sure she's getting this right. "I know I pushed too hard before the Breeders' Cup. I know I wasn't welcome, and I let your father convince me it would be okay."

"Because for Dad hope springs eternal," I say, undoing Kali's tie to the wall and turning her toward Mom, who straightens.

"Maybe so," she says. "But that isn't such a bad thing, July."

"No," I say, because it really isn't. I know better than to be flippant about it. If anything got me through all those years of Mom being gone, it was obsessive hope.

"So I was *hoping*," Mom says, "that maybe we could try again. Only this time, I'll let you and Martina set the ground rules."

I open my mouth and close it again. "Have you asked Martina about this?"

"I . . ." she starts, only for Martina to appear in the stall door.

"Are you coming out sometime in the next decade?" she asks, and then stops, looking between Mom and me like she suspects foul play. "What is going on?"

"I guess I'm testing the waters," Mom says, shifting away from the wall, like she needs to straighten up for Martina. "I want to know if it's okay if I come back to ride in New York."

Martina stares at her for a full beat, a silent wash of emotionlessness that pushes Mom into her next pitch. "Of course, I'll leave this on your terms. I'll have my own place, my own life, and you can be in it or . . . not in it as you see fit."

Then silence. I shift against Kali, who swings her head into the discussion like she has something wise to add. Only she snorts, bowing to rub her face against one pristinely-wrapped foreleg.

"But you'll be riding for Dad," Martina says, her voice sudden in the stall. Mom nearly jumps at the declaration.

"Yes," she says. "Of course, your father and I have an under-standing about that. But only if you're both on board. If you're not, that's fine. I don't want to push. I know I've been guilty of that, Martina. I know it."

Martina works her upper lip between her teeth, considering this like it's a proposal of significant importance. Like it's going to change all our lives. It only occurs to me then that it could. That maybe it already has.

We're here, for starters.

"Fine," she says, shrugging a shoulder like it's nothing when I know it's everything. Letting Mom in is not something Martina will ever do lightly. I let out a breath, and then realize that I've already made my decision.

I'm going forward.

"I'm on board," I say, nodding.

Mom smiles, relief fuzzy around all of her edges. She pushes into me, wrapping me in a hug that's so tight a surprised squeak escapes my lungs. Then she pulls me toward Martina, hauling a confused Kali with her, until she has Martina cuddled close.

"Please let there be no more group hugs in the near future," Martina says, voice muffled against us until she shakes loose, mock-ing a shiver as she ducks out of the shedrow, finished with us and our sentimentality.

"Thank you, July," Mom tells me.

"Hey, it was all Martina," I tell her, and she peers out the stall door at Martina's retreating back, nodding. Then she opens the stall door, and I lead Kali out into the yard.

"Finally!" Izzie shouts, holding up my phone. "Should I start recording?"

"Not yet!" I call back, shaking my head at her enthusiasm. Beck stands next to her, whispering something that is probably devious like *record everything; it's for posterity.*

I mount up, my weight sinking down into Kali's saddle, and set off for the L. Kali swings into a walk eagerly, her ears pricked at the silent tracks. She doesn't expect to find horses out there now, doesn't rush onto the oval like her feet are on fire. At least she knows now what I want of her, which is *not* breathtaking speed.

We walk onto the L, and I push her into a trot to warm up, following one side of the L before managing a somewhat collected turn to trot down the next. I check the brakes, and she drops to a walk, marching on into the bridle with her whole body swinging.

Maybe—just maybe—this will actually work after all.

I bring her to a halt, ask her to round, and loosen the reins once she lowers her head. Then I lean over her neck. The filly bobs her head, chews on the simple snaffle until a little dollop of foam forms on her lips and drops down to the track.

"Today is the big day," I tell her, and Kali's ears sweep back to listen. "Think we can get it in one take?"

"Any day now, Juls!" Beck calls across the track, stirring up a chorus of agreement. I turn and find my audience is lined up against the rail, every one of them watching me intently.

"Should I start, July?" Izzie shouts, lifting my phone. I nod sharply, and she does an excited little bounce on her toes as she taps the record button, holding the phone out and centering it right on Kali, right on me. Collecting the reins, I push Kali into the bridle, asking her to walk on and starting that eternal conversation: *go, but come back to me. Look for me, Kali.*

My filly rounds into my hand like she was born to do it, then lowers her head and takes that first step out into the dirt.

The Story Continues . . .

Book 1: Stay the Distance
Book 2: All Heart
Book 3: Derby Horse

Short Stories:
Whirlaway
Saratoga Summers
Eclipse

All available at Amazon.com or www.maradabrishus.com.

About the Author

Mara Dabrishus is an author and librarian who lives in Cleveland, Ohio. Horse racing is her first great love, but for the past several years she's ridden dressage, learning how to spiral in, half halt, and perform the perfect figure eight. She is also the author of *All Heart*, *Derby Horse*, *Finding Daylight* and two short stories: *Whirlaway* and *Saratoga Summers*.

She can be found blogging about horses, racing, writing and everything in between at www.maradabrishus.com.

Acknowledgments

Where do I start this time? *All Heart* is the product of the hard work of many people besides myself. Erin Smith is my steadfast editor, who presents me with a list of problems to fix with each draft, and without her these books I write would be incoherent. Then there are my beta readers: Natalie Keller Reinert, Kat Simon, Carrie Starkey, and Linda Shantz. You guys made my life easier, and you keep me honest. I am eternally grateful. Gillian Campbell, my copy editor, is worth her weight in frustrating typos. Without fail, there is my family for getting so excited about my new books and stories. Their enthusiasm knows no bounds. And, of course, my husband Mohammad, who cheerfully gets me away from my laptop every so often so I can experience the real world!

Keep In Touch!

Support the Stories

Your opinion is important! If you enjoyed this book, please consider leaving a review on Amazon or Goodreads. Just a few words really help to keep me writing so you can keep reading!

Contact Me:

I love hearing from my readers!

Website: http://www.maradabrishus.com
Facebook: https://www.facebook.com/maradabrishusauthor
Twitter: https://twitter.com/marawrites
E-mail: mara@maradabrishus.com

Printed in Great Britain
by Amazon